HEADLONG

Titles from Cynthia Harrod-Eagles by Severn House

Novels

ON WINGS OF LOVE
EVEN CHANCE
LAST RUN
PLAY FOR LOVE
A CORNISH AFFAIR
NOBODY'S FOOL
DANGEROUS LOVE
REAL LIFE (Short Stories)
KEEPING SECRETS
THE LONGEST DANCE
THE HORSEMASTERS
JULIA
THE COLONEL'S DAUGHTER
HARTE'S DESIRE
COUNTRY PLOT
KATE'S PROGRESS
THE HOSTAGE HEART
THE TREACHEROUS HEART

The Bill Slider Mysteries

GAME OVER
FELL PURPOSE
BODY LINE
KILL MY DARLING
BLOOD NEVER DIES
HARD GOING
STAR FALL
ONE UNDER
OLD BONES
SHADOW PLAY
HEADLONG

HEADLONG

Cynthia Harrod-Eagles

This first world edition published 2018
in Great Britain and 2019 in the USA by
SEVERN HOUSE PUBLISHERS LTD of
Eardley House, 4 Uxbridge Street, London W8 7SY.
Trade paperback edition first published
in Great Britain and the USA 2019 by
SEVERN HOUSE PUBLISHERS LTD.

British Library Cataloguing in Publication Data
A CIP catalogue record for this title is available from the British Library.

ISBN-13: 978-0-7278-8836-5 (cased)
ISBN-13: 978-1-84751-961-0 (trade paper)
ISBN-13: 978-1-4483-0171-3 (e-book)

All Severn House titles are printed on acid-free paper.

Severn House Publishers support the Forest Stewardship Council™ [FSC™],
the leading international forest certification organisation.
All our titles that are printed on FSC certified paper carry the FSC logo.

Typeset by Palimpsest Book Production Ltd.,
Falkirk, Stirlingshire, Scotland.
Printed and bound in Great Britain by
TJ International, Padstow, Cornwall.

ONE

Miching Mallecho

S lider jumped into the car, and Atherton peeled away from the kerb and back into the traffic in a movement so sleek and smooth, a dolphin would have tried to mate with it. 'Where to?' he said.

'Head back towards the Green,' said Slider. 'Don't you know?'

'I haven't been in yet,' said DS Jim Atherton, Slider's sergeant, bagman and friend – lean, fair, and catnip to women. 'I was just leaving Emily's when I got a message to pick you up from outside the town hall, that's all.'

'You're staying at Emily's?'

'Now and then. She doesn't like my house. Too difficult to park.'

'I wondered how you got here so fast.' Emily's flat was in Hammersmith, while Atherton's house was in that part of Kilburn that liked to pretend it was really Hampstead.

'So what's going on?' Atherton asked.

'I don't know much more than you. I was in a meeting with councillors and I got a message.' Slider glanced down at the piece of paper. 'All it says is, "3 Penkridge Gardens. Query accidental death, Edward Wiseman?"'

'*The* Edward Wiseman?'

'Should I have heard of him? Wise man – the sage who knows his onions?'

'I'm guessing it might be Ed Wiseman, famous literary agent.'

'When you put it like that, I seem to have heard of him,' Slider said. 'If it *is* the same one,' he added. 'Wiseman isn't *that* uncommon a name.'

The Tuesday morning rush was almost over, but there was still plenty of traffic about. They hurtled down Shepherd's Bush Road; but Atherton drove with intense concentration and his whole body, so Slider never minded being driven by him. He watched him out of the corner of his eye, the rest of his attention

enjoying the signs of spring – new leaves here, a touch of
blossom there – which made Shepherd's Bush suddenly more
attractive. He felt one of those rare moments of good-to-be-
aliveness, that occurred independently of, and managed to avoid
being contaminated by, the Job.

Ed Wiseman, he thought idly. Literary agent. 'So how does a
literary agent get to be famous, anyway?' he asked after a bit.

Atherton laid the car round the curve of the Green like a lick
of paint. 'Going to the right parties. Being quotable. It's not really
my field, but I think I remember he was a larger-than-life character,
bit of a live wire. The Bad Boy of the publishing world?'

'Something's coming back to me. Isn't he the media go-to man
for opinion on anything to do with the book world?'

'The house expert,' Atherton agreed. 'But if it's accidental death,
what the devil do they want us for? It's not a DCI shout.'

'*Query* accidental death, question mark,' Slider reminded him.
'The devil is in the punctuation.'

'Maybe Someone Up There knows he was famous,' Atherton
said, slipping like a salmon between two cars to enter the white
water of the West Cross roundabout. Someone Up There, of
course, did not mean the Almighty, but the Metropolitan Police
Top Brass – much the same thing to a lowly copper, but without
the connotations of forgiveness and mercy. 'If you're famous, they
get the good silverware out.'

'Don't be bitter, dear,' Slider chided him. 'Left at the end,
and left again. Even the rich and famous deserve our best
endeavours.'

'I suppose it's a case of Ours Not To Wassname,' Atherton
sighed.

'Eloquently put.'

'This is it,' said Atherton, turning into the target road. 'I hope
we can park.'

Penkridge Gardens was on the side of Shepherd's Bush bordering
Holland Park – the posh side. The houses were typical of the
1850's expansion of London. You saw them all over the western
boroughs: tall, handsome, yellow stock brick with white copings,
three storeys with a semi-basement, generally built in terraces to
save space. Number three was in fact an end-of-terrace because,

presumably through some historical or geographical anomaly, number one, the corner house, was detached.

One hundred-and-fifty-plus years represents a lot of history for a building, and in value and status these had gone up and down like a Harrods lift at sale time. At the moment they were on their way up from the low point at which most had been broken up into flats, if they were lucky, and rooms if they were not. There was a certain prevailing shabbiness over the street, but improvement was evidently going on. Some had been bought back into single ownership, and were showing new windows and fresh paint, pristine stonework and – sure sign they had made it safely above the high-water mark – trimmed evergreen shapes in tubs on either side of the front door.

Number three was sending mixed messages. It was in single ownership, but needing attention – nothing desperate, but it had evidently been neglected for some years and was showing wear.

Number one, the detached house on the corner, was undergoing major surgery. It was fully scaffolded, with a sign fixed to it that said D.K. Connor, Building Contractors. High safety-hoardings that screened the site from the street were plastered with warnings: KEEP OUT. DANGER, DEEP EXCAVATIONS. PROTECTIVE HELMETS MUST BE WORN. NO UNAUTHORISED ENTRY.

A skip and various builders' vans were complicating the parking situation. Atherton had to park on the double yellow. 'Deep excavations? The curse of the iceberg strikes again,' he observed as they got out.

London property was expensive, and in limited supply. With these older houses, up was not an option: planning laws protected the look of the street. So the only way was down. It was common to dig out the semi-basement to increase the ceiling height, and extend it backwards under the rear garden, to create a whole extra floor's-worth of rooms. But in some cases – and this seemed to be one – owners were going further, and digging a second basement underneath the first. If the property were valuable enough, and the planning officer could be squared, some even went for a third, so that what was visible of the house was the least part of it – hence the iceberg label.

Slider's architectural sensitivities were offended. These old houses were built with taste, style, and generous proportions, and to undermine them for such ephemera as swimming pool, games room, gym, and/or private cinema just seemed wrong to him. But it wasn't his business what people did with their money, so he merely sighed, 'I wish they wouldn't.' And added, 'Anyway, that's not our house. We're number three.'

But even as he said it, he noted that there seemed to be police activity at both properties – and a lack of building activity where there should be plenty.

Atherton had spotted something else. 'Bandits at twelve o'clock,' he muttered urgently. 'By the pricking of my thumbs . . .' Slider quelled him with a look.

It was their immediate boss, Det Sup Porson, his bald top gleaming in the hazy sunshine, his strange, greenish overcoat flapping about his legs; and leading the way was *his* boss, Commander 'Dave' Carpenter, in a suit so sharp you could peel mangoes with it.

Porson was a tall man, who had, over the years, put the fear of God into generations of underlings; but beside Carpenter he seemed to scuttle in a subordinate semi-crouch like an apologetic crab. Carpenter was big – both tall and muscular – with a head of thick, glossy chestnut hair. Brushed straight back but lifting in its own wave above his scalp, it made him look even taller. And, of course, as borough commander he was big in the spiritual sense, and knew it. He held their lives – or, not to be over-dramatic, their careers – in his perfectly-manicured hands.

Everything about his carriage and expression said 'don't mess with me, boy'. His height allowed him to look down his large, well-shaped nose at almost everyone, and his big chin made looking back up a fruitless activity. Management training had taught him to invite his staff to 'call me Dave', but definite woe would betide the minion who did so. A young detective constable who took him at his word was rumoured to have suffered third-degree frostbite and never smiled again.

Slider had already been on Carpenter's bad side, hadn't enjoyed it, and had hoped to live out the rest of his life avoiding him altogether. Besides, breathing the same air as demi-gods always gave him a headache.

'Slider!' said Carpenter, and smiled. Carpenter smiling was, on the whole, slightly worse than Carpenter not smiling.

'Sir?' said Slider. As every man in uniform knows, you can't go far wrong with one of those. From behind Carpenter, Porson was making a complicated face at him, which seemed to be a combination of apology and warning.

Carpenter halted, blocking out the sun. Slider had never liked being loomed over. The hair rose on his scalp. He felt like a Jack Russell facing a St Bernard. Only in his case, he wasn't allowed to leap up and bite him in the balls.

'I expect you're wondering why you're here,' said Carpenter.

Existentialism at this hour of the morning? Various facetious answers flitted through Slider's mind, but he thrust them down sternly. The only safe answer was another: 'Sir?'

'My wife's cousin is godmother to Calliope Hunt,' Carpenter told him importantly, as though that explained everything. Slider heard Atherton, behind him, snort, and change it into a cough. Fortunately, Carpenter didn't seem to want a response at that point. He went on: 'So you can see why I have to be pro-active on this one. The family don't want any breath of scandal. Leave aside the fact that we're dealing with a high-profile celebrity, so there's bound to be media interest. And media interest is always the wrong sort, as you very well know.'

There was a pause, so Slider inserted another: 'Sir,' into it. The time would come, he supposed, when he knew what the hell Carpenter was talking about.

'I don't want it said that we didn't take this seriously,' Carpenter went on, 'but on the other hand, don't take all day about it. I want it confirmed as accidental death as soon as possible. Do I make myself clear?'

'Accidental death,' Slider repeated. Without the query. Okay. Got it.

'Good man,' said Carpenter, without warmth. 'Carry on.' He swung away to where a young police driver was holding the door of his car open for him, leaving Porson trying to scowl in two directions at once.

He settled on Slider. 'Well, what are you standing there like that for?' he barked. 'You look as if you're laying an egg. I tried to duck this one, but it's landed in our laps, so there's no point beefing. Just get on with it. Make sure there's nothing fishy about it and get back to what we're supposed to be doing.'

Slider picked his way through eggs, ducks, beef and fish, and said, 'I don't know what's going on yet, sir. Query accidental death, is all I know.'

Porson breathed out the give-me-patience, double-nostril gust. 'Deceased lived *there*,' he indicated number three with the jab of a thick finger, 'but the body was found *there*.' Now he jabbed at the builder-benighted number one. 'Capeesh?'

Slider capeeshed quite a bit. Evidently some kind of personal connection existed between Carpenter's wife and the deceased. If it wasn't accidental death, it might be suicide, and most people did not like those they loved to be stigmatised with suicide. Or themselves with having neglected to notice it was about to happen and stop it.

On the other hand, Slider thought, certainty is better than uncertainty. Suicide with a note is at least a full stop. 'Accident' always leaves some questions unanswered, generally lumbering the grieving with an ongoing quest for someone to blame, which only stretched out the pain.

'So the question is *just* accident or suicide, is it?' Slider sought clarity.

Porson looked as though a bad smell had arisen under his nose. 'Commander Carpenter made himself quite clear, didn't he? Make sure it *is* accidental death. And make it quick. We can't afford to waste time on an investigation.'

'I thought that was what I was here for,' Slider said. 'To investigate.'

'A clearing-up process. Don't go pulling any rabbits out of hats.'

Rabbits, yet, Slider thought. 'I just need to know what "make sure" means. At the highest level,' he added, indicating the space Carpenter's car had recently occupied.

Porson scowled. 'I'm the highest level you need to worry about. Do your job, that's all. I'll support you.'

Unclearer and unclearer. 'So you want the truth?' said Slider.

'Don't get clever with me! Just get on with it,' Porson barked, giving him a minatory stare. He turned away, then turned back to say, 'And for Gawd's sake get some bodies in, get some crowd control going. This is not a three-lane circus.'

Porson had a scattergun approach to idiom. *Something* was bound to reach its target.

When it was safe to do so, Atherton moved up beside Slider.

'You actually said "the truth"?' he queried. 'It's not safe to bait your superiors, don't you know that?'

'I must have some pleasures in life.'

'So what *are* we supposed to find?'

'Buggered if I know.'

Now the coast was clear, his own man, DC LaSalle, was coming across, hopefully to fill him in on some of the facts he was woefully short of.

'You know what this is,' said Atherton gloomily. 'This is a poisoned chalice.'

'Should get rid of all the livestock, then,' said Slider.

Chickens, ducks, fish, rabbits. They could do without them. The beef he might keep: a sense of put-upon-ness boosted a copper's adrenaline. It was his usual working environment.

How did someone end up in a building site through accidental death? Even suicide would present the same question: why pop next door to top yourself? Certainty could be hard to come by, and certainty was what Mr Carpenter wanted – as long as it was the right sort.

And who was Calliope Hunt when she was at home?

LaSalle was skinny and pale, with madly bristly ginger hair, like a yard broom upside down. He had a big ginger moustache, too, sprouting out under his nose like a coir doormat. Slider dreaded to think what it must be like for him when he had a runny cold. But he was a decent copper and knew how to give a report.

'Builders arrived at number one this morning, around eight o'clock. Well, the first lot did. They started getting ready to work – you know the way it is. Taking tarps off, setting out tools—'

'Chatting about the footy last night, having a brew,' Atherton put in. 'We get the picture.'

LaSalle nodded. 'Second vanload arrives about twenty past, one of them goes down into the excavations, finds the body.' He had photographs on his tablet. 'This is not the original position. Unfortunately, they moved him, trying to see if he was still alive.' He raised pale eyes to Slider's face. 'They're Polish, so I suppose they didn't know they're not supposed to touch anything. And also, y'know, I think it was a sort of . . . well, being respectful to the dead, guv.'

Slider nodded to the point. 'It might not matter, in the end,' he said.

The photographs showed deceased as a white man in bottle-green cord trousers and a grey sweater, lying on the muddy bottom of the excavations. His back was bowed, his head back at an exaggerated angle, the right arm was bent unnaturally, as though dislocated and/or broken. One leather loafer was missing. 'We found the other shoe down there,' said LaSalle. 'Also his glasses – broken, of course. Well, we're assuming they're his. The builders said they weren't there yesterday.' He held up an evidence bag in which was a pair of brown-framed spectacles, one lens cracked and one side arm detached and bent.

In close-up, the face had been damaged, the nose broken and one cheekbone mashed, but it seemed to have been a handsome face belonging to a man of mature years. The hair was mid-brown, flecked with silver and probably highlighted, thick and a touch on the long side, and the body seemed lean and fit. Trying to be younger than his age and succeeding pretty well, Slider thought.

'The reason he's so crooked,' LaSalle went on, 'the body was lying across a wheelbarrow full of bricks when they found it. I suppose that's why they moved him, to make him look more comfortable, but he was stiff so they couldn't straighten him out. There's all sorts down there, guv, bricks, rubble, tools, machinery. No soft landing. But a barrow of bricks must have stung a bit.' He made a pained face at the thought. He was a nice lad.

'Wait a minute – they're assuming he *fell* onto the wheelbarrow?'

'I'm coming to that, guv.'

Slider nodded. 'All right. When did they call it in?'

'Well, it took them a while to get themselves sorted out. Call was logged at eight forty-seven. Uniform arrived at eight fifty-eight – that was Renker and D'Arblay.'

'Twenty-five minutes before they called it in?' Atherton exclaimed.

'Well – they talk a lot,' LaSalle said with a helpless shrug. 'And what happened was, they were still milling about when the site manager turned up, about eight forty-five, and he took over and made one of them ring it in right away.'

'How come we had the name?' Slider asked. 'Did the builders know who he was?'

'The Polish boys didn't know him, but the manager did. Said

right away, that's the bloke next door. He'd had several conversations with him out in the street, about the building works. And when D'Arblay gets there, he points out to him the window open on the side of the house, right above where the body was. So it looks as though deceased was probably leaning out and done a nose-dive.'

Slider stepped up onto the opposite pavement to get the overall view. Shallow steps went up to the front door of number three, which stood under the usual porch supported by columns. There were two windows on the front façade on each floor. The side wall was right on the boundary between number three and number one, so there were no side windows on the lower floor, but one in each of the upper two floors. The middle-floor side-window, a good-sized sash, was pushed all the way up, and it was the only window that was open. From there, the drop to ground level would be bad enough, but the new excavations had added not only extra depth, but various hazards on the way down and a very unpleasant landing. Quite enough to kill a man.

'Go on,' said Slider.

LaSalle nodded. 'So Hart and me arrives, and we went to number three and rung the doorbell, see if there was a wife or anything around, but there was no answer. We looked up the house phone number online and rung that, but there was just an answering machine on. And then, while we were standing there, this woman arrives, comes up the steps with the doorkey in her hand and she's all, "What's going on?" Apparently, she's his secretary or something. Name of Amelia Hollinshead. Works there, in the house – it's an office as well as where he lives.'

'And should there be a wife?'

'No, he lives alone.'

'Where is she now?'

'Inside, with Hart.' He came to a natural pause and looked at Slider expectantly, ready to take orders.

It looked like accidental death. If the man had been leaning out, perhaps to see what progress had been made next door, and slipped, or overbalanced, he might well strike one or more of the protruding ends of the horizontal scaffold poles on the way down. He imagined him tumbling between hazards like a coin in a dryer, until he smacked down onto the barrowful of bricks, probably breaking his back – if nothing else had done for him already. A catastrophic head wound from the scaffolding, for instance. Plenty there to be going on with.

It looked as though Carpenter would get his wish. Slider need only tie up the ends. 'How far have you got?' he asked LaSalle.

'Well, Dr Laborie pronounced life extinct – she only lives in Addison Road, so she was here in five minutes – but we didn't know what else you wanted.'

'All right,' said Slider. 'Ring the factory and get back-up. We want all the builders statemented, and we'll have to secure the perimeter. And close the road for now.' A traffic situation was building, as drivers slowed to see what was going on. Also, if there were to be more department wheels, they would need to use the road for parking. 'And get a forensic surgeon down here ASAP. Ask for Freddie Cameron if he can come right away. If not – whoever's next on the list.'

'Yes, guv. So,' LaSalle hesitated, 'is there something fishy about it?'

'Just being thorough. He's a celebrity of sorts, and he's got connections with Mr Carpenter,' said Slider.

LaSalle got it at once. 'Oh blimey, one o' them!' he said. 'Right, guv, I'm on it.' And he scuttled off. Nothing like invoking a deity for getting a reaction.

TWO

Nose Dive

As Slider crossed the road, a man detached himself from the group by number one and accosted him. He was in his forties, very weathered of face, with grizzled hair under a hard hat, and a hi-vis waistcoat over his fleece jerkin. His face and eyes were hard with responsibility, and it was no surprise to Slider when he said, 'Craig Flanders, site manager.' He had an Australian accent, also not much of a surprise. Antipodeans seemed to specialise in the more expensive end of construction. 'Are you in charge here?' he demanded.

'I'm Detective Chief Inspector Slider. What can I do for you?'

'I want to know how long my men are going to be held up,' Flanders said irritably. 'I've got a big project on here, for an important client. He's not going to be happy if it's delayed. When can they get back to work?'

'I can't tell you—' Slider began.

Flanders interrupted. Well, you didn't get to be in charge of big projects by being Mr Nice Guy. 'That's not good enough! We've been inconvenienced enough already by this joker's suicide, which I emphasise is nothing to do with us. We didn't ask him to jump into our diggings, and on top of that, getting pointless obstruction from the police when all we—'

Slider interrupted back. 'I can't tell you because I don't know. There are procedures that have to be followed.'

'*Procedures*?' Flanders said it as though it was an outrageous dereliction of duty.

'If it was your loved one, I imagine you'd want to know things were done properly,' Slider said reasonably, and then, seeing Flanders about to protest again, hardened his expression. 'And when it comes to obstruction, if I find you are not co-operating fully with my investigation – you *and* your men – there will be serious consequences. Your client won't be happy about *that*. And why,' he finished, throwing another punch while Flanders was on the back foot, 'do you say it was suicide? What do you know?'

Flanders stepped backwards, lifting his hands. 'Oh, woah, I don't know anything!' he said in a more conciliatory tone. 'I'm just assuming—'

'Assuming?'

'That he came out of that window,' Flanders gestured. 'I mean, there's no way he could have got in otherwise. We got first-class site security here. I want you to make a note of that. When my boys arrived this morning, there was no perimeter breach. Everything locked down tight as a tick, just the way they left it last night when they finished. No way was there any security lapse on our part.'

'Are there any security cameras?' Slider asked.

Flanders looked rueful. 'No, sorry. I suggested 'em, but the client wouldn't swing for the extra expense. Or not at this stage, anyway. He said why bother, when there's nothing to nick?'

'Just your tools and plant.'

'Well, he wasn't bothered about that. And our security is good enough at this stage. Or so I thought,' he added crossly.

'You knew deceased, I understand?'

More back-pedalling. 'Not *knew* him. Recognised him, that's all. I seen him going in and out next door, and he's stopped me a coupla times for a jaw about the work here.' He jerked a thumb.

'Complaining about it?'

Flanders hesitated. 'Not that so much, though he did crack one once about the boys' radio. I got them to turn it down and that was that. I mean, when you're right next door like that there's bound to be friction, but we try to be considerate. That's what it says on our website: D.K.Connor, Considerate Construction. No sense rubbing people up the wrong way. And he was asking one time about the digging moving his foundations, but I showed him the plans and explained it all to him and he was fine with it, no worries.'

'So you had quite detailed conversations with him?'

'Yeah, well, he was interested. What we were doing and how it worked, how we were getting on. Intelligent bloke. Knew how to read a blueprint, too. Maybe he was thinking of doing the same for his own place, I dunno. Very interested in what it was costing, sorta thing, and how it would increase the property value.'

'What did you think of him?' Slider asked.

'How d'you mean?'

'What sort of person was he?'

Flanders looked lost. 'He seemed all right. Quite a pleasant bloke. And bright upstairs, like I said.'

There didn't seem to be anything more insightful coming, so Slider asked, 'Did you see other people going in and out?'

'I wouldn't notice,' said Flanders. 'I'm not here all the time, and when I do come, I'm concentrating on the job. Never gave next door a glance, if you want the truth. I wouldn't have noticed *him*, except he stopped me to talk to me.'

'All right. Thanks.' Slider nodded and turned away.

Flanders put out a hand to stop him. 'When can we get back to work?' he asked. His tone was very different this time – pleading. 'Time is money.'

'You and your men will have to give statements, after which

you can go home. My people will have to examine the site, and that could take all day.'

'So we can start work again tomorrow?'

'If nothing untoward turns up, I imagine so,' said Slider. Flanders seemed to take that as a 'yes'. Stupid Flanders.

Hart, his other sergeant, met him in the hall, her place as babysitter having been taken over by a WPC. She was tall and lean, and had pulled her Afro up into a puffball on top of her head, which made her look even taller. 'She's in there,' she said, indicating the left-hand room. 'I gave her coffee. She seems a bit stunned. What d'you want me to do, boss?'

'Go and supervise the statementing. And make sure uniform's controlling the mobiles. We don't want them sending photographs of the corpse all over the world.'

'Gotcha. What was Mr Carpenter doing here?' The question burst out of her. 'If it was just an accident . . .?'

'Some connection with deceased. Wants to make sure it *was* an accident.'

She absorbed that. 'My money's on suicide,' she decided. 'This place feels dead. We got the answering machine on, but the phone's not rung since I got here. I bet he had money troubles, took the easy way out.'

Slider thought of the wheelbarrowful of bricks. 'Easy?'

'Well, you know what I mean,' she said, and departed jauntily. Ah, the resilience of youth.

The room to the right of the entrance hall had the original marble fireplace, with bookshelves in the alcoves, and was furnished with sofas and armchairs and pictures on the walls. But a coffee table covered with magazines and a chilly atmosphere gave it more the feel of a doctor's waiting room than a private sitting room.

The room to the left had been set out as an office, but quite cosily, with carpet and pot plants, warm lighting and a smell of coffee. It was tidy and clean, with dust covers over the computer's screen and keyboard, and the pot plants looked well-cared for. The secretary was sitting with her hands in her lap, staring at nothing.

'Amelia Hollinshead?' Slider asked.

She hurried to her feet, scanning Slider's face. 'Amy, please.

No one calls me Amelia, except my grandmother, and she doesn't like me.' She didn't smile, though it had the air of a practised joke, as if she said it at every introduction.

'Amy, then. Please sit down. You're Mr Wiseman's secretary?'

'Assistant,' she corrected firmly, as though it mattered. 'Please, what's happening? They said he's . . . That he fell from the window. Is he . . .? He's not really dead?'

'I'm sorry,' said Slider.

She nodded slowly. She looked pale and strained, but was evidently holding herself in control, for which Slider admired her. She was tall and athletic-looking, seemed to be in her late thirties, and had unusually clear, almost transparent skin, that made her look as though she had been polished. If she was wearing any make-up, it could only have been the merest touch on lips and eyelashes, for she looked entirely natural, and luckily had the bones to carry it off. Her hair was dark brown and shiny, drawn back into a severe chignon, and she wore a well-cut skirt suit and low-heeled courts. The garb, combined with the no visible make-up, gave her an uncompromising look. Slider guessed she was efficient at her job and didn't suffer fools gladly, which made him wonder how that fitted with Wiseman's Bad Boy reputation – if, in fact, Atherton was remembering correctly. More questions for later – though with any luck, he'd never need to ask them.

'And this is where you work?' he asked. She nodded. 'Just you? I notice there are two desks in here. Is that one Mr Wiseman's?'

'That was Liana's. There used to be two of us, but she left a few months ago. Ed has his own office upstairs. He lives up there, mostly.'

'What about the room across the hall?'

'That's the clients' waiting room. We have receptions in there, too, parties and so on – for business purposes,' she clarified. 'There's a big kitchen down in the basement, big enough for catering. Ed's office is on the next floor, and his snug, as he calls it, where he sits in the evening.'

'And the top floor?'

She turned her eyes away. 'His bedroom and bathroom. I don't go up there. Strictly private. When you live and work in the same building, you need boundaries.'

'Does he live here alone?'

'Yes.'

This seemed less than helpful. 'He's not married?'

'Divorced. A long time ago.'

'Does he have a current girlfriend?'

'Nobody serious, that I know of.' She hesitated, and added, 'He has a lot of friends, and many of them are women. But I couldn't speak to the state of his heart.'

Fair enough, Slider thought. Working here alone with him for much of the time, you would expect her to be in on his secrets. On the other hand, if he liked to maintain boundaries between work and play, perhaps he'd keep her at arms' length, for his own protection.

'When did you last see Mr Wiseman?' he asked.

'Yesterday,' she said quickly, as though she'd been expecting that one. 'When I left to go home last night. About six twenty, six thirty, give or take. I couldn't say to the minute.'

'And how was he when you left?'

'He was perfectly all right,' she said defensively.

'I mean, what was his mood like? Was he happy, sad, worried . . .'

'None of those. I mean, he was just ordinary, just the same as always.'

'Was he in general a happy person? Good humoured? Easy going? Or was he moody, difficult, exacting?'

She gave a faint smile. 'He could be all of those things. But mostly he's happy. It's his job to get on with people, so he's very charming and easy to talk to, but that really *is* him. I mean, it isn't an act. You can't make people like you, if you're not what you seem.'

'Good point,' Slider said, to encourage her. 'You liked him?'

'Yes, I liked him. I think everybody did.'

'And did he have any particular problems lately? Money worries? Personal problems?'

'None that I knew of.'

He remembered the falling out of the window issue. 'Any health issues? Did he suffer from dizzy spells? Heart okay?'

She looked doubtful. 'He was as fit as a flea, as far as I know. Why do you ask?'

Slider sidestepped that. 'You say you left some time after six. Do you know what his plans were for the evening?'

'He said he was spending the evening reading manuscripts.'

'Here, at home? Was he expecting company?'

'Not as far as I know. There was nothing in his diary. Why, do you think there was someone else here?' she added anxiously.

He smiled at her. 'I haven't got as far as thinking yet. These are just routine questions we always have to ask.'

'But it *was* an accident, wasn't it?' she pressed, anxiously.

'That's what we're here to find out. Don't worry about it. There always have to be questions asked when an unexpected death occurs.'

'Unexpected death,' she repeated, blankly. Her lips quivered.

He was afraid she might be cracking. He distracted her. 'I'm going to go up to have a look at his office now. I may want to talk to you some more afterwards, if you don't mind.'

She looked away with an air of weariness. 'I'm not going anywhere,' she said.

Slider mounted the stairs with Atherton behind him. 'I like her style,' he said.

'Plain and wholesome?'

'Why not? And I admire self-control.'

'Better when they babble. You learn more.' Atherton shivered. It did feel cold up here, but it was presumably a psychic shiver, because he said, 'I'm not liking this.'

'What happened to "ours not to wassname"?'

'I'm starting to wassname. I hope it was obviously an accident. I don't want to be stuck on this for weeks.'

'Why should we be?'

'Poisoned chalice,' Atherton reminded him.

Slider didn't want Carpenter breathing down his neck for weeks – or at all, indeed. 'In and out,' he promised. 'Quick as a bunny. Unless we find a note, there's no reason to think suicide.' They reached the landing. 'Gloves and shoe coverings,' he said. Atherton gave him a look. 'Just basic precaution. Just in case.'

'In case what?'

'It's better to get into good habits,' Slider said. 'Upstairs first, I think.'

Wiseman's bedroom had a double bed, which was unmade, and there was a frowsy smell in the air. On the bedside cabinet on one side there was a used coffee mug and an empty wine glass, on the other a wine glass still containing a little red wine. Further inspection revealed an empty water glass on the windowsill, and another coffee mug, somewhat crusty, standing just under the bed.

'Multiple vessels. Maybe he had company after all,' Atherton said.

'No knowing how long they've been there,' Slider said. 'Maybe he was just a slob.'

A built-in wardrobe covered the whole wall opposite the window, and was mirrored floor to ceiling, making the room look bigger. It was full of expensive clothes, beautiful suits, cashmere sweaters, designer jeans, fine leather shoes. And in the bathroom, there was a variety of grooming products: body creams, after-shave balm, hair-volumising shampoo, hot oil treatments, colognes – even a pot calling itself Dead Sea Mud Facial for Men.

'Blimey!' said Slider mildly.

Atherton was certainly not of the 'real men don't moisturise' school of thought, but even he blinked. 'Vanity, all is vanity,' he said. 'However, please note the soap scum round the basin, spots on the mirror and caps left off bottles and tubes. Seems you're right – he was a slob.'

'I'll take the bathroom cabinet, you take the bedroom drawers. Looking for any medications that might cause dizziness. Or evidence of recreational drugs.'

'Or a terminal illness that might make him want to kill himself,' Atherton said.

But there was nothing of note, only the usual over-the-counter nostrums that a man of mature years might keep about him, and several packets of condoms. 'Which doesn't prove anything,' Slider concluded.

'*Au contraire*,' said Atherton. 'A man who needs that many condoms has no reason to kill himself. I'm coming down for accident.'

The other room on the top floor was a spare bedroom only by virtue of having a single divan bed pushed up against the wall, and a chest of drawers crammed into the corner. The rest of the space was taken up by a rowing machine, a weights bench and a rack containing graded hand weights. A full-length mirror was screwed to the wall opposite it.

'Ah, so this is where he exercises the manly bod, keeps himself in trim,' said Atherton.

'You sound as if it's a criticism.'

'Not at all. Good for him, at his age. Make the most of what you've got, while you've still got it.'

Slider snorted, heading for the stairs.

Wiseman's 'snug', across the hall from his office on the middle floor, had a fireplace that was obviously used, books on every wall that were obviously read, old, saggy armchairs and a sofa that were well sat-in, a carpet worn almost to holes in the most popular spots. There was a faint, old smell of cigarettes, and used ashtrays here and there. On a table in the corner was a tray containing decanters – brandy, whisky, gin. There was a sound system and a good collection of CDs, plus a lot of vinyl – mostly classics and jazz.

'He looked after his records all right,' Atherton noted. 'Nothing left out of its sleeves.' One was lying on top of the turntable lid, as though it had been the last record played, but even that was safely sleeved. 'Julie London,' Atherton said. 'Nice. But everything's turned off. He wasn't listening to music when the end came.'

Beyond this room was a lavatory, and beyond again a tiny kitchenette with a small refrigerator, kettle and coffee machine.

'Very cosy,' said Atherton.

'This is where he holed in, all right. He had everything for his immediate needs without going downstairs.'

'Is that important?'

'I don't know. It just suggests a mindset – that he was very much a bachelor.'

'She said he's been divorced a long time.'

'True. Now for the office.'

'The departure hall,' said Atherton.

'Presumably,' Slider cautioned.

Wiseman's office was on the left at the top of the stairs, above the ground-floor office. It was cold, of course, because the window was wide open. There was moss-green carpet on the floor, a small, cast-iron fireplace, which seemed unused, and the walls were painted cream – what could be seen of them. There were book-shelves floor to ceiling opposite the fireplace, and every other inch seemed to be covered with framed pictures of one sort or another – mementoes of an eventful life, Slider supposed. Even the mantel-piece over the fire was laden with photos, cards and invitations, a pewter mug which seemed to be stuffed with bills or receipts, a trophy of some kind, and a couple of elderly silver sports cups.

Standing with its back to the window, for the light, was a big old mahogany desk with a green leather inlay, and an expensive black leather desk chair – the tilty, wheely sort – pushed neatly in. On the desk was a reading lamp, switched on, and a manuscript apparently in the process of being read: two-thirds in the to-do pile, one third turned face down beside it, done. A pencil lay on the top sheet, and there were scribbled comments in pencil in the margin. A ring notebook lay beside the script, with more jottings on the exposed page. On the other side was a brandy balloon with a fair serving of amber fluid in it. The ashtray on the desk contained the mashed-out stub of a slim panatela and some ash, but the room did not smell of smoking, perhaps because the window had been wide open all night. There was an old-fashioned corded telephone, in the 1960s style, in ivory – the retro colour of choice. There was a wire in-tray containing a pile of mis-matched folders and A4 envelopes, presumably more manuscripts, and a china mug containing pens and pencils.

A second desk of modern make, pushed up against the wall beside the door, took care of the computer, keyboard, and printer/scanner, and also a small portable television.

'Well,' said Atherton at last, 'you can see the scenario. He's sitting there, reading some no-hoper's novel—'

'Why no-hoper?'

'Look at how much he's scribbled on it.'

'If it was hopeless, he wouldn't waste time on it, would he?' Slider objected.

'All right, he's reading a manuscript that needs improvement, gets up to stretch, decides to have a look at how the work's going next door, leans out too far – aided by the brandy, probably – and goes over.'

Slider went over to the window, put his head out and looked down. He was familiar with the urge that sometimes comes over people when they look over a cliff, but there was nothing inviting about the prospect below him, of scaffolding poles, hard edges and metal things. He drew back in and looked around. Something was bothering him, but he couldn't think what it was. He shook it away, for the subconscious to work on.

Atherton took Slider's place at the window and looked down. 'I can't believe it was suicide. It's such a messy way to do it. And inefficient – you're just as likely to end up alive and badly hurt as dead.'

'People commit suicide in needlessly messy and painful ways all the time,' Slider pointed out.

'Usually because they're stupid. Wiseman was an intelligent person. You can always find ways of doing it, less painful ways. And he'd have the imagination to foresee agonising injuries or paralysis.'

'Hmm,' said Slider. 'The overhead light's on, as well as the reading lamp. It must have been dark. So when he looked out, he might not have seen the detail of what was below. Just a chasm. They say that if you look into an abyss for long enough, sooner or later the abyss looks back at you.'

'Very poetic. But I'm not convinced. He knew what was there, whether he saw it or not. It's still accident for me.'

'That window isn't easy to fall out of,' said Slider. 'You'd have to lean your whole body out to go past the point of balance.'

'Well, why not? Maybe he was checking on the state of his brickwork. And he'd just got up from his desk, so he might have been dizzy. Or a bit drunk. You can't say it's not possible.'

'I wouldn't dream of saying that.'

'What's up, guv? It's *supposed* to be accident. Everyone *wants* it to be accident. You're not trying to make it suicide after all?'

'Of course not. There's no note. And he was working – no suggestion he was in a troubled state of mind. It all looks good.'

'Except?' Atherton queried. 'I know that tone of voice.'

'Nothing. I don't know. Something bothered me, but I can't see what it was now. It certainly looks all right for accident.'

'There's absolutely nothing to suggest anything else, so we can get out of here,' Atherton said beguilingly.

'Just take some pictures of the general layout,' Slider said.

While Atherton was doing that, he stood where he was, by the window, and looked round slowly, in case he could spot the anomaly. Despite Wiseman's apparent slobbiness in other areas, the room was clean, the comb-marks of recent vacuuming on the carpet, no accumulation of dust on surfaces. As he moved his head a tiny glint caught his eye, and bending down, he saw a minuscule screw on the carpet, right up against the skirting board under the window. How come the Hoover hadn't picked it up? he wondered vaguely. But there was always a thin strip at the edges that the machine couldn't reach, wasn't there?

'All right,' he said, seeing that Atherton had finished. 'Another quick word with Miss Hollinshead, and we can wrap this up.'

THREE
Can't Help Loathing That Man of Mine

When Slider reached the downstairs hall again, Hart came back in through the front door. 'Doc's here, boss, if you want to speak to him. They're taking the body away.'

'I'll have a quick word,' Slider said.

Freddie Cameron, still in paper suit, though without the head coverings, mask and gloves, was on the pavement, looking at his mobile, as everyone seemed to be these days when they weren't doing anything else. He looked up as Slider approached. 'Morning!' He gestured with the phone. 'Text from the daughter,' he explained.

'Catherine? How is she? I haven't seen her since she was Liesl in *The Sound of Music*.'

Cameron raised an eyebrow. 'That was a few moons ago. And she's Kate now. Thought Catherine Cameron was a bit of a mouthful. Kate Cameron's snappier. She's getting married.'

'Congratulations,' Slider said. 'She won't be Cameron much longer, then, anyway.'

'They don't change their names these days. Causes too much trouble at work.' Catherine was a portfolio manager with J P Morgan. 'He's a bond dealer in the same building as her. Nice chap.'

'So you approve?'

Cameron grinned. 'Since when does approval come into it? But it's nice for Martha and me to feel comfortable with her choice.'

'Big wedding?'

'Sounds that way,' said Cameron. 'They've both got a lot of friends.'

'I hope you've been saving,' said Slider.

'Oh, they'll be paying for it themselves. We offered, but they actually earn more than we do, so it seemed silly to insist. And this way they can have it exactly the way they want. I think some kind of foreign venue is on the cards.' He gave Slider a rueful smile. 'You'll find out.'

'Not for a long time yet, thank God,' said Slider. His daughter, also a Kate, was only twelve. At the moment she regarded boys with an impatient contempt that was a great comfort to him.

'So what's the story here? I didn't call you over, since the body'd already been moved. Rigor is fully developed, so I'd put the death at twelve to eighteen hours ago. Was it suicide or accident?'

'That's what I'm here to find out,' said Slider. 'Presumably the fall did it?'

'It's consistent with a fall from that window. I'll do the post tomorrow, but there's plenty there to cause death – head injuries and a broken neck, to name but a few.' He gave Slider a canny, penetrating look. 'Not a sensible way to choose, if it was suicide.'

'No,' said Slider. 'We rather hope it was an accident.'

'That's what I supposed. A man with connections, I gather. Not sure how you'd prove it either way – but that's your problem.'

'Thanks,' said Slider.

'So, I'll be off on my appointed rounds, then, and let you have the report tomorrow. Good luck.'

As he headed for his elegant grey whisper of a Jaguar, someone else jumped out of a bile-green Yaris and pranced towards Slider, a gleam of authority in her eye. It was the PR guru from headquarters. He sighed inwardly. He knew Lily Saddler was a stayer, because she had outlasted the previous commander, Mr Wetherspoon, and he admired her for that, but he couldn't like her. She was small, Glaswegian and hard as polished enamel, and though he had been assured she had charm when schmoozing the press, he never saw any of it. She was convinced that her job was more important than his, which was hard for a DCI to take. Unfortunately, when it came to celebrity corpses, the Brass tended to agree with her.

He got his word in first. 'I can't spare you long. I've got an interviewee in there getting cold.'

'You've got a witness to the fall?' Saddler asked quickly, her sharp crow's eyes pecking holes in Slider's skull to get at the juicy thought processes inside.

'Not as far as I know. Person who worked with him. Possible last person to see him alive.'

'Oh.' She was disappointed. 'Well, make sure you don't tell her more than she tells you. We don't want any *more* leaks.'

'Who's talking about leaks?' Slider said, letting the insult to his professionalism slide past. There was never any point in arguing with the Saddlers of this world.

'*Somebody* told the press Ed Wiseman was found dead. Why d'you think I'm here? Dave is very unhappy about it.' The chummy use of Carpenter's first name was meant to display her power to Slider, the PR equivalent of a baboon's bottom. He bet she wouldn't call him Dave to his face. 'So let's make sure there are no more slip-ups. Do you know the cause of death yet?'

'Falling out of a window onto a wheelbarrow full of bricks,' said Slider.

She gave him an impatient look that said, *Strike one*! 'I'm quite well aware of that. Can I say it was accidental death?'

'That's one possible interpretation of the facts so far,' he said.

'*One* possible interpretation?' She seemed about to say more, but studying his face, fell silent a moment.

'All right,' she said at last, 'I'm going to issue a statement along the lines of, "Ed Wiseman was found dead at his home this morning in what appears to be a tragic accident." Any objections to that?'

Would I dare? Slider asked silently.

Failing of an answer, she snorted in an annoyed way and said, 'Just so long as nobody on your side contradicts that.'

'Aren't we all on the same side?' he asked innocently.

Strike two! 'Say nothing more than that to any media person who approaches you. Those words exactly – don't improvise. And don't let anyone else on your team say *anything*. Not even "no comment". Do I make myself plain?'

'Quite,' he said. 'I have to go now.'

He gained the top of the shallow steps before her voice reached him. 'And if I was you, I'd make damn sure it *was* an accident before the end of the day.'

He stopped and turned round. 'What *are* you suggesting?' he said sternly.

She didn't flinch. 'The media won't be held off by a "looks like" for more than a day – two at the most. If we don't confirm, they'll start speculating. I want to kill this tomorrow at the latest. I want it to be a non-story.'

He gave her a thoughtful look, turned and left without a word.

Atherton was waiting in the hall. 'What did Wee Jimmy Krankie want?'

'Who?'

'Scottish comic character. Look it up online. With that helmet hair, she's the spitten image when she smiles. Have you ever seen her smile?'

'Actually, no,' Slider discovered. 'I don't think she likes me.'

'You *are* a PR nightmare,' Atherton allowed. 'But I don't think she likes any of us. I tried to get on her good side once, but I fell off the other side without finding it.'

'You didn't ask her out?' Slider said, horrified.

Atherton gave him a look so cool you could have kept a side of salmon on it for a month. 'What *do* you think of me? What did she want, anyway?'

'I'm to say it appears to be a tragic accident. You lot are to say nothing.'

Atherton shrugged. 'Are we going to talk to the Hollinshead woman now?'

'Yes – I'm sorry it's taken so long. Is she still holding up?'

'Extremely well. Probably hasn't sunk in yet.'

Watched over impassively by WPC Lawrence, Amy Hollinshead was still sitting staring at nothing, but she looked exhausted. It would be sinking in right about now, Slider thought, and he pitied her. She had lost not only someone she had worked with closely for years, and probably admired, but also her job – and while he had no idea how easy it was in the publishing world to get a new one, it meant a violent disruption to her life.

'I won't keep you much longer,' he said kindly. 'Just a few more questions.'

'You've seen his office?' she said, looking up anxiously. 'Does it – did he really fall out of the window?'

As opposed to jump? Slider imagined the question. 'It looks likely that that's what happened.' She closed her eyes a moment as if in pain. 'You said that he didn't have any medical conditions that you were aware of, that might make him overbalance?'

'He was fit and well, as far as I knew,' she said faintly.

'Did he drink a lot?'

That sharpened her. 'He wasn't a drunk,' she said.

'But he obviously did like a drink,' said Slider. 'Decanters in his snug. And a glass of brandy on the desk.'

'Yes, he liked a drink. Lots of people do. But I never saw him the worse for it. He just got smilier. Never bad-tempered. Never unsteady, or slurring his words, or anything like that.' She was defending him like a lioness her cub.

Slider switched course. 'Tell me about yesterday. Was he in the office all day?'

'No, he had lunch with Cathy Beccles. She's rights manager at Wolff and Baynes. The publishers.' He waited, and she filled in the silence. 'That's quite a big part of his job, keeping in with editors and rights directors and so on, all the people who can affect the progress of a book, or an author.'

'What time did he get back?'

'About half past four, quarter to five. I'm not sure exactly.'

'Isn't that rather a long lunch?'

'Not really. About the usual. They were old friends.'

'Then I suppose it would be quite a boozy lunch,' Atherton put in smoothly, very much matter-of-fact. 'I know those sort of occasions.'

'Well, they *had* alcohol,' she said doubtfully. 'I could smell it on his breath when he came in. But he wasn't drunk. And Cathy would have had to go back to work, so they wouldn't have been drinking hard.'

Slider took it back. 'And what sort of mood was he in when he got back?'

'Oh, fine. Cheerful. Just normal.'

'Then what did he do?'

'Got changed. Did some emails, some paperwork. We talked a bit about routine business. Then I went home.' Another shadow flitted across. 'And that was the last time I saw him.'

'What was he wearing?' Slider slipped the question in.

'Wearing? Well, a suit to go up to Town, of course. Then he changed into cords and a sweater,' she answered. She examined his face. 'Bottle green cords and a grey cashmere sweater, if it matters?'

'Was that what he usually wore to hang around the house alone? He didn't dress down more?'

'You mean, slob clothes? No,' she said, with a hint of reproof. 'He wasn't made that way. He was always smart, whatever he was doing. Why do you ask?'

'It was what he was wearing when he was found, and I was wondering what he did during the evening, after you left. He looked smart enough to have been going out again, or having company in.'

'I told you, he said he was reading manuscripts all evening. And there was nothing in his diary about a visitor.'

'Still, someone might ring him and come round. Or he might go out later – for something to eat, for instance?'

'He didn't eat much in the evenings,' she said, 'and especially not if he'd had lunch out. He was very careful of his figure. His health in general. He was very serious about keeping fit and well.'

'Yes, we saw his exercise gear in the spare room upstairs,' said Atherton.

An arrested look crossed her face. 'What is it?' Slider asked.

'He could have had a visitor, of course,' she said in a distant voice, as though she was thinking about something else. 'I think he'd have mentioned if he knew someone was coming round, but someone might drop in. As you say.'

'You thought of something just then,' Slider persisted. 'What was it?'

She shook her head, tried to smile, found it painful and stopped trying. 'It was when you mentioned . . . Upstairs. His private space.' She gave a little gulp. 'I just suddenly realised – I'll never see him again. It's hardly sunk in yet. I can't . . .'

That sentence didn't seem to go anywhere. He watched her for a moment, chewing her lip. Then he asked, 'You've worked for him for a long time?'

'Thirteen years,' she said. 'Before that I was an editorial assistant with Random House, but after four years there, it all began to seem too . . . corporate. I wanted more hands-on contact with books and authors. I saw an advertisement for a job with Wiseman & Cantor, had an interview, and they hired me right away.'

'Cantor?' Slider queried.

'That was Reggie's maiden name. Regina Cantor, Ed's wife. Ex-wife, I should say. She was an agent too. After they divorced and she left the partnership, he went back to just Wiseman, but it was still Wiseman and Cantor when I joined.'

The questions had settled her, and he rose to go, thanking her for her co-operation. 'Lawrence here will take down your statement, and then you're free to leave.'

'That's all right,' she said vaguely. She looked a little dazed. 'If you need to ask me any more questions . . . *Anything* you need. Ed was . . . such a wonderful person. I want to help.' She met his eyes. 'You don't think it was suicide, do you? He seemed happy. I can't bear to think he was unhappy, and hiding it. It *was* an accident, wasn't it?'

To avoid answering that question, Slider asked one of his own, that he should have got in earlier. 'Oh, by the way, did he wear glasses? Contact lenses?'

'Glasses, but just for reading,' she said automatically. 'Why do you ask?'

'We found a pair. What did they look like?'

'Just ordinary, rather old-fashioned. Brown frames.' He showed her the photograph on the tablet. 'Yes, that looks like them.' She seemed shaken.

He had reached the door when she said abruptly, 'Can I see him?'

He said, 'He's been taken away now. I'm sorry.' But he wasn't. He thought of the battered face. She should be spared that.

When they eventually returned to the car, Atherton said, 'Clearly Hollinshead was in love with her boss.'

'Steady,' said Slider. 'Clearly she liked and admired him.'

'No surprise if she did. He was supposed to be Mr Charisma. Anyway, it looks like accident, so that lets us off the hook. At least, there's no evidence of suicide. I presume that will please Mr Carpenter.'

'He might want us to look through Wiseman's papers to make sure he didn't have any money problems or health worries – any reason to top himself.'

'If he doesn't *want* it to be suicide, he's better off not having us dig any further, isn't he? I mean, you can always find *something* in a person's life that wasn't hunky-dory.'

'Hmm,' said Slider absently.

Atherton glanced at him. 'What?'

'I don't know,' Slider replied. A pause. 'Just . . . something.'

'A consummate answer. Want to drive?'

'No, I want to look him up on Wiki. I really don't know anything about him.'

'I'm quicker at that than you. You drive, I'll Google.'

Slider grunted, but agreed. He eased the car out of the parking spot.

Atherton started scrolling. 'Well, look at this,' he said. 'Conjunctivitis.com. That's a site for sore eyes.'

'Get on with it!'

'Ok. Wiki, then: Edward Falcon Wiseman.'

'Falcon? Named after Scott of the Antarctic?'

'Who knows? Age sixty-seven.'

'He looks good for it.'

'Yes, and it puts all those condoms into context,' Atherton said. 'Born in Cheltenham, father Leo Wiseman, literary agent. Mother Miranda Hastings, actress.'

'Never heard of her.'

'Me neither. Probably gave it up to become a mother. Oxford University, Classics degree. Editorial jobs at Faber, Heinemann, Chatto & Windus, and then joined his father's firm, the Leo Wiseman Literary Agency.'

'Imaginative name.'

'Later they had professional differences—'

'What were they?'

'Doesn't say.' Atherton scrolled on. 'So he left and set up on his own. Married Regina Cantor, also an agent, went into partnership as Wiseman & Cantor Literary Agency. Children Olivia, thirty-seven, Ivo, thirty-five. Among his clients are John Grisewood. Spy stories. Le Carré-esque,' he explained kindly to Slider.

'I know that. I've heard of him. I'm not a complete philistine.'

'Martin Pusey. Maritime adventures. Nelson's navy.'

'I *know*.'

'Virginia Foulkes.'

'Don't know her.'

'History mysteries. Regency detective stories.'

'*What?*'

'It's true.'

'How do you know? Don't tell me you read that sort of thing.'

'Ex-girlfriend Lucinda used to read them.'

'Did they even *have* detectives in Regency times?'

'Who knows?' Atherton shrugged. 'Detective Dandies. Forensic fops. Beau Brummell with a bloodhound. Lucinda seemed to like them.' He scrolled on. 'And Guest Halliday, author of the Kay Tortelli medical examiner mysteries.'

'I know about *them*,' said Slider. 'Every case solved by forensic experts alone. You'd never know detectives existed,' he concluded bitterly. 'Except to flounder about, baffled, and be rescued from humiliation by the giant brains of the scientists.'

'So she was one of his. I'm impressed!' Atherton said. 'I doubt if he had money worries, in that case. He must make a fortune out of her alone.'

'Really? I don't actually know how literary agents work.'

'They negotiate all the rights and get a percentage of everything the author earns. And remember, the Kay Tortelli stuff's been on television.'

'I know. Irene used to watch them.' Irene was his first wife. 'But I think she did it just to annoy me. I don't think she really understood them.'

'I saw a couple of episodes,' Atherton admitted. 'I was particularly fascinated by the women's long pointed fingernails, wondering how come they didn't pierce through the latex gloves.'

As they passed Porson's room, the Old Man called out, 'Slider. In here.'

'No, Slider out here,' he muttered. But he went in anyway. Atherton went on down the corridor.

Porson was standing by the filing cabinet, reading something laid out on the top. He had a pathological dislike of sitting down. Slider remembered reading somewhere that Tudor people had slept sitting up because they thought that if they lay down flat, God would think they were dead and whisk their souls away. And then they would be.

Less welcome was the sight of the borough commander, sitting in Porson's seat behind his desk. He looked up sharply as Slider came in. 'Report,' he snapped.

Slider picked his words carefully. 'We didn't find a suicide note.'

'Good!'

'His assistant says everybody liked him and he didn't have any health problems or money worries.'

'Good!'

'She also said he liked a drink. And there was a glass of brandy on the desk where he was working.'

'Even better. So you can wrap it up, then. Accidental death. Finish it tonight.'

'I have to wait for the post-mortem report tomorrow.'

Porson stirred a little, restively, but Carpenter positively scowled. 'What the devil did you call for a post-mortem for?'

'In the case of an unexpected death, sir—'

'There has to be an inquest. There doesn't have to be a post-mortem!'

'I'd have thought all concerned would be glad of the reassurance, sir,' Slider said delicately. 'Just to tie up all possible ends.' He swallowed. 'And I'd like to call in SOC.'

Carpenter exploded. 'What the hell for?'

'Some nice fingermarks in the right position on the window-sill would clinch it.'

'Rubbish! Wouldn't prove a thing! His own fingermarks in his own house? What the hell's the matter with you? I give you one simple thing to do . . . I sometimes wonder about your sanity, Slider, I really do.'

Slider bore it meekly. Bosses had to berate those below them, otherwise how did they know they were bosses? Fish gotta swim, birds gotta fly, brass gotta make you wish you could die . . .

'Don't even *think* of spending any further money on this,' Carpenter concluded. 'And get it wrapped up tomorrow.'

He waved a dismissive hand, and Slider oozed out. Porson followed him, and in the corridor stood close and said quietly, so that Carpenter wouldn't hear, '*Is* there something wrong?'

Slider couldn't answer. He just felt uneasy. But he couldn't mention that to Porson, who could be scathing about 'hunches' if they didn't fit in with his budgetary constraints. And Porson was a man who took to constraints of any sort like a cat to water.

'No, sir,' Slider said. His private niggle would either resolve itself, or it wouldn't.

Porson gave him a long, speculative look. He knew his Slider, and on the whole trusted his instincts, but letting him run with them could turn out very inconvenient to all around him, as he had discovered on previous occasions. And anyway, you couldn't do everything. You had to prioritise. 'Post-mortem we have to have, now you've ordered it,' he said, 'but as soon as the report's in, wrap this up, so I can get Mr Carpenter off my . . . set his mind at rest. And get back to something important. Who's the next of kin?'

'Ex-wife, sir. Local police are informing her.'

Porson nodded dismissal, but as Slider turned away, he said, in the same quiet voice, 'Find out who leaked to the press. I was with Mr Carpenter when the Saddler woman gave him the news, and he wasn't pleased. That's how I got lumbered with it. If it was one of yours, I want to know.'

'Yes, sir,' said Slider. 'I don't like leaks either.'

'Nip it in the bug,' Porson said. 'Before it nips you.'

His people drifted in to report. None of the neighbours had seen or heard anything. London neighbours traditionally kept their eyes to themselves, and given that the fall could only have occupied a couple of seconds, they'd have had to be looking in exactly the right direction at exactly the right moment, so it wasn't surprising.

Site security seemed tight, and as far as one could determine the builders had knocked off between five and five thirty, though as Amy Hollinshead had seen him after six, that didn't add anything.

Hart came to his door. 'Anything else for me, boss? I'm off, otherwise.'

'You've written up the builders' statements?'

'Yeah, not that there was anything to 'em. Except that they said they'd never seen that window open before. We asked if deceased had been in the habit of looking out at the works, and they said not that they'd noticed.' She looked restless. 'Not that

that proves anything. I don't suppose they look up from their work that often. Bit of a non-starter, all this, innit?'

'It's supposed to be. Disappointed?'

'Well, if he's dead anyway, he might as well give us a bit of fun while he's at it.'

'That's a deplorable attitude. Oh, by the way – any idea who it was that tipped off the press?'

'Yeah, boss, it was one of the builders,' she answered at once.

'I thought they were Poles and didn't speak English?'

'They all speak a bit. But one of 'em was born over here, so he speaks it like a native. And apparently the site manager wasn't the only one to recognise Mr Next Door. This one's phoned his wife before even Uniform got there, she's got straight on to the papers, and once they've got the address it's easy enough to find out the name and realise he's a celeb – of sorts. I'd never heard of him,' she concluded scornfully.

'I see. Well, there was nothing you could have done about that. I'm glad it wasn't one of us.'

'Kidding? We wouldn't dare. We all know how you feel. And after the Holland Lodge business . . .' The leak enquiry after that case had taken longer than the original murder hunt.

Slider didn't want to be reminded. 'Don't probe the ulcer, sergeant. We were on a slippery slope there.'

She gave him a sassy grin. 'We got away with it, though. We're all still here. 'Cept I'm going home now. G'night!'

FOUR
China Syndrome

Atherton was the last. He appeared at Slider's door, still looking, even after a day's work, groomed and elegant. Slider, feeling grubby and rumpled, wondered how he did it. Probably had himself laminated. He remembered how, when he was a child growing up on an Essex farm, there had been a girl at junior school like that. Yvonne Manners. Never a hair out of place, whatever they'd all been doing. No one had liked her.

'You're the Yvonne Manners *de nos jours*,' he told Atherton. 'I bet you never even sweat.'

'In the first place,' Atherton said, 'I don't sweat, I perspire. And in the second place, I don't perspire. Emily's free tonight. Fancy meeting up later for a meal? We could meet halfway in King Street. Have a curry at Potli.'

'Can't,' Slider said. 'Joanna's at home with George tonight. Dad and Lydia are away.'

'We'll come to yours, then? Pick up a take-away on the way.'

'All right. I'll check with Joanna.'

He rang her, and she said she'd got a casserole on the go, but it would keep until tomorrow. 'It's always better the second day. And I'd like the company.'

'She says yes,' he translated to Atherton.

'Good. Will Yvonne be there?'

'I thought you weren't listening.'

'I'm always listening. Who is she, anyway?'

'A girl who never sweated.'

Emily was a freelance journalist, and being in the words business was the most interested of all of them in Ed Wiseman. 'I met him once,' she remembered as they passed the containers of curry around. 'Must be eight, ten years ago. At an awards dinner. Guest Halliday had just won the big crime novel award for the first Tortelli book, and there was a lot of griping by the native writers because it had gone to an American, and not to one of them. To add insult to injury, she didn't even turn up to the dinner. He had to receive the prize on her behalf, as her agent. Made a very funny speech, though,' she concluded. 'Almost won round the antis.'

'What was he like?' Joanna asked.

'Lean, athletic – always laughing.'

'What was he – a dolphin?' said Slider.

'And sexy,' Emily went on. 'Oh boy, was he sexy! When he gave you one of those looks, you could feel your insides melt.'

'Right here, beside you,' Atherton complained mildly. 'I *can* hear you.'

'Before your time, my pet,' Emily told him. 'I don't enquire into your distant past.'

And not so distant, Slider thought, but he didn't say it aloud. Joanna caught his eye and he knew she knew what he was thinking. Atherton was a serial romancer. Joanna had opined that Emily really ought to sew his trousers up before she let him out in the morning.

'He flirted with me most professionally,' Emily went on. 'I enjoyed it.'

'Apart from *that*,' Atherton said, 'what do you remember about him?'

She frowned in thought. 'Not from meeting him, but by reputation he was a roisterer in his heyday. Used to get thrown out of nightclubs, him and Lionel Tippet and somebody else. Who was it? I'll remember in a minute.' She drummed her fingers on the table to help memory along. 'Murray Pauling, that was it! They were a gang. I think the three of them were at uni together. Called themselves—'

'Let me guess: The Three Musketeers,' Atherton interrupted witheringly.

'Actually, no, smarty-pants. It was the something club.' Her phone appeared in her hand like magic and she rattled away like machine-gun fire. 'The Claret Club, that was it. Apparently like the Bollinger, but with more refinement.'

'And who *were* the other two?' Joanna asked, just beating Slider to it. 'I mean, what did they do?'

'They were all in the publishing world. Tippet was an editor – with Hodder, I think – and Pauling was with Mirador and then started up his own publishing house, New Avalon.' She reached for the rice. 'It's a shame Ed Wiseman's dead. The world needs charmers like him.'

'He sounds like a bottom pincher,' Atherton grumbled.

'I wouldn't know. But if he did, he'd do it with style. So, you just have to decide if it was accident or suicide, is that it? Anyone want some tarka dal?'

'It's cruel, eating otters,' Slider said, passing it on. 'Any views, suicide-wise? You're the only one of us who ever met him.'

'I didn't *know* the man. He flirted with everyone, charmed everyone, was always full of life and fun. But that can be a cover-up for a deep loneliness.'

'Thank you, Dr Joyce,' said Atherton. 'Or he might have been exactly what he seemed, and just leaned out too far.'

Emily grinned. 'You're jealous. I like it!'

Later they retired to the drawing room to be comfortable, and when Slider went back to the kitchen to get more beers, Joanna followed him. 'I'm worried about those two,' she said.

'I don't think he's really jealous,' he said, surprised. 'It's just play.'

'I didn't mean that. I think they've got a deeper problem. She wants a baby, and I don't think he's up for it.'

Slider raised his hands defensively. 'I can't possibly get involved in that sort of discussion. I work with the man.'

'I know. I don't expect you to comment. Anyway, it's the modern problem, isn't it? Woman wants baby, man wants to stick with his old freewheeling life. Only the woman's got a hormone deadline to meet.'

She sounded so low about it, he put down the bottles and put his arms round her. 'Do you think about it often – the miscarriage?'

'I wasn't thinking about me,' she said, giving him a squeeze, 'but thanks for worrying. This Wiseman business – it's not going to mean long hours, I hope?'

'No, it should all be cleared up tomorrow.'

'Because remember you've got George this weekend. I'm working.'

'I remember.'

He didn't have a good night, and gave up on it at six, leaving Joanna sleeping to go downstairs and make a cup of tea and put on the radio. Not music – the news programme. He could tune out voices, but music could too easily become an earworm. Wiseman's name caught him back from his thoughts.

'Ed Wiseman, the well-known literary agent, was found dead at his West London home yesterday in what appears to be a tragic accident. Over a long career, Wiseman represented many famous authors, including John Grisewood, Martin Pusey and Guest Halliday.'

And then it was on to the sport. Lily Saddler had done a good job of restricting interest, Slider thought. Without his inconvenient doubts, it could all be closed down today with the minimum of disruption.

Joanna came into the kitchen, yawning, her hair in spikes. George followed her, frowning in concentration over a Transformer robot, trying to get it to turn into a sports car.

'Breakfast?' he asked her. 'Scrambled eggs, bacon, toast?'

'Are you offering or asking?'

'I'll make it.'

'How nice. All of the above, then, please. I'll make the tea. Come on, Boy, let me put you in your chair.'

George was too preoccupied to object. 'He keeps being a robot,' he complained as Joanna heaved him into his booster seat. Now he was running around everywhere, he was getting to be a chunky child, not fat, but a solidity of bone and muscle. 'He won't be a car.'

'Let me see,' said Joanna, reaching.

George pulled his hands and the toy away. 'Daddy do it.'

'Of course, because Daddy's a man and understands mechanical things,' Joanna said, going to put the kettle back on. 'And they tell you gender bias is learned, not innate.'

'That sounds unusually sharp, from you,' said Slider.

'I'm tired. We'll have to get separate beds if you're going to practise for the marathon all night,' she said.

'Eh?'

'Thrashing legs at all hours. No more curry and beer before bedtime for you, my lad.'

'Sorry. It wasn't that. I had something on my mind.'

'I know you can't help it, but I have sessions. I have to be on top of my game.'

'Oddly, so do I,' he said, and then wished he hadn't. It sounded sour, and effectively stopped conversation. They never quarrelled, but there was something almost approaching an atmosphere in the kitchen, and that was the last thing he needed.

Swilley was reporting to him on a case she'd been working, a 'carer' stealing from the houses she visited, when LaSalle came in with a mid-morning cup of tea for Slider and said, 'Is there anything else you want me to do on the Wiseman business, guv?'

'He was quite a big wheel, wasn't he?' Swilley said. 'I saw him on *Have I Got News For You* a while back. He was good. Accident, was it? Had he been drinking?'

Slider stared at her for a moment, thoughts working. Then he said, 'Can I run something by you? Both of you,' he added, as LaSalle made to leave.

'Sure, boss,' said Swilley. 'Is something bothering you?'

'Yes, and I don't know if it's really something, or I'm getting it out of proportion. Before she left some time after six o'clock, Wiseman told Amy Hollinshead that he was staying at home all evening, reading manuscripts. There was a manuscript on his desk, half-read, with scribbled notes on it. The reading lamp was on, and there was a glass of brandy on the desk beside the manuscript. The window behind the desk was pushed right up. One of those tall, old-fashioned sash windows. The position of the body is consistent with his having fallen out of it to his death.'

'So that looks all right,' Swilley prompted helpfully.

'Possibilities: one, he'd got up for a break and a stretch, looked out of the window to see how the building next door was getting on, leaned out too far, and overbalanced.'

'Right,' said Swilley.

'Two, he heard something, some sound from outside, went to the window to look out, leaned too far and overbalanced.'

'Right.'

'And there is possibility three, which is that he was overcome with despairing thoughts, got up and went to the window, and looking down into the abyss, gave in to them and threw himself out.'

LaSalle looked worried. 'Are we thinking it *was* suicide now, then?'

Swilley saw this was not the point. She flapped her fingers at LaSalle to still him, and said, 'Yes, boss, with you so far. What's the problem?'

Slider twiddled his pen between his fingers, frowning at it. 'His desk chair was pushed right in under the desk. If you get up for a break, or to look out of the window because you've heard some-thing, you don't push the chair back in, do you? You leave it out because you're coming back.'

Swilley was thinking. 'He didn't need to push the chair in to *get* to the window, did he?'

'No, the desk was well towards the middle of the room. There was plenty of space to pass behind, even with the chair right out. It wouldn't be in the way at all.' Slider showed her the layout on his tablet.

'It might have been a reflex action, maybe?'

Slider looked up at her. She wasn't arguing with him, just being thorough. 'Most people getting up from a desk shove themselves backwards as they stand, pushing the chair away behind them. And unless there's a particular reason to, do they really then go round behind the chair and push it back in before getting on with what they got up to do?'

LaSalle said helpfully, 'But what if he'd decided to kill himself? If it was sudden overwhelming despair? He could have been sitting there for hours, not working, just brooding over his problems, then finally he jumps up and just does it.'

'It still seems an odd thing to do, to push your chair back in.'

Swilley nodded. 'It's a matter of "what's wrong with this picture", isn't it? But it would be hard to make it the basis of a case.'

'I know. And there's something else,' Slider said. 'His glasses were found with him in the basement diggings. But according to Hollinshead, he only wore them for reading. I can't see in any of those three scenarios how he would look out of the window with them on. You can't look at distances through reading glasses. He'd take them off automatically as he stood up. They should have been lying on the desk with the manuscript.'

'Maybe he took them off, but was still holding them in his hand,' LaSalle offered.

'Even then, he'd need both hands to push the window up. He'd surely have put them down somewhere.' He watched LaSalle rehearse the action in mime. You pushed a sash window up with your palms. Glasses held in the hand would get in the way.

'So what's your thinking, boss?' Swilley asked.

He sighed unhappily. 'I'm thinking that someone *wanted* us to think that he was working on that manuscript, got up for a stretch, leaned too far out of the window and fell. The brandy was a little stage dressing – to suggest that perhaps he'd had too much to drink, which helped him lose his balance.'

'You think it was staged?' Swilley said.

'By somebody quite good, but not good enough.'

'And that means you think . . .?' said LaSalle.

'That he didn't fall,' said Slider, 'he was pushed.'

Porson poked his head round the door. 'I've just had Mr Carpenter on the blower again. Have you signed off on that Wiseman thing yet, and if not, why not?'

'I haven't heard from Freddie Cameron yet,' Slider said.

'Oh,' said Porson, withdrew, then snapped his head back through like a tortoise spotting a wild strawberry. 'What?' he positively barked.

'Sir?' said Slider warily.

'I know that face of yours. What are you cooking up?'

Slider hesitated, but answered. 'I have doubts about its being an accident.'

Porson put both hands up in a warding-off gesture. 'Oh no. Oh no, no, no. Do not do this to me.' But he waited, receptively, until Slider explained his two niggles. His eyes narrowed, but he did not immediately bellow. He was, above all else, a policeman. After a silence, he said, 'You can't go in front of a jury with just "he pushed his chair in" as evidence.'

'I know,' said Slider. 'But that's not to say there isn't more to find. If I'm allowed to look.'

Porson shifted his feet like a nervous horse. 'I don't know . . . We can't be wasting our time. Limited resources . . . On the other hand, he's high profile . . . If it turned out there *was* funny business and we missed it . . .'

Slider waited. He didn't particularly want to be thrown in the deep end of a poisoned chalice without a snorkel, but he knew, because he knew himself, that it would always nag at the back of his mind. The chair and the glasses didn't make sense, and in a torrid world he needed things to make sense.

Porson finally met his eyes with something like melancholy. 'Can't sign off till you hear what Cameron says. That gives me a few more hours to think about it. But these celebrity cases can be tricky. It can cut both ways, as the Chinaman said when he gave his father a two-edged knife. It'll probably be better all round to call it an accident.'

Better for who? Better for them, perhaps. Not for Wiseman. But he was past caring, wasn't he? *What's dead can't come to life, I think.* It was just the little matter of Truth, Justice and the Metropolitan way. Cheesy as that sounded, it did not behove coppers, however exalted their rank, to stop taking it into consideration.

And Porson knew it. He sighed. 'Let me know when you've heard from Cameron,' he said, and stomped away.

Slider came back from a meeting to his office to find Freddie Cameron bending over his desk, scribbling on his jotting-pad. 'What an unexpected pleasure,' Slider said. 'A man in a decent suit.'

Cameron straightened up, still immaculate after a day of carving corpses. Another Yvonne. It must be something to do with breeding – Freddie was cut glass from accent to shiny shoes. 'I was just writing you a note,' Cameron said. 'I happened to be passing on my way home, so I thought I'd pop in and tell you the news in person.'

'How civilised,' Slider said. 'I'd ring for sherry, but this is a luxury-free zone.'

'So I see,' said Cameron. 'You can't even offer a visitor a chair.'

'I don't have visitors. But I do have a very fine windowsill.'

'I'll stand, thanks. It's Wiseman. That's a copy of my findings—' he nodded towards the manila envelope he'd put on the desk – 'but in essence, it was the blows to the head that killed him. At least two forceful blows to the left side of the head with a heavy, blunt instrument, resulting in comminuted fractures of the os sphenoidale and the os zygomaticum and causing, inter alia, a catastrophic cerebral haemorrhage under the parietal bone. It was the bleed wot dun it,' he translated at the end. Even his cockney was exquisite.

Slider was trying to picture it. 'So,' he said slowly, 'he hit his head on the way down? On those protruding scaffolding poles, maybe?'

'I think not,' said Freddie, giving him an unnervingly kind look. 'The other injuries, broken neck, collarbone, humerus and so on, which were consistent with falling from a height onto a variety of unforgiving surfaces, were all post-mortem. Considerably post-mortem.'

Slider looked unhappy. 'He hit his head on the way down and then lay dying?'

'You're not listening. I said they were *post*-mortem. In my professional opinion, he was dead when he went out of the window. The blows to the head killed him almost instantly. The trophies he collected from the fall were neither here nor there. I'd say he was dead at least an hour before them.'

Slider stared. 'So it wasn't accident. Or suicide.'

'Unless he'd worked out a way to whack himself on the head while suspended in mid-air, no, I don't think it was suicide. And if the original blow was an accident, someone went to considerable trouble to cover it up.'

'Damn,' said Slider. 'I *knew* there was something wrong with it.'

'Then I've proved you right,' Cameron pointed out.

'I didn't want to be right. I'd always sooner be happy than right.'

Freddie smiled the serene smile of the man who delivers the bad news and then goes off to dine, secure in the knowledge that it's no longer his problem. 'Bad luck, old chap. Anything more I can do?'

'Tell me he had a fatal disease, so it was a mercy killing.'

'Nope. He was fit and healthy, very good musculature for a man his age. No sign of drug use. Stomach empty apart from a little wine—'

'Not brandy?'

Freddie smiled. 'I didn't analyse it. It *smelled* like wine. But there's no pathological sign that he was drugged or poisoned. Do you want a tox screen? I've taken his fingerprints and blood type, of course.'

Slider shook his head slowly like one goaded. 'This is not going to make me popular. Mr Carpenter particularly wanted it to be an accident.'

'Did he, indeed? Does that make him a suspect?'

'You're not helping, Freddie.'

'I'll go. Just let me know in your own time what tests you want me to send off for. Meanwhile – goodnight, sweet prince. And flights of anguish sing thee to thy rest.'

'They'll do that, all right.'

Porson gave him a bloodshot look. 'I might have known.'

'It isn't my fault, sir,' Slider pointed out.

'Just let me have a moan, all right?' He stamped up and down a bit, and then said, 'What do you need?'

'I'll have to put my whole team on it,' Slider said. 'The house secured. Full SOC work-up. He didn't hit himself on the head, so someone must have gone in there later that evening. Maybe they left traces.'

'No CCTV cameras nearby?'

'Sadly, not. But we may find the weapon, if it was dumped.'

'If it was me, I'd've dumped it on the building site next door.'

'That thought had occurred to me,' Slider said sadly. 'Plenty of heavy blunt instruments there to be going on with.'

'You'll have your work cut out,' Porson grunted. 'Any idea of motive?'

'Haven't got that far yet, sir. I'm told everybody liked him.'

'Well, everybody bar one,' Porson pointed out.

FIVE

The Regina Monologues

Atherton was singing, an old policeman's ditty, 'Don't ever hit a suspect with a shovel, it leaves a bad impression on his brain.'

'What have you got to be cheerful about?' Slider growled. He was driving.

'The game's afoot. It's exhilarating. The roar of the greasepaint, the smell of the crowd . . .'

'You're a victim of circuses,' said Slider.

'Why are we going back to the house?' Atherton enquired.

'I'd like to have another look at the departure lounge.'

'It's a bit dark, calling it that.'

'You said it first. Anyway, death *is* dark.'

'They say death is but a sleep,' said Atherton hopefully.

'But it's a lot harder to wake up in the morning,' said Slider.

SOC had finished with Wiseman's study, and Bob Bailey, the SOC top dog, reluctantly agreed they could go up.

'Did you find anything?' Slider asked.

'No blood,' said Bailey.

'The fatal blow didn't break the skin,' Slider said, 'so I didn't expect any.'

'Well, we haven't found anything that looks like a blunt instrument, so presumably chummy took it with him.'

Slider remembered the tiny screw, and asked about it.

'Yeah, we got that. Bagged it. Looks like it might've come out of a pair of specs.'

'Wiseman's glasses were broken,' Atherton said. 'One side arm was off.'

'It ought to be possible to match the screw to the specs,' said Bailey.

'I'm not sure that would add anything,' Slider said. 'Except that he was wearing them when he was attacked.'

Bailey lost interest. 'I got the rest of the house to do,' he said accusingly. 'Millions of fingermarks. Anything in partic I'm looking for?'

'Someone else was there that evening,' Slider said. 'Evidence of that someone, where they went and what they were doing.'

Bailey snorted. 'How about a signed confession while I'm at it? You don't want much. What d'you want to look at the office again for, anyway?' he went on in a complaining voice. Civilian experts came in two flavours, the ones who felt privileged to help the police, and the ones who liked to throw their weight around and show them up. It was curious, Slider thought, how few of the former he came across. 'You've got photographs.'

'No substitute for the naked eye,' said Slider.

The bookshelves, as they had previously noted, were full of books, which turned out on closer inspection to be pristine, and mostly hardbacks still in their dust jackets.

'Copies of titles Wiseman agented,' Atherton hazarded.

'Except for these,' Slider said. There was a whole shelf of *Wisdens*, cheerfully yellow, as recognisable as old friends. 'Some of them are historic,' he said, eyeing the dates. 'Could be worth a bit. I wonder what the connection was. He didn't agent them, surely.'

'Of course not.'

The rest of the walls were covered in photographs, posters for books, framed dust jackets, letters, press cuttings: his life measured out not in coffee spoons but in evidence of public notice. The anatomy of the deceased, exposed and undefended now. When death was unexpected, you lost control over what would be left behind for the next man in to judge you by, what image you would project to the cynical eye of the world. It put a whole new perspective on that *Reader's Digest Condensed Book* on your bedside table.

In the photos, a younger, darker-haired Wiseman, usually in evening dress, was snapped with various people, some of whom Slider recognised. Those he didn't mostly had a dazed expression of having been unexpectedly tapped on the head with something less than lethal, like a whole salmon perhaps, so he supposed they were writers who had just won some award or other, or were being honoured in some other way. Famous or not, Wiseman's arm was invariably round them, and his grin was huge, attractive and life-affirming.

Atherton drifted up behind him, and said, 'Oh, look, that's Lady Jane Flamborough. You know – big historical biographies.'

'I've heard of her. She's got a lot of diamonds,' Slider observed.

'She's a lot of rich,' Atherton said. He scanned more photos. 'Tactile chap, wasn't he?'

'You noticed?'

'He's even got his arm round John Grisewood, look, and *he*'s no cuddly bear.'

'Oh, is that who that is?'

Atherton gave him a look. 'I told you, cold war spy stories.'

'I know who John Grisewood *is*,' Slider said with dignity. 'I've just never seen a picture of him before.'

'No, I suppose most authors don't get to be recognised in the street,' Atherton agreed.

'Perhaps they wouldn't want to be,' said Slider. He looked some more. 'All this stuff is quite old,' he remarked.

'I suppose he'd run out of room for new stuff,' said Atherton.

'He could have swapped in.'

'With an arrangement like this, you tend not to start messing with it. Once it's up, it's up.'

'True, I suppose,' Slider said. 'You stop even seeing it after a while. But there is one space he could have used.'

Under the shelf of *Wisdens*, displayed on the wall among the frames, were four battered-looking cricket balls, displayed two by two, one above the other, each nestling on a separate round bracket – the sort of thing that might have held a tooth-mug. Presumably they meant something to Wiseman: what with the *Wisdens*, it seemed he had an interest in the game.

'Maybe he played when he was younger,' Slider said.

'Maybe he handled cricketing memoires,' Atherton offered.

'Anyway, there's a space.'

Between the pairs of balls there was indeed a remnant of unused wall – enough to have hung a couple more frames.

'Maybe there was something there at one time,' Slider said. At the top of the space, in the shadow of the shelf, was a wall-mounted spring clip.

Atherton shrugged it away. 'What I've been thinking is that if he was reading at the desk—'

'We don't know he was,' said Slider. 'That's just what we were supposed to think. He could have been anywhere in the house.'

'What about the tiny screw by the window?'

'Villain could have dropped it when he was throwing the glasses out. We mustn't make the mistake of buying the bit of theatre uncritically.'

'All right. But it's a fact that someone whacked him, which would be easier if he was sitting down.'

'Or was bending his head, examining something. He'd have his glasses on for that. Or he could have been reading in bed. We don't know what time it happened or what time he went to bed. What was your point?'

'Only that it was probably someone he knew. Rather than an intruder.'

'There were no signs of a break-in,' Slider agreed. 'I was rather assuming it was someone he knew, and that he let them in.'

'So we want someone with a secret grudge,' said Atherton.

'Why secret?'

'Would you let in your worst enemy, late at night, armed with a baseball bat?'

'He might have pushed his way in and walloped him right there in the front hall,' said Slider. 'The thing is, if this scenario in the departure lounge was a set-up, we really don't know anything about "how". We're going to have to do it backwards, starting with "who".'

'So we want someone tall, strong and cunning,' said Atherton. 'Or less tall, more cunning, and with a winning personality who could get the victim to sit down nicely to be clobbered.'

'We've got to look at phone records and computers, see if he was contacted by someone for a visit – he didn't necessarily tell Hollinshead everything. And his finances.'

'Good thinking. If it isn't passion, it's usually money,' said Atherton.

'And the more cunning,' Slider said, 'the less likely it is to be passion.'

'And what are *we* doing?'

'I'm going to pay a respectful visit to the ex-wife. You're the literary expert, so you're going to exert your charms on the person he lunched with on his last day.'

'Cathy Beccles, rights manager at Wolff & Baynes,' Atherton supplied.

'Right. Find out what was on his mind, who he was involved with, whether he mentioned any plans for the evening. Hollinshead said they were old friends so they might have chatted.'

'Must have, I should have thought, to make lunch last that long.'

'Oh – and find out who Calliope Hunt is. I'm sick of that name cluttering up my mind.'

The ex-Mrs Wiseman, formerly Regina Cantor, was now married, Slider discovered, to Simon Haig, the author. He didn't need Atherton's helpful intervention to place him. Simon Haig and Quantum went together in the mind: *The Quantum Files*; *The Quantum Enigma*; *The Quantum Sanction*; and so on. Spy thrillers. Slider had never read one – he didn't have much time for reading, and when he did read a book, he liked something where the plot unfolded in a straight line and the action didn't jig back and forth between characters, times and sometimes even dimensions. He had enough obscurity and complexity in his job: he had no capacity to spare for it in his leisure pursuits.

Gascoyne, however, was a fan, and was considerably excited when he learned Slider was going to Haig's house and might possibly meet him – so excited, Slider was obliged to cool him down by asking witheringly if he wanted his autograph. Gascoyne's bright, boyish smile indicated that he was on the brink of saying yes, before he controlled himself and said, 'I don't collect autographs. Not anymore. Just when I was a kid.'

'What was your best one?' Swilley asked from her desk. It was not clear if she was trying to be nice, or trying to trap him for purposes of ridicule.

'I had Roy Hattersley's,' Gascoyne admitted. 'And Mike Rutherford. Of Genesis. At least, I think that's who it was. I couldn't really read it. I saw him in Archer Street and he was in a hurry, so I didn't like to ask.'

Swilley evidently decided this was beyond parody and went back to what she was doing. Slider also turned away, and heard Gascoyne behind him say wistfully, 'I suppose a signed copy of a Quantum book's out of the question?'

The Haigs, if that's what they called themselves, lived in a flat in one of those tall dark-red buildings in Barkston Gardens, a side street off the Earl's Court Road. The lady of the house was alone, and let him into a flat which had been altered beyond recognition from its sombre Edwardian beginnings. It was on the top floor, and had had access to the leads, and the outside space had been turned into a narrow terrace, with potted shrubs and a view over the communal gardens. All the rooms on that side had been knocked together into one and the whole wall was now sliding glass doors, letting in the light. The large room was sparsely furnished over beige wall-to-wall carpet, with fat cream leather chairs and sofas, glass coffee tables, an entire wall of books, and an ultra-expensive sounds-and-viewing complex on another wall. An open archway showed a tiny but very modern kitchen beyond, with a breakfast bar and two tall stools looking onto the terrace.

Swilley had done a quick recce online and told Slider that a flat of that size in that road would go for around two mill these days. Of course, there were lots of people who had lived in them for thirty years or more, and it did not follow that the Haigs were millionaires; but seeing what they'd done with the place, Slider instantly concluded that they were not hurting at all. And given the Quantum books, no wonder.

Mrs Haig, who instantly corrected him, saying, 'I don't use my husband's name – I'm Regina Cantor. For business reasons. Please call me Reggie,' welcomed him with a serene smile and offered him coffee. 'It's all ready to go – I only have to switch on.' He accepted. She was short and plump with tightly curly grey-black hair and intensely dark eyes in a soft pale face, like big raisins in an uncooked bun; but she was well-corseted and expensively dressed, and moved and spoke briskly, so the overall impression was of efficiency and success, allied to an underlying kindness. A good combination for an agent, he supposed.

The coffee smelled good, and when they were seated on one of the big sofas with cups, he sipped appreciatively, then began by saying he was sorry for her loss.

She nodded, sad, but not overwhelmed. 'It was a shock, I must admit. So unexpected. But it's a long time since I moved on from Ed, so you needn't treat me as a grieving widow. When we parted ways, I made a determined effort to detach myself emotionally from him. There was no other way of coping, because we still had business with each other for some time afterwards.'

'And did you succeed?' Slider asked. He was glad she was prepared to conduct the conversation on this free and easy level – it would make his life easier.

'In detaching myself? On the whole. Ed wasn't someone you got over easily. One is always a *little* bit in love with him. I suppose I always shall be. But I haven't been weeping into my pillow – though it was disconcerting to have him go in that way. Falling out of a window? You don't expect people to die from falling out of a window. But they said there were excavations next door, which made it a much longer drop – is that right?'

This was the tricky bit. 'I'm afraid we suspect now that it wasn't an accident.'

She looked startled. 'Suicide? No, I can't believe that. Ed was too much in love with life to kill himself.'

'Not suicide,' Slider said. He waited for her to filter it. Her dark eyes searched his face.

'You're not telling me someone *pushed* him out?'

'I can't go into the specific details, I'm afraid, but we are proceeding on the basis that he was murdered. I'm very sorry.'

'Good God,' she said blankly. She processed the information for a few moments, took a sip of coffee, and squared her shoulders. 'That's horrible. Unbelievably horrible. How can I help?'

'Talk to me about him. The more I know about him, the better I understand his life, the easier it will be for me. Tell me about you and him. How did you first fall in love with him?'

'Instantly,' she said. 'That's the way it was with Ed. I met him at a party. He was with Chatto then. I was a junior agent at the Anthony Halligan agency. It was a launch for one of our authors. And there was Ed – tall, dark, full of fire. It seemed to radiate out of him – you could almost see it, like a corona.' Her face had softened with recollection. 'He took it upon himself to charm me – I don't know why – and I was charmed. Fell instantly, head-over-heels in love. Like tumbling down a mine shaft.'

'And was it mutual?'

'Hard to say, with Ed. When you were with him, he made you feel you were the only person in the world that mattered. But as he was like that with everyone . . .'

'He was insincere?'

'Oh no,' she hastened to defend him. 'That's the thing you have to understand about him. He really meant it – at the time. He loved people. Just too many of them.' She shrugged. 'It took me years of marriage to understand that, and many more years to accept it. It was just the way he was. You couldn't hate him for it.'

Perhaps someone did, Slider thought. 'But he married *you*,' he said, 'so you must have been special.'

She smiled. 'Thanks. I hope I was. After that first meeting, we went out a few times, but I didn't fool myself it was anything serious. But then he joined his father's literary agency, and I started to see more of him.'

'He had professional differences with his father, I believe?' Slider asked from the depths of his Wiki knowledge.

'That collaboration was never going to work,' she shrugged. 'Leo was a difficult man, reserved, a perfectionist, impatient of informality, while Ed was a free-flowing, seat-of-the-pants, impulsive, chameleon person. Agenting really was his milieu, because he got on with everyone, had a natural empathy, instinctively knew how to get the best out of people – and that included getting good deals from publishers. But he didn't like the hard graft behind it, the paperwork, the detailed stuff. Leo loved all that. They *should* have been a good partnership – probably would have been if they hadn't been father and son. But Leo wanted

Ed to be like him and couldn't accept the ways in which he was different. They rubbed each other up the wrong way all the time. It was bound to end badly.'

'He left,' Slider suggested.

'Yes. It hadn't lasted long – only two years. And I knew it was coming, because by then we were dating regularly, and I was the dumping ground for a lot of Ed's complaining. I'd met Leo, and frankly couldn't see how it could work at all. So I wasn't surprised when he said he wanted to set up his own agency, and asked me if I'd like to come in with him. I had quite a few of my own clients by then, and my areas seemed a natural fit with his. But it was a big jump, financially, and I said I'd have to think about it. And while I was thinking, he asked me to marry him, too.' She gave Slider a ravishing smile, that told him a lot about what she had looked like when she was young. 'Which convinced me,' she concluded.

'And was it hard?'

'Financially? Yes, at first. We set up in Floral Street – Covent Garden?'

'Yes, I know it.'

'In an office above a perfume shop, with a tiny flat on the floor above, very cramped and a bit primitive. There was no central heating, no double glazing. Draughts and traffic noise. Love in a cold climate! But we made ends meet, just about. And then he signed Virginia Foulkes and I signed Jane Flamborough, and Jane brought us John Grisewood – they were old friends and he wasn't happy where he was – and we were off to the races. I had Olivia – our daughter – the following year and Ivo two years later, but luckily agenting is something you can do while pregnant, and even when I had to take time off, I could still do the office work, which Ed was never keen on, so it all worked out. It was a bit cramped in Floral Street with two babies, but when Olivia was five, Ed's father died and left us this flat, so we were able to move, and keep Floral Street just as the office.'

'This was Leo Wiseman's flat?'

'Yes, the family home. It was where Ed grew up. Of course, it didn't look like this back then – all small dark rooms and heavy mahogany furniture. But we were glad to get it, furniture and all.'

'So Leo must have forgiven Ed at the end?'

She shrugged. 'Ed was all he had. Ed's mother had died a long time before, and Ed was the only child. There was no one else to leave things to. And Leo didn't hate Ed – he was his son. He was irritated by him, annoyed with him for some time after the split, but they mended fences when the grandchildren came along. He adored Olivia – Leo did. I used to drop her off with him at week-ends sometimes, when I had things to do. But it was sudden, Leo's death – he was only sixty-six – and Ed was devastated. I think he felt he hadn't had time properly to make up, and to tell his father how much he loved him. He threw himself into his work, building up the business, and succeeding brilliantly. I suppose his very success was at the root of the trouble.'

'Trouble?'

'Do you really want to hear all this?' she said, seeming to come back to reality with a bump. 'I mean – all this personal stuff. I don't want to bore you.'

'Please – I'm not bored at all. As I said, the better I understand him—'

'All right, but I'll need some more coffee. You?'

'Thanks.'

This time she brought a plate of biscuits as well, and settled herself in the corner of the big sofa, one leg tucked under her, as if making herself comfortable for the long haul.

'Being married to Ed might have been my dream, but it wasn't one long picnic,' she began.

SIX

Brat Worst

'Ed was a wonderful person – warm, funny, kind – great company, a wonderful lover and a brilliant father,' said Regina Cantor. 'He just wasn't a very good husband.'

'In what way?' Slider asked.

She ruminated a moment. 'You have to understand, the seven-ties and early eighties were the golden age of publishing. Editors had almost complete autonomy to buy the books they liked and believed in.'

'Don't they now?'

She gave a short laugh. 'Not quite! Everything has to go through committees of accountants and analysts. You see, back then, the numbers of books sold, compared with today, was phenomenal. Quite ordinary paperback fiction might sell twenty or thirty thousand copies. The same book now, you'd hope to sell three or four thousand. So there was money and scope to publish a wide range of fiction. Now they're all hunting for the one bestseller that will pay all the bills.'

'Surely publishers would always be hoping for a bestseller,' Slider said, trying to understand.

'Yes, of course. But *then* it was only part of the picture. *Now* it's everything. It's all about trends – trying to guess what the next one will be, or desperately trying to jump on the last one to pass by. There's got to be something to hang the PR on, you see. I'm always having perfectly good, well-written fiction through my hands that I have to turn down because that's all it is. No market hook. I know I won't be able to sell it.' She gave herself a little shake. 'But I was talking about *then* – the golden age. It was dynamic, exciting, everyone was making money. There were long lunches, launch parties, conferences, book fairs. There was a lot of drinking, a certain amount of cannabis, and a *lot* of sex. And everywhere you looked, there was Ed, having a hell of a good time.'

'Ah,' said Slider. 'You're saying that he . . .?'

'Ed's fatal flaw,' she said, 'was that he tended to sleep with his young clients. Actually,' she corrected herself, 'they didn't even have to be all that young.'

'That must have been difficult for you,' Slider said neutrally. Sex was so often at the bottom of everything: jealousy, betrayal, hurt. Revenge.

'I've tried over the years to understand. Ed was full of the juices of life, and they overflowed. He never meant to hurt me. He just couldn't help himself. He was always desperately contrite when I found out and was upset. And to do him justice, he never intended anything serious by it. He never wanted to be married to anyone but me. But in the end,' she sighed, looking away, 'it wore me down. I loved him, you see, so despite the dulling effect of repetition, it went on hurting. In the end, out of sheer self-defence, I had to leave him. Once Ivo was out of uni, I told him I wanted a divorce.'

'How did he take it?'

'He was devastated, begged me to change my mind, made all sorts of promises I knew he couldn't keep. I had to harden my heart against his pleading.' She looked distressed at the memory. 'But it was the best thing for both of us, really. I'm sure he was happier afterwards, able to go back to his carefree bachelor life.'

'So the split was amicable?'

'Oh yes. I told you Ed was kind. He gave me everything I asked for. Both the children were off our hands, so they weren't an issue. By then, we had the house in Shepherd's Bush to work from, and the children used the flat upstairs there as a pied-à-terre. I said I'd like this flat and Ed could keep the house. We also had a cottage in Wales, and we sold that and split the proceeds. And we kept the partnership going for almost another five years while I gradually extracted myself. Then I met Simon, and wanted to get married again, so that was the spur to cutting the final threads.'

'And you've remained friends?'

'Well,' she said, 'there's no animosity between us, and when we do meet it's on affectionate terms. But we don't see each other much. It's just if I happen to bump into him on the professional circuit. We don't have cosy lunches or anything of that sort. I told you, I had to detach myself from him emotionally. Ed was all too easy to love, and having got over that particular sickness, I wasn't going to risk being infected again. And,' she added, growing brisk, having been reflective, 'Simon certainly wouldn't like it if I had anything but an arm's length relationship with him.'

'He's jealous?' Slider asked, slipping the question in blandly.

But she looked at him sharply. 'Simon is quite fêted enough on his own account not to feel his ego shaking when Ed's mentioned. But no man welcomes his wife's ex into the nest, does he?'

'And your children – how did they feel about him?'

'Oh, they adored him, of course. He had that magnetism – and as I said, he was a wonderful father, always ready to play with them, take them on outings, make magic for them. And by the time we divorced and they had to learn he had feet of clay, they were grown up. More or less. They . . .' She hesitated. 'They were upset of course. But they got over it.'

He sensed something else under the words and waited; and when she didn't go on, he asked, 'Where are they now?'

'Olivia's married and lives in New Zealand. Works for a publishing house there. Ivo lives in Los Angeles. He agents film scripts.' She raised her eyes to his. 'Both happy and settled, you see, with good careers.'

But far away, he thought.

'Do you see them often?' he asked. He saw she didn't like the question.

'We Skype,' she said shortly.

Old illusions can persist in spite of experience, and Atherton had subconsciously been imagining the premises of Wolff & Baynes as a tall, narrow Victorian building in Bloomsbury, full of handsome staircases and marble fireplaces, and employees quietly beavering behind solid mahogany desks. It was disappointing to find them occupying one floor of a massive featureless glass cube near Waterloo. It was open plan, bright, modern, and smelled faintly, agreeably of books, of which there seemed to be dozens lining every sub-divided working cubby. The only thing that had translated from his vision was the hush. Publishing workers seemed to have the natural reserve of librarians.

Cathy Beccles had been not only willing but eager when he telephoned her to make the appointment. Now she met him at the lift doors, and led him through the open plannery, where a vast herd of employee browsed quietly on words, peaceable as buffalo. She conducted him to a glass cubicle off to one side, with a sign painted on the door saying MEETING ROOM 2. It was furnished with sofa, chairs, small round table, and a bar with cupboards above and below, on which stood a coffee machine and an electric kettle, and into which was set a small sink for water and for washing the cups.

'It's sound-proofed,' she told him, with faint anxiety as he watched the glass door sigh closed behind them. 'We'll be quite private in here.'

On the open plain, he could see the necessity of such a conversation cave. The walls, however, were all glass; Atherton assumed it was to stop employees having sex on the sofa. Or perhaps only a sneaky nap.

Cathy Beccles offered him coffee, and he accepted, more for her sake than his, because she seemed nervous, or at least ill at ease. She was very small and slight – you might even call her thin – with mild brown eyes in a long, pale face and thin, limp, mouse-coloured hair that hung down on either side to jaw level as though it hadn't the energy to do anything more enterprising. She was wearing a knee-length, dark-brown, wool skirt, and a beige cashmere cardigan over a white shirt; no earrings, but a plain heavy gold chain round her throat; no rings on her fingers, but well-kept hands and perfectly-manicured nails, painted in what he took to be ballet-slipper varnish.

He was intrigued by her. At first glance she was a nothing, instantly forgettable, the sort of person the eye slipped over without remark, looking for something more interesting to rest on. Neat and tidy were the adjectives you'd naturally apply to her. But on second glance, there was an understated – oh, definitely understated – elegance about her. Not glamorous or expensive elegance, but just something about the way she stood, the way she allowed her face to tell its own story without the help of paint, the care she took of her hands. A glance down confirmed she was wearing well-polished court shoes. Slider, he thought, would have expected that. One of his rules was that you could tell a person by their shoes, and how they looked after them.

When they were settled, she looked searchingly into Atherton's face and said, 'I read something on the web. That you were treating Ed's death as suspicious. I suppose your coming here confirms it. It means you think he was . . . murdered?' The word seemed hard for her to say, as it was for many people. It sounded absurdly melodramatic when applied to real, everyday life. It was the stuff of TV drama and sensationalist fiction. In real life people you knew did not get murdered.

He said, 'I know it's hard to believe. Everyone feels that, and with good reason. There's only around six hundred intentional homicides a year out of a population of sixty-five million, so the chances that you'll ever come across one are tiny. It's good for us to remind ourselves of that sometimes.'

'I suppose you come across them more often than ordinary people,' she said. 'That must be hard. Does it make you depressed?'

Ve vill ask ze qvestions! He smiled at her. 'I'm supposed to be interviewing you.'

'Oh, sorry,' she said. 'Lifelong habit. Trying to figure people out.'

'You're in the right job, then.'

'I am?'

'Novels are all about what makes people tick, aren't they?'

'Well – yes, I suppose so.' She watched him docilely now, waiting for his questions; but the eyes, he thought – the eyes were a thinker's.

'You sell rights, I understand,' he said. 'What exactly are rights?'

'The extras surrounding a book. You have your basic hardback and paperback. But then there's ebooks and other digital formats – that's big nowadays, of course. Book club versions. Serialisation. Translation into foreign languages. Film and TV. Merchandising – that can be big with books that make it into film. You know, like Star Wars games and action figures.'

He nodded. 'I know what merchandising is.'

'So my job is to sell as many of those and wherever possible. It can make a huge difference. Rights can make more than the basic book does.'

'So you're an important person to know?'

'I wouldn't say that,' she said. 'But I'm good at my job. I think I bring value to the company.'

If anyone notices. On the way through to the glass box, he had noted that most of the other employees he passed were young, in their twenties or early thirties. He wondered about her age. It was hard to tell, her face being so smooth and unlined, but now he studied her, he thought she must have twenty years on the oldest of them. Was she an outsider? Did these bright young things allow their eyes to pass over her unheeding? And did she mind? These lean lads with their whippy waists and designer stubble, these girls with their magazine-shoot make-up and long glossy hair . . .

If he were on the hunt – of course, he told himself hastily, there was Emily now, so he was not – but if he *were* on the hunt, how tired he would be of all that hair! The time and effort spent on its care and maintenance, the intrusiveness of it, the constant tossing and swinging and grooming and brushing – it was like having a girl bring her pony with her on a date. No, he'd make it a rule only to date short-haired girls. They'd have so much more attention to spare for him . . .

He realised that Cathy Beccles had her eyes fixed patiently on his face, as if perfectly used to having minds wander away from her. He straightened himself out guiltily.

'You had lunch on Monday with Ed Wiseman,' he said. 'I understand you were old friends.'

'I've known Ed a long time,' she said. He gave her a 'go on' nod, and she did. 'I was an editorial assistant at Mirador when Ed was just starting his agency. We met at a launch and it went from there. When you work in publishing, you get to know the leading agents. And it's *their* business to know *you*.'

'This friendship has endured a long time. Was it *more* than friendship?' She looked down at her hands. 'He was a very attractive man. I've heard stories—'

She sighed and interrupted him. 'We had . . . From time to time. Over the years. He was married, of course. To Reggie. Nowadays, it would be considered bad form, I suppose, but there was a lot more of it back then.' She still wasn't meeting his eyes. 'And somehow, with Ed, it was as if ordinary rules didn't apply. He . . . you didn't—'

'You had an affair with him?'

Now she looked up, faintly shocked. 'Oh, not an affair! Nothing that serious. Just sometimes, when we met at a fair or something . . .'

'You slept together.'

'Rights used to involve a lot of travel. Nowadays it's all done on line, but back then I was hopping over to New York and Tokyo and so on . . . Agents travelled too. When you're staying in a foreign hotel, you're glad of the company. Having a few drinks or a meal together leads to . . . to . . .'

This was painful. He let her off the hook. 'I understand. And you've always remained friends.'

She smiled, and he saw that she was not, in fact, plain at all. 'He was very loyal. Once you were his friend, you were always his friend.'

Atherton remembered something that was said about

Charles II with regard to his mistresses: that he never discarded, only added to his hand. He was getting a good idea of Ed Wiseman's character.

'So when you had lunch with him on Monday, was that for business, or was it purely pleasure?'

'It was always a pleasure to have lunch with Ed. But he had a business reason for asking me.' A shadow crossed her face briefly. 'He wanted help with a book.'

'Why does that trouble you?' Atherton asked quickly.

'It isn't a very good book. I happen to know it's already been rejected by Translit and Welling House. He sent it to me, asked me to read it, then arranged that lunch. He wanted me on side before he pitched it to Wolff, I suppose, because he knew they would be sticky. He thought if I said it had tremendous sub-rights potential it would tip the balance.' She shrugged. 'Flattering in a way, to imagine I have that much influence. But I don't think he's been thinking straight about this particular book.'

'And what is it? What's wrong with it?'

'It's called *Headlong*. A psychological thriller by Calliope Hunt.'

'Calliope Hunt!' said Atherton. He'd got to it at last, and without even asking.

'You've heard of her?'

'Should I have?'

'She's done a bit of modelling and a bit of presenting on local TV. This is her first novel.'

He shook his head. 'I was just thinking it was a good name.'

'And *Headlong*'s a good title, but that's as good as it gets. The plot's confused, inconsistent, and frankly unbelievable. And the writing's bad – stilted. She has no talent for characterisation or dialogue. The sad thing is that Ed knows all that, or he wouldn't have been calling in favours.'

'If it's that bad, why was he bothering with it?'

Her eyes shifted away. 'I suppose he thinks there's some mileage to be made on the success of *Gone Girl* and *Girl on the Train*. It's obvious that that's what Calliope was hoping, because the original title was *Girl Headlong*.'

'So what's the real reason he was bothering with it?'

'What do you mean?' She coloured slightly.

'You know there's something else underneath. You can't hurt

him now by telling me,' said Atherton. He had already guessed, of course. Ed Wiseman had been sleeping with Calliope Hunt. The question was, who else knew.

She thought a moment, as though debating whether to cough up. Then she said, 'I suppose it can't hurt now, as you say. Ed was in love with the girl. He was infatuated. OK, she was young and attractive, and I'm not surprised he was sleeping with her. He did tend to bed his female clients. Sort of a bonus, I suppose.'

'For them or him?'

'Good point. But females were never unwilling to be seduced by Ed. He was – just plain gorgeous, I suppose. But this was different. He was letting his professional judgement be clouded. He was determined to get her book published, however bad it was. And she struck me as a dangerous person for him to disappoint.'

'In what way?'

'Spoilt. Self-obsessed. Entitled. A little bit of modelling and TV have gone to her head. She thinks the world revolves around her and everyone's there to do her bidding. She'll throw a wobbly if Ed doesn't come up with the goodies – I mean, she would have, if he hadn't,' she corrected herself, her face registering the hurt of the past tense. 'I've only met her once, when Ed brought her to a book launch in Holland House Orangery. She made a huge fuss about the canapés, were they gluten free and organic and so on, demanded they go and make something special for her, wanted some obscure mineral water they didn't have – you know, extracted by hand from snow-fed Tibetan springs, that sort of thing. And when she couldn't get what she wanted, she went shouty crackers and threw a glass of water over one of the waitresses, who was only doing her job, poor thing. Everyone was so embarrassed. Ed had to calm her down and take her away to supper in some expensive restaurant in Notting Hill. It was awful to see how enslaved he was by her, because he must have *known* she was no good.'

'Well, perhaps he didn't,' Atherton suggested. 'Isn't that the point of infatuation?'

'I suppose you're right,' she said unhappily.

'So what was the outcome of the lunch on Monday? What did you tell him?'

'That I couldn't help him with the book,' she admitted

reluctantly. 'I hated to do it, but I really couldn't go to the board and recommend that piece of—' The word *shite* hung unspoken between them. She was too much of a lady to say it aloud.

'And what was his reaction?'

'Disappointed, of course. He begged and pleaded, used all his best wheedling on me, but I had to stand firm, however hard it was.'

'You'd have done it for him, but not for *her?*' Atherton suggested.

A red spot appeared on her cheek. 'Not even for him. I'm not that shallow.'

'I'm sorry. So what was his mood when you parted?'

'A bit quiet, as you'd expect. I suppose he wasn't looking forward to telling her it was a "no".'

'When was that going to happen? I suppose he'd tell her as soon as possible?'

'I'm not so sure. He hadn't given up. He said something about trying Avalon – though if he'd thought there was a chance there, I'd have expected him to have tried them first. But if he still had hopes, why tell her about the disappointment until he had to, and risk bringing the storm down on his head? I wouldn't be a bit surprised if he didn't tell her about our lunch at all.' She seemed to remember suddenly what all this was about. 'You can't think it was *Calliope* who did this?'

He was treasuring the description of Ms Hunt going 'shouty crackers'; and bashing the head of Ed might well be the result of some wild and momentary anger by someone unused to thinking about consequences. Also there was the intriguing fact that Mr Carpenter, whose wife had a connection, had been desperately keen to have it called as quickly as possible as an accident. It would be nice to stick a pin in his balloon.

But to Cathy Beccles he only said, 'I'm not thinking anything at the moment. Just trying to gather information. What time did lunch finish?'

'About a quarter to four, four o'clock. I couldn't say to the minute.'

'Long lunch.'

'Ed's always were. And he did a lot of persuading. Attempted persuading.'

'And he left in a gloomy mood.'

'Oh, I wouldn't say gloomy. He was down for a bit, but he perked up. Ever the optimist. He was back to normal, really, when I left him.'

'And did you go home then?'

'Back to the office. I had things to do, calls to make. I was here until about half past seven, then I went home.'

'And stayed home? Do you live alone?'

'I've never married,' she said meeting his eyes steadily. 'Typical spinster.'

'I don't think you're typical at all,' he said gallantly. 'So there's no one who can vouch for your whereabouts on Monday evening?'

'I'm afraid not,' she said, with absolute calm. He could read her. She didn't kill Ed Wiseman, and it was not possible for anyone to think she ever would, so why should she worry about having no alibi? It was impressive. Atherton was impressed.

'Can you think of anyone who may have wanted to do him harm?' he asked.

'Not specifically,' she said. 'I suppose there may have been people who were irritated by him – not at the time, not when they were with him, but in retrospect. He did *use* people, though in the nicest way. And there's always jealousy – as a motive, I mean. He was handsome, charming, successful, every woman he met fell for him. A lot to be jealous about there, I'd have thought.'

'But no one in particular springs to mind? Think about it – I'm in no hurry.' He smiled, to suggest he was enjoying her company.

She smiled back. 'You're a little bit like him, aren't you? A smooth operator. Except that in Ed's case, he meant it. He always meant it. That's what made him irresistible. No, I can't think of anyone who would have wanted to harm him. Except possibly Calliope – but I hasten to say, I have nothing against her. It's just that she's the only person I know with enough of a sense of entitlement. But whether she could ever have gone as far as to kill him . . . I suppose someone in a rage might shove someone hard enough for them to fall under a train, for instance, without ever meaning it to go that far. I don't know how it was done, of course. If it was slow and deliberate it would be a different question.' She looked at him with raised eyebrows but he didn't respond. 'I can't help you,' she said. 'I'm sorry.'

'You've helped a great deal,' he said.

'Now *that*'s an alarming thought,' she said.

SEVEN
The Plot Sickens

They met back at the factory to compare notes. 'Well, I'm glad you've got the Calliope Hunt business sorted out,' said Slider. 'Can we have a look at her?'

Everyone was interested. Hart brought images up on her computer and they crowded in. LaSalle said, 'Wow, fit as a butcher's dog!'

Fathom, leaning in over Hart's shoulder, whistled. 'Hot totty!'

Hart shoved him back impatiently. 'Dickhead!'

McLaren had a look and dismissed her. 'She's got nothing on my Natalie.'

Hart snorted derision. 'Yeah, right!' They heard all too much about McLaren's Natalie.

He was unmoved. 'I don't like skinny birds you can cut yourself on,' he explained calmly. 'And she's got no boobs to speak of.'

'You like full fat milk, eh?' Fathom said, chortling at his own wit.

'And they said Neanderthals were extinct,' said Norma witheringly, from her own desk. 'Here, boss, I'll find you something without drool on it. Here we are. She's actually got a Wiki page. Mm. Not much on it, though. Hertfordshire girl. Born in Welwyn. Went to Queen's Walk School, Hatfield. Won a modelling competition age seventeen. Had pictures in *Girlzine* and *Bliss*. Presented on *Inside Out* for BBC East for a while. Nothing recent.' She stopped.

'That's it?' said Atherton. 'Or were you giving us the highlights?'

'You got the expanded version,' said Norma. 'Hardly a stellar rise. She's twenty-two now. Done nothing for eighteen months, give or take.'

'Except write a book,' said Atherton. 'And ensnare Ed Wiseman. I wonder how long the book took to write. Ensnaring Wiseman would be instantaneous. Was there anyone the man wouldn't bonk?'

'That's rich, coming from you,' said Swilley, trying more searches.

Surprisingly, Atherton didn't come back with anything, and glancing at him, Slider saw he had slumped into thought.

'I wonder why Mr Carpenter was so keen to protect her from scandal,' Slider said. 'Doesn't sound as if she's a sensitive flower. Or has a sensitive career, one that could be ruined by media exposure.'

'We don't know who her parents are,' Swilley said, still clicking away. 'They might be posh. I mean, they called her Calliope, for goodness' sake. And she went to a private school. Posh people just don't like being in the papers.'

'But she's not really likely to have killed him, is she?' Gascoyne put in. 'I mean, a young girl from a good home—'

'Have you ever *been* to the pictures?'

Atherton came back from his reverie. 'I'd like to have a look at her book. Could be some clues in it. At that age, a first novel's bound to be autobiographical.'

'What do you know about it?' Norma jeered.

'It's just logic,' Atherton retorted. 'At twenty, twenty-one, all you know about is yourself.'

'Dun't have to be her that done it,' LaSalle argued. 'Killed Wiseman, I mean. Someone could've been trying to protect her. Father, brother, someone that doesn't like her being exploited by an older man.'

'It sounds as though she was the one doing the exploiting,' said Atherton.

'They might not see it that way. She's twenty-two, he's going on seventy. It wouldn't thrill me if it was *my* daughter.'

'I bet it would if it was Mick Jagger,' Fathom said. 'He's, what, seventy-something, and he's just had a kid with some twenty-something bird. People don't care about that sort of thing any more. Not if the bloke's famous.'

'Some people might,' Slider said. 'But if we're going to look into that possibility, we're going to have to be very careful. The commander won't like us blundering in asking for alibis from his nearest and dearest. And we'll have to have a lot more reason to be asking than anything we've got so far.'

'Well, she was obviously a big factor in Wiseman's life right at the end,' said LaSalle.

'So let's find out what other factors there were,' said Slider. 'Telephone records, emails, finances, just for a start. Meanwhile—' he looked at Atherton, who seemed to be in a brown study again – 'I think another chat with Amy Hollinshead is in order.'

Atherton jerked to life. 'Oh, right. Want me to get her in?'

'No, I'd like to see how she is at home. You can come with me, add your silent observations.'

Amy Hollinshead lived in a conversion flat in a long road near Lancaster Gate station. She buzzed them up, and met them at her door looking pale and unexpectedly glad to see them. Slider thought she must have been at a loss, having no work to go to, to take her mind off things. She would probably just be glad to have someone to talk to about the horrible, upsetting business; to talk to about Ed.

She was in the present-day mourning garb of grey tracky bottoms, a vast cable-knit beige sweater, and thick pink socks – clothes for sitting on the sofa mainlining hot chocolate and box sets, but at the nicer end of the spectrum: the trackybots looked designer, and the socks cashmere, and her hair, pulled back in a scrunchie, was clean and shiny.

The flat was on the first floor of an early Victorian terrace, so had pleasantly high ceilings, and the main room was a good size. It had French windows onto the tiny balcony, which probably made up for having to have a kitchen counter and breakfast bar in the corner of your living room. The floorboards were sealed and varnished, and partly covered by a large Turkish carpet of the sort you generally had to inherit. Perhaps she came from a wealthy family. There was a massive leather Chesterfield, much scarred and softened by age, lots of books, a couple of very modern lamps; everything looked clean and up-market-plain.

The rest of the flat, from Slider's experience, would consist of a small bathroom and one bedroom, and even this reduced accommodation would probably cost twelve to fifteen thousand a year. He'd love to know what Ed Wiseman had been paying her.

A Cyprian cat stalked up to him, tail rigidly erect, and when he bent to offer a finger, it wiped its cheek along it in a friendly manner, purring like a Volvo.

'You don't mind cats?' she asked.

'I like all animals,' Slider said. The cat walked on, through the gap in the part-open French windows onto the balcony, and leapt lightly, terrifyingly up onto the high narrow iron rail, where it sat, impossibly balanced, to watch the world go by. 'Isn't your heart in your mouth when he does that?' Slider asked.

'It used to terrify me,' she said, 'but I've got used to it now.' Her voice had lost its music. It was flat with pain.

'We'd like to ask you some more questions,' Atherton said, 'if that's all right.'

'I've got nothing else to do,' she said. 'Please sit down.' She folded herself into a corner of the Chesterfield with one leg under her. She had forgotten to offer them coffee – not that Slider wanted any, but it was indicative of her state of mind. She had not yet sunk to going unwashed, but all was not well with her. 'I heard something,' she began. 'That you think . . . you're treating it as suspicious.' She gave Slider a hungry, searching look. 'Does that mean . . . you think he was—'

'All we know so far is that he didn't fall, or jump. Someone else was involved.'

She looked aghast. 'I can't believe it,' she said. 'How . . .?'

'I can't go into that at the moment. And I'd be glad if you didn't spread this any further.'

'No, of course not,' she said automatically. 'That's terrible. Terrible. Who would want to hurt him?'

'We thought you might be able to help us with that.'

Her eyes widened. 'Me?'

'You might know if he had any enemies. Anyone who might want to do him harm.'

She swallowed. 'But why me? You should ask . . .' Her pause was long.

Slider said, 'Unless you can think of anyone who knew him better.'

'I wouldn't say I *knew* him,' she said cautiously.

Atherton intervened impatiently. 'You saw him every day. You worked with him for thirteen years. You knew what was going on in his life. All right, you've said everybody loved him, but everyone has people who just don't get them. Or who are annoyed by them. Or who have conflicting interests. We need you to think carefully about that.'

Interestingly, she seemed to find Atherton's abrasion comforting. She pulled herself together and thought. 'There was an incident,' she said slowly. 'Someone who – but it wasn't really anything,' she back-pedalled. 'I don't want to drop anyone in it—'

'Just tell us,' Atherton said. 'We won't jump to conclusions, I promise.'

'Okay, I told you Ed was going to be reading manuscripts all evening. It's a big part of our work. I share the reading with him – one of my many tasks. We get half a dozen scripts a day. Ed's unusual in accepting unsolicited work. Most agents won't any more. There's so much dross, you can get swamped. But Ed likes the thrill of the hunt. Usually you can tell on the first page that it won't do, but sometimes there's something you can work with. And if you do happen to hit on that one diamond in the rough . . . Well, it's . . .'

'Exciting,' Atherton suggested, to keep her going. 'So what was this incident?'

'Well, you get some complete idiots sending you the most awful rubbish. It's too easy, now everyone's got a PC. But the worst of all, in my experience, is the fantasy stuff. Imaginary worlds. It's always "an epic battle between good and evil".' Her sing-song tone marked the inverted commas. 'And the strange thing is that the heroes have amazing Star Wars-type weapons, but they still ride on horseback and dress in animal skins. Weird!' She shook her head in wonder. 'The trouble is, the writers get so involved with this world they've imagined, that they can't bear any criticism.'

Atherton saw where it was going. 'And there was one idiot in particular?'

She nodded. 'This man, Brian Langley, he'd sent us two scripts over the years, and they were both unpublishable – practically unreadable. The usual castles and dragons stuff, but they were also very violent, worryingly so. And misogynistic – quivering maidens chained up in dripping dungeons with rats running over them, that sort of thing. Ed hated them, but being Ed, his rejections were always polite. Maybe that was the problem. Maybe he ought to have spelled it out, instead of just saying it wasn't for him. But a couple of months ago we got another script, only this time he brought it in person.'

'Oh?' said Atherton significantly.

She looked into his face. 'He was really frightening. Enormous – over six foot and massive with it, like a . . . like a bouncer, you know? A sort of thick, meaty face, as if he'd spent his life being punched. All red. And little mean eyes.'

'What happened?'

'Well, he wanted to give the script to Ed in person, but he wasn't in. I promised to give it to him, and I did. But last Friday this Langley came back, and he was angry. He came barging in and demanded to see Ed. I would have put him off, I didn't like the look of him, but just at that moment Ed came downstairs, and this man rushed at him and grabbed him by the arm and shouted he was Brian Langley and he'd had enough of being messed around and fobbed off, and he was bloody well going to make sure Ed read his book if he had to stand over him all day. Only he didn't say "bloody".'

'I understand. What did Ed do?'

'Oh, Ed was magnificent. He was calm as an iceberg. He said, "You're quite wrong, Mr Langley, I *did* read your book," and then he started quoting from it – not the actual words, I mean, but the names of characters and describing bits of the plot.'

'Amazing!' Atherton said, since her tone of voice seemed to expect it.

'Well, it was,' she said eagerly. 'Have you any idea how many books he reads in a year? And to remember the details of that dreadful rubbish! He has an amazing memory. And he was so cool and collected. This huge man, roaring at him, grabbing him with hands like, like *hams*, practically lifting him off the ground . . . I was terrified, but Ed didn't show a thing, just talked to him in a normal voice, talked him down, until the man let him go. And all he did then was straighten his jacket and invite Mr Langley into the next room for a chat. Asked me to bring them coffee.'

'He must have been very confident in himself,' Slider put in.

'In his ability to keep the peace.' He'd have made a good policeman, he thought.

She glanced at him, then back at Atherton. 'When I took the coffee in, I was still shaking, I was ready to call the police at the slightest move, but there was this huge bruiser sitting there in silence, his eyes fixed on Ed's face, while Ed told him exactly why we couldn't take on his book. He said the vogue for violent literature had passed, and while it might come back one day, there was no sense trying to buck the current trend, and was there anything else Mr Langley could write, had he thought of children's fantasy fiction?'

'What?'

She nodded. 'I thought he was making fun of him – which would have been very scary – but afterwards, he told me he'd just wanted to get him to write something completely different, get him into a different mindset. And he said . . .' She paused.

'Yes?'

'He said that as we didn't handle children's fiction, if Mr Langley wrote a children's book he could send him round to Reggie and let her deal with him. Reggie always did the children's stuff when they were in partnership, you see.' She gave an unwilling smile. 'It was a joke, of course – I think to cover up how scared he'd been. This Brian Langley was a marine once, so he was very strong and had all those fighting skills, and it wouldn't surprise me if he hadn't got what-d'you-call-it, PTSD, as well. I mean, his scripts were very *odd*.'

This, thought Slider, was almost too good to be true. A violent ex-soldier with a grudge? 'How did the incident end? How did you get rid of him?'

'Well, he drank his coffee and talked to Ed a bit more about his books, describing his favourite bits and saying how good they were, trying to persuade him, you know. And Ed listened patiently and kept repeating that he couldn't sell them and why. And in the end he got up and shook Mr Langley's hand, which made *him* get up to leave. I heard Ed say, "Think about what I've said. You need to try a completely different kind of writing." And he went. But I don't think he was really convinced. I saw his face as he passed the door, and it was . . . well, dark. Scowling, sort of.'

'And that was last Friday?' Slider asked.

'He wanted to pass this violent writer off onto his wife?' Atherton asked at the same moment.

'I told you, it was a joke,' she excused him hastily. 'He and Reggie were okay. There was no ill feeling.'

'And what about Simon Haig? Was there ill feeling there?'

'Oh, no, I'm sure not,' she said. 'That thing was a long time ago. At least three years ago.'

'What thing?' Slider asked.

She looked from him to Atherton, slightly disconcerted. 'I thought you knew. I thought you meant when Simon punched him.'

'Why did Simon Haig punch Ed Wiseman?' Slider asked patiently.

She put her hands to her cheeks. 'I shouldn't have said anything. I thought you knew. I don't want to get Simon into trouble.'

'Nobody's in trouble,' Slider said. 'I'm just collecting information. The more you tell me, the clearer a picture I'll have.'

'Well, Simon's a sweetie,' she said anxiously. 'Or – not exactly a sweetie, but he's perfectly nice and I'm sure he'd never—' She intercepted Slider's look and straightened up. 'Simon punched Ed outside the Ivy one evening. It was in all the papers at the time. You see, Ed had taken Marina to dinner there – Marina Haig, Simon's daughter by his first marriage? It was only dinner, but of course, Ed has a reputation. And I think it was more surprise than anything. Simon was just going in with Oliver Knudsen – the film producer? – and he didn't know they were there, and Ed walked out with Marina on his arm and they came face to face, and I think Simon just lashed out in surprise.'

You don't hit people outside a fashionable restaurant in central London just because you're surprised to see them, in Slider's experience. There must have been some history there.

He tried the blunt approach. '*Was* he sleeping with her?'

She looked away. 'I wouldn't know. He never said anything to me.'

Atherton caught his eye and with a quirk of his expressive face managed to convey, *so much for Mr Wonderful being loved by all. That's two people hating him. How many more?*

Slider phrased it more tactfully for Wiseman's number one fan. 'A man as talented and good-looking as Ed was bound to ruffle a few feathers, I should have thought. It wasn't necessarily his fault, but men do get jealous, even when there's no reason to. You've done very well so far, Miss Hollinshead. Is there anyone else you can think of who's been upset by his . . . shall we say, glamour?'

She looked at him cautiously, as if checking whether he was making fun of her, and then shook her head, pushing her hands up her sleeves defensively. 'No. I can't think of anyone,' she said, a touch sulkily. 'You seem to want to make him out to be a monster.'

'Not at all,' said Slider soothingly. 'Everyone I've spoken to has said he was a very attractive person, in every way.' It was almost true. He tried a new tack. 'You said there used to be another assistant – Liana?'

'Liana Karev,' she agreed, looking indifferent. 'What about her?'

'Why did she leave?'

'There wasn't really enough work for her. Ed had to let her go.'

'Was she upset about that?' Atherton asked.

'No. She had another job to go to. He waited until she'd found one. He was a kind and considerate employer!'

'So there were no hard feelings,' Atherton persisted.

'Look, she was getting married anyway. They were going to live south of the river, so she wanted a job further in, easier to get to than Shepherd's Bush. Ed gave her a reference and she got a place at Translit, at Victoria. There were no hard feelings. All right?'

'Have you heard from her since?'

'No. I wouldn't have expected to.'

Slider took it back. 'You say there wasn't enough work for her. Was the business slowing down? Was it in trouble?'

'No, not in trouble. It's not a matter of that. Ed wanted to take things a bit easier, that's all. He's sixty-seven. Not that you'd know it – I mean, he's amazing, so full of energy and drive! Anyway, sixty-seven is nothing nowadays, is it? It's the new forty-seven.'

'He was thinking of retiring?'

'Of course not. He'll never really retire.' She seemed not to have noticed the irony of that statement. 'He wanted to take more time to enjoy what he was doing, instead of dashing about like a mad thing. Relax more, concentrate on his favourite authors. So he hasn't been taking on so many new names.'

'Calliope Hunt was new, wasn't she?'

A shadow passed over her face. She sighed. 'Yes,' she agreed. 'And she is taking up a lot of our time.'

'In what way?'

'Well, she needs a lot of hand-holding. Some authors do. Ed's good at that sort of thing – he's a real people person. I work with some of the authors, too, helping them with rewrites and so on – I was in editorial before I changed to agenting, which was one of the things Ed hired me for. But some of them practically need you to be a mother to them, or a father. Ed was genius at that. He had so much patience with them.'

'And you didn't?' Slider suggested.

She frowned. 'The thing is . . .'

'Yes?' Slider encouraged.

She sighed again. 'You don't mind the time and effort spent if the book's worth it. I just don't think *Headlong* is a good book. There's been so much re-writing already – Ed and I have both had a go at it, as well as Calliope – and I don't know that it's made it any better. It has no . . .' She searched for a word. 'It's like an exercise in writing,' she began again. 'If you have character x and character y and setting z, and plot features a, b and c, you must have a bestseller, right? But somehow it doesn't work like that. If it did, computers could write books. There's something else, some element – it's hard to quantify, but you know when it's there. Basically, you have to *believe* in a book. And I don't believe when I read *Headlong*.'

'So why does Ed persist with it?' Atherton asked.

'I suppose he sees something in it that I don't. He's much more experienced than me. One has to trust his judgement.'

Slider asked the next question before Atherton could. 'What do you think of Miss Hunt herself? Have you met her?'

'Oh yes, she's come to the office many times. She and Ed work on the script together in his office. He's asked me for my input on occasions, but I don't think she welcomed my involvement. I suppose I wasn't as positive about the book as Ed. But I had to be honest – I'd be no use otherwise, would I?'

'Quite. What did you think of her as a person?'

'Very pretty. And confident. She'd be very good in front of the cameras, for PR purposes – and that's a big part of a book's success these days, being able to promote it.'

'But? You were going to say "but".'

'I thought she was shallow,' she said in a dissatisfied tone. 'I thought that came out in her writing. It felt to me . . .' A long hesitation.

'Yes?'

'I don't want you to think I'm just being bitchy,' she said, with a plea in her eyes, 'but it felt to me as if she only wanted to get published for the fame and attention. As if it was the next thing to do in her media career. That's why there was no *feeling* in the book. Do you think I'm horrible? I mean, I don't really know her. She might be a wonderful person, just not very good at expressing herself.'

'I'd have thought being good at expressing yourself was a must for a writer,' Slider said mildly.

'Not always, I'm afraid,' said Amy Hollinshead, with infinite regret.

EIGHT

One Nightstand to Remember

They got up to leave, and thanked her for her time. She said, 'Anything I can do.'

The cat hopped down from the balcony rail to see them off. Slider bent to stroke it, and said, 'I meant to ask you, what was the cricket connection?'

'Cricket connection?'

'A full collection of *Wisden* in his office.'

'*Wisden*? Oh, you mean all those yellow books.' She shrugged. 'He was interested in cricket, I suppose. He always listened to the radio when the test match was on, that sort of thing,' she said with the complete indifference of someone immune to the game. 'Went to matches sometimes at, whatsisname, Lord's.'

'And the memorabilia?'

'You mean the cricket balls? I think they were from some important matches that he'd been to. Souvenirs, you know? He did tell me once, but I don't really remember. It wouldn't mean anything to me. I've never seen the point of cricket – though I like tennis. I watch Wimbledon, and I play a bit. Cricket's like rounders, something they make you play at school.'

Outside, going back to the car, Slider said, 'Rounders! What an appalling attitude. That's no way to talk about the king of sports!'

'I thought horse racing was the king of sports,' Atherton objected.

'No, that's the sport of kings,' said Slider. 'And I don't agree with that anyway. It's cricket. That young woman has a lot to learn.'

'Women generally don't see the point of sport at all. Emily goes out of the room if I try to watch a game. Unless it's rugby and Wales are playing – she's got a thing about Leigh Halfpenny.' He shook his head sadly at the shortcomings of women. 'It's always about personalities with them. And not only in sport.'

'A valuable insight, sergeant,' Slider mocked him. 'Well, at least we've got something to work with.'

'A mad marine and a jealous husband-stroke-father. And I'm wondering about the sacked secretary. Was it really as harmonious as she claims? She was very eager to defend her old boss, so maybe he needed defending.'

'Evidently, since he ended up dead,' said Slider.

Porson listened with a slight lifting of gloom to the Wiseman catalogue of ill-wishers. 'Though I'd sooner it was just one,' he said at the end. 'One nice juicy suspect. Too many thieves spoil the broth. It all gets . . . wafty.' He waved his hand to indicate vague veils of suspicion.

Wafty. Slider liked it. So much of his life was wafty so much of the time. It was the bits in between that had the hard edges and sharp corners you hurt yourself on, but sometimes the waft hid them until it was too late.

'So we've got some lines to follow up, sir,' he said.

'Yerrss,' said Porson thoughtfully. 'I'll pass that on to Mr Carpenter. Of course, he knows it's got to be investigated now.'

The Calliope Hunt connection was one of those sharp corners. 'Do we know exactly what the problem is, why he was anxious about it?' Slider asked.

'There's no mystery there,' said Porson. 'This cousin of

Mrs Carpenter's, who's godmother to the Hunt girl, she's a Lady
something. Her husband's a JP, they're uppity folk in the county,
big nobs, the sort that hates publicity. And Mrs C's not only her
cousin, they're very close, so she's with her on that.'

'But how did they hear so quickly that Wiseman was dead?
That's what worries me,' Slider said.

'Oh, I get you. No, they didn't. See, Lady Wotsit'd been worried
already about the Hunt girl and Wiseman being seen together,
because of the age difference and so on. She could see it turning
into a story. And she'd shared her concerns with Mrs C, who'd
passed them on to the commander, so he was already fully aware.
So when word reaches him that Wiseman's done the big header,
the first thing he thinks is, gotta stamp on this, shut it down
before the cat's out of the bed.'

'I see.'

'Now it's a suspicious death, it's even more crucial to keep the
girl out of it, and I don't see you've got any call to get after her,
from what you've told me.'

'I've other lines to follow first,' Slider conceded. 'But there's
no way of suppressing the news.'

'No leaks!' Porson barked in alarm.

Slider shrugged. 'It's not a matter of that, sir. Even if it's not
in the papers, there's no way to control the social media. And
everyone who knows anything will be putting their little bit up on
the web. It'll be all over the country in no time.'

Porson seemed remarkably unmoved by the prospect. 'Not our
problem. Just make sure nothing's got our fingermarks on it. And
let's hope some proper evidence turns up when the SOC report
comes in, and not just all this . . .' He waved his hand again.

'Waft,' said Slider.

'Right,' said Porson, and waved him away.

Slider went, remembering the Reverend Dr Spooner, who was
supposed to have tried to compliment a fellow don on the shafts
of wit that issued from his mouth. Those were the sort of wafts a
policeman knew all about.

'But none of this means anything,' Swilley complained. 'People
have disagreements with people, they don't necessarily go and kill
them.'

'It's better than no one having disagreements with him,' said Gascoyne reasonably. 'And I like the sound of the big bloke, the marine.'

'But there was no break-in,' said Slider. 'Would Wiseman have let in an enraged Brian Langley? At night?'

'I suspect he was daft enough for it,' said Atherton. 'Not so wise his ego wouldn't tell him he could talk him round. People like him can never grasp that there might be some people in the world who really just don't like them.'

'You're so like him,' Swilley sighed.

'In what way?' Atherton enquired icily.

'A few conquests in the bedroom, and you think you're the Messiah.'

'Well, he does know about the second coming,' said McLaren.

Gascoyne, put out by the near-blasphemy, tried to divert attention by asking seriously, 'What exactly is the secret to your success with women? I've read that if you make them laugh . . .'

'No. It's Pernod,' said Atherton.

'Eh?'

'On the first date, you make sure they drink Pernod.'

'What are you talking about?' Swilley said impatiently.

'It's well known,' said Atherton, 'that absinthe makes the heart grow fonder.'

Now it was Hart's turn to intervene. 'I'm liking Simon Haig,' she said loudly to get their attention. 'Wiseman'd let *him* in all right. And he's got form – bashing him outside the Ivy.'

'A long time ago,' Slider pointed out.

'Yeah, but you don't know what Ed's been up to recently. Or who. Could still be doing the daughter. Could even be doing the wife. And even if not, if the Regina woman's still fond of him, that'd rankle. After a long brood, Haig comes round to say, leave my wife-stroke-daughter alone, and Ed comes over all now, now, my good man, and Simon loses it and lamps him. I would,' she concluded frankly.

'Well, we'll certainly have to follow up on it,' said Slider. 'On all of them.' He was starting to feel like Porson. One good, juicy, lone suspect would be a relief.

* * *

Bob Bailey called in with the preliminary report, and to have a leer at Hart, whom he fancied. To his disappointment, she wasn't in the office, so he had to make do with Slider, who, frankly, didn't have the legs.

'Well, it's a mess,' Bailey said, of the crime scene. 'There's latents all over the house, like you'd expect, of the victim and the woman, and a lot of older stuff in the downstairs areas, which I gather were in the nature of a public place. But there's nothing fresh of anyone new in the room with the open window. Upstairs, well, there was definitely someone else there recently. In the bedroom. You noticed there was a wine glass on both bedside tables?'

'We did. But given the general lack of tidiness in the bedroom, they could both have been his.'

'The empty wine glass, there's his marks all over it,' said Bailey. 'The one on the other side, the one that had some wine left in – that was more interesting. It had his marks, one clear set, like as he might have made handing the glass over after he'd poured.' He demonstrated on the open air. 'No other fingermarks on the glass itself, but a lot of smears on the stem. So she's picked the glass up by the stem to drink.'

'She?'

'Holding by the stem's what women do. It's dainty. Men aren't dainty.'

'It's a bit of an assumption . . .'

Bailey grinned. 'Nah! The lip latents on the rim weren't male. Too full. They were definitely female.'

'Oh, so you've got lip marks?' Slider brightened. Cheiloscopy was an improving science, and lip prints were accepted in court these days as conclusively as fingerprints.

'Don't get excited. There's several overlying each other. She's drunk each time off the same place. I don't know yet if I can get a clear photograph, clear enough for identification. But it's definitely a female's been on that side of the bed. And,' he added with relish, as having left the best until last, 'there's semen on the bottom sheet. He's had someone up there the last day.'

'Well, that's useful to know,' Slider said, though it wasn't as much help as it would have been had it been a female murder victim. The semen, one supposed, would be Wiseman's. Though, of course, one should never assume. 'You'll get it typed?' he asked.

'Course. On it. But he wasn't known for batting left-handed, was he? So it's gonna be his all right. Tell you one thing, though,' he added kindly as he prepared to leave. 'Semen on the sheet means he was riding bareback. Which means it wasn't a one-night stand. Not casual.'

Slider saw the point, as did Atherton when he repeated it to him. A condom wasn't only for birth control, but for the prevention of communicable disease, of which everybody these days was prudently aware.

'Quite,' said Atherton. 'A casual encounter always means a condom. Sex with no condom means a long-term relationship. With trust. Which points possibly to Calliope Hunt.'

'Or lover or lovers unknown,' Slider added, to bring him back to earth. 'We don't know how many people he was carrying on a current relationship with, unknown to each other. It might even have been his ex-wife.'

'I think his ex-wife might have been a bit more cautious,' Atherton said dryly, 'given that she definitely knew how promiscuous he was.' He looked cheerful for a moment, and then frowned. 'It's opened up the books, hasn't it?'

'We don't know,' Slider pointed out, 'that it was the woman in the bed who killed him. Violent blows with a blunt instrument are more a masculine method.'

'True,' said Atherton. 'Suppose he was diddling someone's wife and they caught him in flagranté? No, that wouldn't work. No break-in. They'd have had to have a key.'

'Flagranté could just mean she was in the house without a good excuse,' Slider pointed out.

'Husband suspicious, calls round, Ed opens the door, husband sees wife in the background, or hears her voice, and does a berserker.'

'In the hall?'

'He could have been killed anywhere in the house,' Atherton reminded him. 'If the falling-out-of-the-window was staged. Though carrying him upstairs or downstairs would have taken some strength. Most likely he was killed in the departure lounge.'

'It's still all speculation,' Slider sighed. 'Wafty.'

'I know,' said Atherton, with a frustrated jerk of the head. 'Why couldn't the idiot have installed security cameras?'

*   *   *

Friday dawned sweet and balmy outside, more like summer than spring. Sunlight, pale gold and innocent as lambs, poured down the street and pooled beguilingly in the gardens, promising scents to noses deprived all winter.

Inside, things in the kitchen were less benign. Joanna had listened tight-lipped – not a usual expression of hers – as he talked about the case over his eggs and bacon.

'So if it's now a murder case, that means you're going to be busy.'

'Well, yes,' he said cautiously, alerted by her tone. 'You know how—'

'No weekends off, I suppose?'

He caught on. 'I'm sorry,' he said. 'I know I was supposed to be looking after George tomorrow.'

'So what are you going to do?' she asked uncompromisingly.

'Me?' He saw that was not a wise question to pursue. 'Who do you usually call? I mean, don't you have a list, for when Dad can't be here?'

'Even if I have – so what?'

'Well, couldn't you ring round?'

'Oh no! I'm not doing your job for you. You got yourself into this mess, you can get yourself out of it.'

'Jo, don't be like that.'

'*I'm* not being like anything. *You're* trying to wriggle out of your responsibilities and chuck them at me.'

'It's our son we're talking about, not some onerous—'

'*Our* son. That means yours and mine. You conveniently forget the bit where he's yours whenever it suits you. Why should organising childcare be my responsibility?'

He saw the hazards looming in any answer he was likely to give. *Well you always have in the past*. Nope. *You're the mother. It's the mother's job*. Double nope. Instead, he said, trying to sound reasonable, 'My job *is* important.'

'I have a job too. And unlike you, I can't call in sick.'

'You're not suggesting—'

'Suggesting nothing. This is for you to sort out.'

'But if I can't find anyone?'

'You'll have to take him in with you. Anyway, I can't stand here talking about it. I've got to get him off to pre-school, and then I've got rehearsal ten to one. I'll see you later – if you're back before I'm in bed.'

'Jo, don't be like that,' he called after her as she stalked out. 'Jo, please – we never quarrel.'

'I'm not quarrelling,' her voice floated back.

He finished his breakfast – or his dust and ashes, as his mouth told him it had become. She reappeared in the doorway with George, adorable in a red woolly coat and matching Fair Isle mittens, in her arms. He beamed at his father. 'I've got glubs,' he confided.

'So you have,' said Slider. 'Very handsome ones.'

'On strings, up my sleebs. So Mummy says I won't lose them.'

Joanna interrupted the seminar. 'Say goodbye to Daddy,' she instructed. 'He's looking after you tomorrow.' And whisked him away.

'I don't know what's got into her,' he said to Atherton. 'She's never unreasonable about that sort of thing.'

'Last straw, camel's back? Worm turning? That sort of thing?' Atherton offered, leaning on the doorframe. 'It happens. They put up with an awful lot from us, one way or another, and every now and then it's too much. I shouldn't worry about it.'

'I have to worry. I have to find someone to look after George. I suppose Emily . . .?'

'In Brussels this weekend. For the summit.'

'Oh,' said Slider. 'Anyway, we put up with a lot from them, don't we?' he grumbled.

'Hm,' said Atherton. 'Not so much. Okay, they're away a lot, out in the evenings, it's hard to get schedules to co-ordinate, but it all works out, and that's probably because *they* make it work.'

'All right for you. You don't have children.'

'Children!' Atherton had a light-bulb moment. 'There you are – ask Irene to have him.'

Irene was his ex-wife. 'Away,' said Slider. 'Bridge weekend.'

'So who's looking after Matthew and Kate?'

'Cousin of Ernie's, who lives near the hotel they're going to.'

'Well, then?'

'I think that connection is getting a bit too tenuous, don't you? My ex-wife's second husband's cousin?'

Atherton shrugged. 'You may be scraping the bottom of tenuous before you're finished.'

Slider rubbed his head and groaned. 'Mary Poppins, where are you when you're needed?'

He had to get on with some work, but he was left puzzling why Joanna had been so snarky about it, when usually she was as reasonable as pie. They *never* quarrelled. Was she unwell? But she seemed all right – blooming, in fact. Apart from the snark. That was as bad as the waft for disrupting a well-organised life.

Swilley came in with the telephone log. 'On the landline, during the last day, the calls seem to be business-related. He had a short call from Cathy Beccles – presumably confirming their lunch. He had one from a solicitor called Duncan Grieves, six twenty-eight to six forty-one – that's the last, no more after that. And just before that, Virginia Foulkes called from six oh-one to six twenty-five. On his mobile, he had one to and one from Calliope Hunt, both quite long. Others are probably also business, or maybe combined – a short one from someone called Murray Pauling, someone called Petra Grace from a company called Simon Manning, a Maura Sambourne, who's an editor at Mirador, and interestingly, a BBC producer called Erica Beasley – I've looked her up, and one of the programmes she's producing is one called *Money Mart*, whose presenter is Marina Haig.'

'So he might still have been having contact with her,' Atherton said, perched on the windowsill, contemplating the crease in his trousers. 'That would piss off Simon Haig. Can we put him back on the list?'

'I didn't know he was off the list,' said Slider.

'I didn't know there was a list,' said Swilley.

'There is now. And Simon Haig is on it. I don't like him. He's smug,' said Atherton.

'I didn't know you knew him,' said Slider.

'I don't, but his books are smug. And I've seen him on Melvyn Bragg's *Write Now* programme – he's such a luvvie, he makes Martin Amis seem approachable and populist. He makes me want to punch him.'

'Steady,' said Slider. 'You can interview him, not punch him. And we need to have a word with Virginia Foulkes. She might know something about his state of mind.'

'Her call was after Hollinshead left,' said Atherton. 'She was the last person apart from the lawyer to speak to him. He might have mentioned expecting a visitor.'

Hart had drifted up and had been listening, fiddling with strands of her voluminous 'fro, today hanging – or rather standing out – loose round her head. 'Two long talks with Calliope? I bet she was coming round. Here, boss,' she added with a chirpy grin, 'how about this? She was round Ed's house bonking him, and Mr Carpenter comes round looking for her, throws a berserker and wallops him. That would account for why he wanted us to make it accidental.'

'Those are the sort of thoughts best kept to yourself,' Slider said sternly.

'Could happen, though,' she asserted, unabashed.

Slider shook his head at her, and turned back to Swilley. 'Look into all those calls, eliminate all the business, try to find out anything that's known about his state of mind or plans for the evening. Meanwhile—'

'Oh, let me go and interview Marina Haig,' Atherton begged. 'She's gorgeous.'

'Too rich for your blood,' said Slider. 'We'd never get you back. Didn't she go out with Prince William at one time?'

'I promise I won't let that go to my head. I'm no throne ranger.'

'Hm,' said Slider. 'All right. It's a pity we can't talk to Calliope. But somebody had better track down Brian Langley and find out what he was doing on Monday night.'

'I will,' said Hart. She intercepted his doubtful look. 'I'm not made of paper, y'know.'

'No, but I think your talents will be better used elsewhere. McLaren can go. He'll speak his language. And I'll go and have a chat with Virginia Foulkes.'

'Keeping the best for yourself?' Hart grinned.

'That's why I'm the boss.'

The room cleared and he called Swilley back, rather shamefaced. 'Um – you're off this weekend, aren't you?'

'Was supposed to be. But I'm assuming you'll want me in,' she said. 'It's okay, I could do with the overtime.'

'You sound relaxed about it,' he said. She shrugged, waiting for the point of his questions. 'So what will you do with little Ashley?'

'Tony will be home,' she said.

'And what would you do if he wasn't? I mean, if it were last minute – do you have a list of people to call?'

She gave him a puzzled smile. 'Are you in some kind of trouble, boss?'

He gave in. 'I'm supposed to be looking after George. Joanna's working, and now she's pissed off because I asked her to fix up a sitter for him. She says I've got to do it.'

'Tony gets mad with me that way sometimes. "There's two of us in this marriage" sort of thing. It'll pass.'

Slider nodded dolefully, hoping his male helplessness would trigger whatever the female version of chivalry was.

Swilley took pity. 'Would you like Tony to have him? He won't mind, and Ashley'll love it. She's always wanted a little brother. She'll go mental.'

'That's tremendously kind of you.'

'No sweat,' she said. 'Look, can you bring him in with you? Tony's taking Ashley to Toddle Town – it's an indoor playground for toddlers,' she elucidated. 'You know, slides and climbing frames and bouncies and all that sort of thing. It's in Hammersmith. He can pick George up from here on the way.'

'God, that would be a boon,' Slider said. 'Would he really do that? But how about later?'

'We'll fix something up. Don't worry.' She grinned. 'Makes you realise, doesn't it?'

She didn't elaborate. He knew she meant – makes you realise how much worry your wife saves you in normal times.

'Yes,' he said contritely.

NINE

Science Friction

DC Maurice McLaren was not given to introspection, and had little imagination, which was not always a bad thing in a copper. It meant he was not open to subtle appeals to corruption: if you wanted him to do something illegal or against the rules, you'd actually have to spell it out, which would land you right in the stickies when he told you he wasn't interested, that he liked his job and his boss and wasn't about to crap all over either.

It also meant that he had no fear, and would go up against much bigger men or unsuitable odds without even thinking about it. So when he looked up Brian Langley and saw a man-mountain with a record of violence, it didn't bother him. Langley was six foot three and weighed sixteen stone, and from the photographs that wasn't sixteen stone of fat. McLaren was five foot eleven and on the whippy side; but in a fight he was lightning quick. His mentor and relief sergeant when he had first been in uniform had told him there should only ever be one punch thrown in a fight, it should be his, and it should end it. Speed would beat brute force – that's what McLaren would have believed if he had ever thought about it. In reality, he had been a copper for a long time, and knew how to handle situations, so he never did.

Langley's criminal record was for drinking and fighting: half a dozen arrests over the years, but no court appearances – always let off with a caution. His address was in Fulham. His early arrests gave his occupation as tool fitter for Braxton Engineering in Battersea. The later ones showed him as unemployed.

'Living on the dole and writing his fantasy novels,' Atherton interpreted, looking over McLaren's shoulder as he happened to be passing. 'Probably sitting in his bedsit in his underpants with the curtains drawn, surrounded by posters of half-naked alien warrior maidens with green skin – the loser!'

McLaren didn't disagree. He'd seen SF geeks like that. Interestingly, though Amy Hollinshead had said he was an ex-Marine – presumably because he had told her so at some point – there was no record of him in any of the services, so it looked as though that was a fantasy too. And also surprisingly, he had no online accounts, no Facebook, Twitter or the like. His only appearances were in the chat room of the Fulham Science Fiction & Fantasy Fanzone – which boiled down to FSFFF and sounded like an angry cat – where he argued obscure technical points about characters in books, about whether their weapons could really work or their craft could really fly, and so on.

Atherton had moved on, and it was Fathom standing behind

McLaren now, a meaty, slightly sweaty lad, still on a learning curve. He looked at the image of Langley that McLaren had brought back up, and said, 'Izzat the bloke you're going to interview? Not going on your own, are you?'

McLaren gave him a ribald look. 'No, I was going to get me mum to hold me hand.'

Fathom missed that one. 'He looks well tasty,' he said slowly. 'You might need help. D'you want me to come with?'

'I'm just going to ask him a few questions,' McLaren said impatiently, 'not go ten rounds with him.'

'Yeah, but . . .' said Fathom.

'What?'

'Well, some of the lads downstairs,' Fathom said reluctantly, 'they reckoned since you got together with Natalie – well, they reckon you might've lost your edge.'

McLaren rose so quickly, Fathom sprang back and almost lost his balance. 'Me? Lost my edge? I got more edge than . . . than . . .'

'A stellated dodecahedron,' Atherton suggested, passing back the other way.

'What's that?' Fathom asked suspiciously. Brainy ponces like Atherton, in his experience, were apt to make fun of you if you left them an opening.

Atherton hadn't paused. 'A very edgy thing,' he threw over his shoulder.

'Yeah, that's me,' said McLaren.

He grabbed an Airwave from the rack by the door, and left.

The place Langley lived in Fulham was the upstairs half of a tiny Victorian terraced cottage that had been divided by developers, probably with their breath held, into two self-contained flats. McLaren knew very well what it would be like inside, because he currently lived in the downstairs half of an identical house in Putney. The victim of two failed marriages, it was all he could afford.

As he waited for someone to vacate a parking space so that he could get in, he pondered a moment on that business about edge, and whether there could be anything in it. Now he'd got Natalie, he was happy, and that was a very strange sensation for him. Women, from his experience of two wives and multiple girlfriends, were sharp, uncomfortable things – alluring, but affording no rest, like a bed with broken springs. They watched you, judged you, criticised you, told you with that withering sarcasm how far short you fell of their ideal of manhood.

And they changed the rules all the time, so you never knew from day to day what was going to get you into trouble. You could say innocently, 'You look nice in those trousers', and they'd be on you, like a terrier grabbing a rat. 'What d'you mean, in these trousers? What's wrong with the ones I was wearing yesterday? You think my bum looks big, don't you? Why don't you just say it, you think my bum's enormous. I suppose you want me to wear a dress. I know you, you want me in stockings and suspenders. I suppose that WPC tart you're always drooling over wears suspenders. And a thong, the dirty trollop.' And so on. They'd be all soft and lovey-dovey while they were trying to get you to marry them, and as soon as you got within tasting distance of that nice bit of cheese, *crack*! Down came the metal spring and broke your back.

But Natalie . . . Nat . . . Nat was different. She seemed actually to *like* him. Not some version of him she was going to try to change him into, but *him* – which he found pretty difficult to believe, because when he removed the necessary outer layer of machismo needed for the Job, he didn't think he was much of a catch. He wasn't handsome, young or rich, he couldn't talk like Atherton, and he'd developed some pretty ropey bachelor habits over the years, like eating cereal out of the packet and drinking straight from the kitchen tap. And farting ad lib.

But Nat was round and warm, she drank beer and played darts, she laughed at his jokes, she liked his mates, she knew what the offside rule was, and she seemed extremely partial to his stringy bod. Too good to be true? He was aware that his colleagues didn't think she was any oil painting, but she seemed beautiful to him – a woman without scorn in her eyes or acid in her tongue.

He was happy. Did that make him less of a force? An irritated motor horn behind him snapped him back to reality, and he slid into the now-vacant parking place. And at the same time, his mind snapped back into copper mode. Thoughts of home and women fell away as cleanly as a mould rapped with a mallet, and it was DC McLaren who got out of the car, and walked along towards the house, his mind subconsciously noticing and processing everything about his surroundings.

The little house, built for railway workers in the 1880s, had an unloved appearance now. What had been the front garden was covered with stained concrete, on which stood two wheelie bins and a squashed KFC box. The decorated tiles of the front path were cracked and several were missing, the front door was battered, the windows dirty, and the original brickwork of the façade, yellow London stock with soft red trim, had been covered long ago with lumpy Tyrolean and painted a gloomy shade of beige, like cheap coffee ice cream. Rented, McLaren concluded, and from a landlord who didn't care.

There were two bells by the door, neither labelled, so he rang both, long and loud. The door opened, but it revealed a short, thin, elderly man with an oppressed expression who could not possibly be Langley. Behind him McLaren could see a tiny snippet of hall with a door, open, on the left to the downstairs flat, and a closed door straight ahead covering the stairs to the top flat.

'Police,' said McLaren. 'I'm looking for Brian Langley.'

'Upstairs. Top bell,' said the man irritably.

'Is he in?'

'*I* don't know,' the man said as if it were an outrageous question. 'If he's not, he's down the Dunstan. Practically lives there. Don't ring my bell again.' He shut the inner door with a slam, but McLaren's copper's sixth sense could feel him lurking behind it, waiting to see what developed.

McLaren rang again and, since he was already in the hall, pounded good and hard on the inner door. He felt Langley coming rather than heard him – the heavy footsteps on the stairs sent a vibration right through the floor. Then the door opened.

Christ, he *was* a big bugger, McLaren thought. Big and muscular as a bull, in a cocoa-brown jumper and mustard-coloured trousers. His hair was shaved close up the sides of his head, but on top it was cut back to aggressive upright bristles, which had a gingery tone. His hand, so meaty there were dimples on his knuckles, held the edge of the door, ready to slam it. The other drummed an irritable tune on the frame with a signet ring.

'Brian Langley?' McLaren asked, but not as if he had any doubt.

'Who wants to know?' Langley growled. Meaty was the only word you could apply to that face; so meaty, the eyes seemed sunk in and small, the nose an insignificant nub; the fleshy chin was so deeply cleft it looked like a pixie's bum.

'Police,' McLaren said. 'I'd like to ask you a few questions.'

Langley stared a moment, calculating. 'I don't have to talk to you.'

'Yeah, you do, chap,' said McLaren easily. 'Otherwise I'll think you got something to hide.'

More calculation. Langley said, without expression, 'Upstairs.'

McLaren followed him up, or rather followed the enormous muscular bottom which was just about at eye level. Upstairs, the original two rooms (these places were built before the working classes had bathrooms) had been knocked through and then re-divided, so there was a small room at the back with a closed door, that McLaren guessed was the bathroom, and the rest of the space was now an open-plan bedsitter with a sink and an electric ring in the darkest corner by way of a kitchen.

The place was clean and tidy, but smelled of cigarettes, and underneath there was a thick, feral smell of feet and sweat that clogged the throat and made McLaren's neck hairs stand up in sheer reaction. There was also a faint, savoury smell of hashish, which he mentally filed for future reference.

There was a desperately cheap beige carpet, and the walls would have been magnolia if you could see them; but they were covered with film posters from fantasy movies, and with bookshelves packed tight with books and DVDs. There was a single bed with a cheap Indian cotton bedspread, a gas fire with a chipped ceramic mantle probably dating from the 1930s, and the rest of the available room was taken up by a desk on which stood computer keyboard, two screens, and printer and speakers. Before it was an old office chair on wheels whose seat sloped at an unnatural angle, presumably from having had to swivel Langley's bulk back and forth on a daily basis.

Atherton wasn't far wrong, McLaren acknowledged; there was nothing for him to do up here but sit at his desk working on his books or watching DVDs on the computer screen. There wasn't even anywhere else for him to sit. He'd have to eat his food and read his books at the desk, or sitting on the bed. It was not cosy. It was barely human. It was not a room to fill a visitor with confidence, and McLaren's professional eye had immediately picked out, without ever looking at it directly, that Langley did indeed have a baseball bat, propped in the corner between the window and the gas fire. His neck hairs had another workout.

Langley was standing in the middle of the room, his hands down by his side flexing and unflexing with tension. McLaren halted, aware of the open stairs behind him – good for legging it, bad for getting thrown down.

'Well?' said Langley.

'Ed Wiseman,' McLaren said, equally gnomic.

Langley scowled with anger. 'That bastard!' he said. 'Typical snobby, middle-class, bloody, arty-farty, privileged bastard!'

It was a lot of adjectives. McLaren was impressed. 'What did he do to *you*?' he asked.

'All that crap about "the market not being right".' He put on a mincing tone to show the words were a quotation. 'It's his bloody job to sell books, isn't it? Blokes like him *make* the market. No, I wasn't good enough for him, was I? If I'd've been some ponce called Sebastian from the good old alma mater, it'd've been a different story!'

'He turned down your book,' McLaren suggested.

'If you bloody know, why're you bloody asking me?' the bull bellowed.

'You know he's dead, don't you?' McLaren asked.

A stillness came over Langley. The hands clenched and unclenched still, but it was a wary bull. Thinking. 'Saw it in the papers,' he admitted at last. His feelings overcame him again, and he burst out with, 'Good bloody riddance!'

McLaren distracted him. 'Why did you say you'd been in the army?'

He looked surprised by the question. He had to think a minute. 'I thought it'd make him take me seriously. That sort is all Eton-Oxford-and-the-Guards. It was true, anyway. Nearly. I *wanted* to join the army, when I was a kid. My old man wouldn't let me. Then it was too late.'

'What, you were too old?' McLaren asked. As far as he knew, you could join right up to age thirty-two.

'You got to go in young to make a career of it,' said Langley, which seemed a slight evasion.

'Your book – that's not about soldiers, is it?' McLaren said. Keep changing direction, keep them unbalanced.

'No. Well – yes. In a way.' His face was not built to show much in the way of emotion, but he did seem to perk up. 'The Seers, the wise people of the planet Arimalia, they're trying to protect the galaxy from the warlike hordes of the Vorga, and they've got to find the Amulet of Horg, which will protect them, before the Vorgassi get to it. So they call in the Mercenaries of the White Plains, because the Seers aren't fighters, it's against their creed. It's a battle between good and evil, you see, and—'

That was enough of that, McLaren thought. Change direction again. 'Where were you on Monday night?'

It didn't trip an answer. The light faded, Langley's face congested. 'Why're you asking me that?' he said.

'Just answer the question. Monday night, between – oh, say, six o'clock and midnight?'

'I don't have to tell you that,' Langley said with growing indignation. 'Where d'you get off, coming here asking me questions?'

'What's the problem, chap?' McLaren said lightly. 'If you've got nothing to hide, there's no reason not to answer. Where were you, anyway?'

'Get out!' Langley yelled.

'No need to get antsy. Answer the question and I'll go. Where were you Monday night and what were you doing?'

'You fuck off! Mind your own fucking business!'

'You mind your language. Got some special reason for not telling me? Like you were out and about doing something you shouldn't?' Langley's face boiled but he didn't answer. 'Come on, chap, make this easy. Down the Dunstan were you? Lots of blokes there to give you an alibi? Or were you down Shepherd's Bush maybe. Having a word with your friend Ed Wiseman?'

The massive fist coming McLaren's way was fast, but he was quicker. He caught it in his left hand with a tremendous smacking noise and a jolt that went all the way up into his shoulder, but he used the counter-coup to whip out a blow with his right to the tip of the pixie's bottom, not enough to hurt either of them, but enough to catch Langley off-balance. He reeled backwards, more in surprise than anything.

'That's assaulting a police officer,' McLaren said. 'You're just stacking up trouble for yourself, chum. You wanta watch that temper of yours.'

Langley had steadied himself by the footboard of the bed, and now without looking he reached back and grabbed the baseball bat, pushing himself upright in the same movement.

McLaren didn't wait to see where this was going. There were situations you were better off observing from a distance. He ran down the stairs, slamming the bottom door behind him, and keying the Airwave as he shot out into the street.

It was always easier to question a man at the station, on your own ground, where you knew the layout and he was at a disadvantage. Not that McLaren thought in those terms. He simply reflected with satisfaction that the bastard had dropped himself right in it now.

TEN

The Time of his Wife

Virginia Foulkes lived in one of those solid white-stuccoed houses in Regent's Park Road, which could call itself Primrose Hill or Regent's Park as the fancy took it. According to Atherton, a lot of luvvies lived in Primrose Hill, and since she was married to Oliver Knudsen, the film and TV producer, Slider supposed they would go with Primrose Hill, even though, with the windows open, they were close enough to hear the lions roar in London Zoo.

He always liked to know what level of entitlement he was dealing with, so he looked up similar properties on the Internet, and found they were selling for between six and seven million. Of course, the Foulkes/Knudsens might have owned the house for yonks, since before the Russian-inspired property boom; but it still suggested a certain affluence. Popular novelist, plus film director that even Slider, who rarely went to the pictures and never stayed for the titles, had heard of; he shouldn't be surprised.

The area was very agreeable on a fine spring day, with a mist of green spreading over the trees in the park, municipal beds of tulips pinking up, blossom trees in gardens beginning to unfurl.

A squirrel bopped across the road in front of his car and shot up the peeling trunk of a gigantic, graceful plane tree. A black cat was baking its fur on a windowsill as he pulled up, and gave him one slitty yellow glance, before going back to the important day's work of sleepin' in the sun.

He rang the bell, and the door was opened somewhat precipitately by a very tall, very large man, with a fighter's body under a suit so bespoke and expensive it looked as though it could take messages, arrange conferences and run a personal organizer for its owner as well as command respect for him from all he met. It was the custom-built private Learjet of gentlemen's wear. It fitted him like a . . . well, like a suit.

Above the collar was a very clean, big-featured face and a very large bald head. The eyes were sharp and imperious and the face looked angry, though Slider, who had encountered a lot of anger in his years as a copper, decided this was the artificial sort that was designed to subdue minions and deter them from arguing. The face's owner was used to getting his own way.

Slider got his word in first. 'Detective Chief Inspector Slider, to see Virginia Foulkes.'

The faint, grey brows contracted, the eyes glinted as they raked him down. 'So, you've come to bother my wife with questions about that jackass?' he snapped.

'Sir?' Slider said. You could never go far wrong with that.

'Ed so-called bloody Wiseman! What a waste of space the man was! Well, come in, come in, if you must. I have a meeting to get to, otherwise I'd stay and make sure you don't upset her.'

'I won't upset her,' said Slider.

'So I should bloody well hope!' Knudsen barked. He turned and stalked into the house, and Slider followed, politely closing the door behind him. 'Ginnie! Darling?' Knudsen bellowed into the depths. 'Your policeman is here! Come and take him off my hands!' He turned back to glare at Slider while he waited, as though he suspected he might nick the silver if he turned his back.

And then Virginia Foulkes appeared, paused by Knudsen and said, 'Go. Go. I'll take it from here.' She stretched up and kissed his cheek. 'Do buzz off, darling, I'm quite capable of talking to the police without bursting into tears. Go, do your thing, win awards.'

He returned her peck somewhat sheepishly, gave Slider one last glare, and strode off further into the house, presumably heading for some back entrance, garage and car – or possibly helipad, who knew?

She came towards Slider smiling, and said, 'Don't mind Oliver. He's rather a guard dog when it comes to me, with anyone he doesn't know well.'

Slider took the hand that was offered, which was cool and dry and firm. 'No need to apologise for loyalty,' he said.

'Oh, he's loyal all right!' she said with a laugh, but didn't elaborate on the comment. 'Come through into my study. It's the pleasantest room in the house when the sun shines. Which is why I bagsed it, much to Oliver's chagrin. But he has his studio now – down the garden, but too grand to be called a shed. It's soundproofed and has every mod con and electronic gadget known to man, so he loves it devotedly. It can be hard to get him out – except when he has to go to work. I don't know really why we have this big house. If it weren't for visiting me, he'd probably never set foot in it.'

She talked on lightly, in a pleasant, musical voice, requiring no response from him. He knew this ploy. It was a way, which he had met before, of establishing control over a situation, usually encountered in the more mentally nimble. It came of a need not to say the wrong thing – but what the wrong thing was varied from situation to situation. He wondered what hers was.

Meanwhile she led him along passages – parquet floors, white walls, fine artworks, muted downlighters – and into a large, bright room with French windows onto a garden, mainly lawn, with surrounding, sheltering shrubs. This being inner London, it was not big, but it was green and pleasant, and with Regent's Park across the road at the front, gave the house a bosky setting. At the bottom was a long white building, presumably the studio.

The walls of the room were lined floor to ceiling with bookcases. There was a white marble fireplace with an enormous gilt-framed antique mirror over it. The ceiling was painted a soft, rusty red and pocked with downlighters. The carpet was dull red, there was a leather sofa and chairs, and an enormous partners' desk on which sat the computer screen and keyboard where presumably she composed her novels. The atmosphere was cosy and quiet, with the dark, bookish look of a gentleman's library, but the view of the sunny garden and the light coming in through the French windows made it anything but sombre.

She was watching him looking round at it, and smiled, and said, 'Yes, this is where it all happens. The factory for *mes histoires*. Nice, isn't it?'

'Very,' he said.

'I love it. I joke about Oliver's studio, but I love mine every bit as much as he loves his. Come and sit by the doors. There's real warmth in the air today.'

There were two tub chairs, upholstered in a faded hunting tartan, facing the open French windows, with a low round table between them, on which sat a paperback book and a glasses case. He took one chair and watched as she came round to sit in the other. She was, as he knew, about the same age as Wiseman, which meant in her sixties, but though not tall she had a neat figure and moved like a much younger woman, with an unconscious grace, as a cat does. Her face was remarkably unlined, her make-up subtle, and she had what novelists used to call 'good bones', with deep-set, grey-green eyes, and a good head of loosely curly hair of a colour between ash blonde and grey. Altogether, he thought, she was attractive enough for her age not to matter, or at least not to be the thing you noticed about her. Add to that a winning smile, and an expression in the eyes that said, 'I know men, I like them, they amuse me', and you could see, Slider thought, that she had led a full, rich emotional life. She would be easy to talk to, and that would be her stock in trade.

One of them, anyway.

She had sat, and now remembered, 'Oh dear, I didn't offer you anything. Coffee, tea? A drink?'

'I'm fine, thank you, Mrs Foulkes.'

'It had better be Virginia,' she said, 'since we shall be talking about personal things. About my darling Ed. Oh dear.' Her mouth turned down and she put her hand over it and looked away. Then she turned back to him, recovered. 'Don't worry, I'm not going to break down. I had my cry, when I first heard. Now I'm more angry than anything.' Her eyes sparkled. 'Because they're saying on the web that it wasn't an accident, that he was killed on purpose. And if I can help you find out who did it – that *is* what you're here for, isn't it? He wasn't ready to go. Someone stole his life from him. And him from me. I want that person punished.'

'You were fond of him,' Slider said.

Her lips trembled a moment. 'I've loved him for most of my life. Since we first met. That doesn't mean I had any illusions about him, ever. But love knows all and forgives all, doesn't it?'

'And did he love you?'

'Oh yes. I understood him, you see. That made me a rare commodity.'

'Your husband said he was a jackass.'

It didn't upset her. She smiled. 'Yes, husbands mostly did think that.'

'He was, surely, a sexual predator? Not an admirable thing to be?'

'Oh dear, is that what you think of him? No, no. You don't understand.' She thought a moment. 'When a man has sex with a woman, we tend to think of him *taking* something from her. But in fact, with Ed, every time, he left a little of himself behind. It was the women who were predating *him*.' She looked to see if he was believing her. 'He never had to force them, you know,' she said reproachfully. 'They were all over him. Every woman wanted a little piece of Ed. They pecked him to death, my poor lamb.'

'I'm afraid I find that—'

'Hard to believe?'

'Isn't it every man's dream to be desirable to lots of women?'

'Is it *yours*?' She said it with a hard but humorous look directly at him. He didn't answer – of course, it *wasn't* – because they weren't here to talk about him. She went on. 'I've known a lot of men in my life, and I never knew one who didn't really just want to be loved properly by one woman.'

He thought of Atherton, and wondered if she could possibly be right. 'You're a romantic novelist, I believe?'

Now she laughed. 'You think that was a sales pitch?'

'No. But perhaps you might have a certain way of looking at the world.'

'Oh dear. I can see you don't know much about writers. But why should you? In fact, I write Regency detective stories, so I don't know what that says about my mindset. There is a bit of romance in them, too. But what I write about is people, and they're much the same in any age.'

All very nice, he thought, until someone loses an eye. When she talked about 'people', she meant a very different set from the ones he had been encountering since he first joined the Job, who would have to work themselves up the social ladder to be gutter trash.

But she might be quite acute about those on her own level. She might be useful to him. 'Tell me about Ed Wiseman.'

She needed no encouragement. 'I met him at Oxford. He was at Balliol. I was a Hildabeeste – St Hilda's,' she translated to his blank look. 'Where I was a bit of a fish out of water. They were all desperately academic, and I was a good-time girl. I met Ed on a frolic and we hung out together, along with Gus and Lionel. We were a posse, the four of us. Happy times,' she sighed.

'That's Lionel Tippet and Murray Pauling?' She nodded. 'Why do you call him Gus?'

'That's his nickname. Everyone calls him Gus now, but we originated it. Because he was always saying *de gustibus non est disputandum*. He got hold of the phrase at an impressionable age and thought it suited him. It was his signature, like Terry Pratchett's hat.'

'That's a very sophisticated way of getting a nickname.'

'We were sophisticated creatures. So we thought. We drank black velvet. We read Iris Murdoch. We smoked pot. We believed in free love.'

'And did you practise it?'

She made a moue. 'What a question! But since we're being frank: Ed and I were lovers. Li was too fried, even in those days, to manage sex at all. He was always more interested in drugs than any of us. He's dead now, poor Li. He became a very successful editor, specialising in science fiction – SF fans the world over know his name. He used to go to the conferences and everything. They loved him. I suppose it was the one career he could have made a success of, while in a state of altered consciousness. But it took its toll in the end and he died of a heart attack at forty-nine.'

'And Gus Pauling?'

'Oh, he's frightfully respectable. And successful. He worked in publishing too, then started up his own imprint, New Avalon, made it fly, bought up a lot of little independents, so he's now the boss of what they call a publishing empire. Has a lovely wife, two lovely children, a lovely house in Hampstead and a lovely farmhouse in the South of France. Everything just as it should be.'

'Were you and he lovers at Oxford?'

'No, Gus never made a play for me. I thought he just didn't

fancy me, but I came to realise quite soon afterwards that the reason was he had a secret burning passion for Ed.'

'I thought you said he was married?' said Slider.

'Yes, married with two lovely children. Not everyone is liberated, you know. He'd tie himself in knots to prevent anyone finding out. The poor lamb is so far in the closet, he's practically in Narnia.'

'He and Ed were still friends at the end,' Slider suggested, remembering the phone call.

'Oh yes. Still close. Ed was very loyal, you know – once he loved you, he always loved you.'

'But he didn't marry you,' said Slider.

'Accident of timing,' she said with a shrug. 'I wasn't what he was looking for, then. And, frankly, I had other priorities than marriage. By the time we could have got together in that way, he'd already married Reggie. And, before you ask, no, he would never have divorced her for me. Loyal, you see.'

'But they *were* divorced.'

'That was entirely Reggie's doing. She was sick of him and she'd got a new man lined up.' She sighed again. 'It's a pity. He and I would have been good together. Reggie just wasn't built the right way.'

'She didn't like his infidelities.'

'Infidelities,' she chuckled. 'What a dear little word! But if she'd loved him properly, there wouldn't have been infidelities.' She saw his sceptical look, and said, 'Let me explain about Ed. His mother died when he was twelve years old. That's a terrible time for a boy to lose his mother. You see, for a man to be able to relate properly to women, a mother has to love her son, and then let him go. Ed's mother died, so he was never let go. He never got to the end of the process. He had no siblings, and his father was a cold man – not bad or cruel, but he had no time for people or emotions. He sent Ed off all alone to boarding school, then to university, intending him to take over his business. So when I met Ed, I wasn't what he needed. He was still looking for his mother.'

'And that's why he married . . .?'

'Reggie. Yes. And by the time he grew out of wanting Mama, it was too late.' She grinned. 'Puberty hit him about age thirty-three and he was off to the races! A port-and-lemon in every girl.

Poor old Reggie couldn't cope. Eventually she met Simon Haig, decided he'd be the right antidote, and shoved Ed out of the door.'

'Your husband and Simon Haig are friends, I believe?'

'How did you know?'

'They were together that evening when Simon hit Ed outside the Ivy,' said Slider.

'Oh, that! I wish I'd been there.'

'Do you?'

'Men hitting each other when they're not used to it is always comic. It's not like in films – well, I'm sure I don't need to tell you that. Simon punched Ed, and then the two of them reeled about cursing, Simon clutching his hand and Ed clutching his jaw. It was a toss-up who was hurt more. And Marina flung herself sobbing into Oliver's arms shrieking "Make them stop! Make them stop!" Pure pantomime.'

'Was it?'

She changed tack slightly. 'I'm afraid Oliver might have had something to do with it. I suspect him of egging Simon on. He has a misplaced sense of humour sometimes. Simon's not really the punching sort – much more likely to take out an injunction. But Oliver wouldn't object to seeing Ed flattened.'

'Is *he* not the punching sort?'

'Oh, he's quite capable of it, if provoked.'

'By a man sleeping with his wife, for instance?'

She paused a moment, looking at him. 'Goodness, you don't pull your punches, do you? Oliver didn't like Ed, but that was just a clash of personalities. It had nothing to do with my sleeping with him. Oliver has his own little peccadilloes,' she went on, with a sharpness in her tone. 'His little actresses and production assistants. I turn a blind eye to his, and he turns a blind eye to mine. It's a civilised marriage.'

'So you were still sleeping with Ed?'

'Now and then. It wasn't a big thing any more. We both had busy lives. Occasionally, when we met, and it happened that way, we would get together. But what we felt for each other never changed. We were each other's best friend, if you like.'

'So he told you his problems?'

'He told me everything. Mostly on the phone – as I said, we didn't meet very often.'

'You rang him on Monday.'

Her mood was further dampened. The smile had all gone. 'I suppose I shouldn't be surprised that you know that.'

'What did you talk about?'

'This and that. What friends talk about.'

'Specifically?' She didn't answer, staring at her hands. 'It may be important,' he urged gently. 'You must realise that knowing what was on his mind on the last day of his life—'

She winced at the words. 'If you must know, he was talking about Calliope Hunt. Again.'

'*What* about her?'

'About how wonderful she was and what a wonderful career she was going to have. And her wonderful bloody book.' She looked across at him. 'You know about Calliope Hunt and her book?'

'I know that Ed was handling it for her.'

She snorted. 'That wasn't all he was handling! And, by the way, there's a long tradition of the casting couch, and not only in Hollywood.'

'You think she was sleeping with him to get her book published?'

'Or possibly the other way round. He was promising to get her book published in return for getting into her knickers. Though I'm sure she didn't wear them. She looks the thong type to me. No good can ever come of consorting with a girl who wears the sort of underwear you could floss with.'

She was using humour to hide her hurt, he thought. She had not liked that relationship. Jealous? She had loved Ed all her life – had she still hoped they might get together? And was there an echo for her, with her husband's 'peccadilloes'? The use of the expression 'casting couch'. . . . She was an attractive woman, but he knew, as every sensible person did, that there was a difference between a man of sixty-nine and a woman of sixty-nine, however relatively fit they were. Ed and Oliver could get all the nymphettes they wanted with no trouble: wealth and power made up for age in a man. But what could Virginia Foulkes get? Not even Ed?

'Perhaps it was a good book,' he suggested.

'He was besotted with her,' she retorted sharply. 'The poor bloody imbecile. Completely cross-eyed goofy. The book was rubbish. Yes, I have read it,' she anticipated. 'Ed emailed me the first version, before he started rewriting it for her, before he got so involved.

I told him it was rubbish, but he started burbling about hidden depths and diamonds in the rough, and I thought his judgement had gone, his brain had gone soft. I wondered if he was smoking weed again. But after a few more conversations, I realised it was just an old man's last hurrah.' Her voice hardened further as she went on, 'He thought she was going to marry him, the idiot.'

'He wanted to marry her? It wasn't just about the book, then?'

'I told you, he was cuckoo about her. It was pitiful.'

'Why pitiful?'

'Because he was never going to get that book taken on by anyone. And as soon as she realised that, she'd drop him.'

'Perhaps she loved him?'

Do me a favour, said her eye-roll.

'So what was his mood like, during that last conversation you had with him?'

'I wish you wouldn't keep calling it "the last",' she said irritably. 'There's no need to rub it in. He was talking about Calliope Hunt, so he was cock-a-hoop. Very jolly. He'd just had lunch with Cathy Beccles – so there was probably wine taken,' she added facetiously. 'And he said she was going to speak up at the next acquisitions meeting for Calliope's book. Cathy Beccles of Wolff & Baynes?'

'I know,' Slider nodded.

'I can tell you now, she wouldn't. Whatever she might say over lunch, Cathy's got her head screwed on right – even if she is still carrying a torch for Ed. And,' she added, narrowing her eyes, 'if he'd got as far as begging favours from Cathy, who's a rights bod, not even an editor, he was desperate. His little dream bubble was about to pop.'

'Did he *sound* desperate?'

'No, as I said, he was jolly. I suppose the Calliope creature was coming over and he was looking forward to hot gratitude sex from his teen queen.'

Jealous, he thought. 'Did he say she was coming over? That evening?'

'No. He didn't say when he was seeing her. In the end I got fed up with the burbling and said I had to go, I had work to do, and he said, "me too" and we rang off.' She stopped abruptly and then added, looking at her hands again, 'If I'd known that was the last time I'd hear his voice . . .'

He braced her with a question. 'Where was your husband on Monday evening?'

She looked up with a quirk of a smile. 'Oliver? Is he First Murderer now?'

'Just routine, ma'am,' Slider said.

'He was out. Away. Filming somewhere in Essex – that place with all the old beamed houses.'

'Lavenham?'

'That's the one. Shooting a new episode of *Brimstone*. Have you been watching it?'

'I don't get to see much television.'

'I look forward to telling Oliver that,' she said with a taut laugh. 'You haven't missed much. I watched the first episode just to show willing, but it's too violent for my taste. Why has everything got to be so violent? They say it doesn't affect people, but I know it does. You must know it too,' she said, looking at him shrewdly. He restricted himself to a non-committal nod. 'I sometimes wonder what sort of a nation we're building, when our young people get fed that stuff from the time they're weaned. Even Calliope's rotten little book had a nasty sadistic seam under what she laughably called the plot. Violence everywhere. It's always a relief to slip back into my Regency world.'

'No violence there?'

'Well, you might get a pistol shot in the dark, or a rapier through the heart,' she admitted, smiling, 'but it's always done with impeccable good manners.'

He smiled back. 'And where were you on Monday?'

'Routine again? I was here, working. I'm in the last third of a book so I rarely do anything else.'

'And in the evening?'

She thought for a second, and then said, 'Here as well. I worked on a bit longer after I'd spoken to Ed. Finished about eight o'clock. Then there was just time to get some supper, listen to some music, watch the news and go to bed.'

So, no alibi, Slider thought. He brooded a moment.

She prompted him. 'Is that it?'

'Just one more question. Can you think of anyone who might wish Ed harm?'

'Apart from the husbands and boyfriends of all the girls he was *schtupping*? I'm joking,' she added, waving a negating hand. 'I mean, people don't do that in real life.'

'If he was in any trouble, do you think he would tell you?'

'Probably. I was his "person". Who else would he tell?'

'Did he have money troubles?'

'Not that I know of. My money came through regularly. He didn't have so many new authors lately, but we old war horses keep going, and he gets his cut of everything we earn. And he had a fairly simple lifestyle. He owned that house, he didn't pay Reggie anything and the children were off his hands.'

'Calliope Hunt might be proving a bit expensive?' Slider suggested.

'Well, yes – there was Calliope Hunt. And there's no knowing what excesses she might push him to. All I can say is, he didn't mention any troubles of any sort to me. He was happy and optimistic on Monday – the *schmuck*!'

De mortuis, thought Slider, *and then some!*

ELEVEN
Jab Well Done

Hart's interest in Liana Karev sharpened when she telephoned Translit and discovered that she hadn't been in to work since Monday, and hadn't telephoned, either, to say she was sick. From the HR department she got her address in Wandsworth, and headed off to sniff her out. It turned out to be a flat in a bright new block built on the site of a defunct factory in the town centre, handy for the Overground to Victoria, where Translit had its offices.

When Liana opened the door, her interest faded a little with the realisation that she was obviously pregnant, so less of a suspect for a violent attack with a blunt instrument. She was dressed unbecomingly in stretchy sweatpants, a baggy T-shirt with YALE UNIVERSITY printed across it, and bare dirty feet. Her face was pale, her eyes and nose pink, as though she'd been doing a lot of crying, and her hair had not been brushed in what looked like a couple of days.

Hart's spirits rose again when she showed her warrant card and got as far as, ''Allo, love, police,' and Liana gave a frightened shriek and tried to slam the door on her. There was a reason policemen wore tough shoes. Hart's foot was in the way before she'd even thought about it, the door jerked out of Liana's hand, and Hart said soothingly, 'Don't get your knickers in a twist, girl. I just wanna talk to you.'

'He didn't . . . I didn't . . .' she gibbered. 'He's not here! I don't know anything! Oh, *please* go away!'

Hart eased her backwards, got herself into the passage and shut the door behind her. 'Not likely, love. Don't throw a fit, there's nothing to be scared of. You look a mess. Let's make you a cup a coffee first. You had any breakfast?'

The nurturing treatment seemed to work. The young woman calmed down a few notches, though she continued to watch Hart like prey at a raptor's convention. *A born victim*, Hart thought with impatience she didn't show. She always felt that women who didn't stand up for themselves let the side down. But she'd grown up the sole girl in a family of boys, which she acknowledged gave her an advantage.

She eased Liana into the tiny kitchen, which was modern and newly fitted out, but with the sort of units that would soon show their age. Developer's Cheap was the brand. She put the kettle on and slammed two slices into the toaster, then turned on the cowering girl with as motherly a smile as she could muster and said, ''Ow far along are you, then?'

'Twenty weeks,' Liana answered, and burst into tears.

Hart gave her a couple of tissues and said, 'Is that what you've rowed about?'

Liana blew, and said in wobbly tones, 'How d'you know we've rowed?'

'Girl, you been blubbing, you've not gone in to work, and the first thing you've said to me is "he's not here". I can see you've had a row. Where is he, then?'

'I don't know!' she wailed. 'He won't answer his phone.'

'You tried 'im at work?'

'He's self-employed. He fixes computers on site. I don't know where he's supposed to be, and I wouldn't dare try and ring his customers – it'd make him mad. But I'm scared he's . . . he's done something.' Her eyes, enormous with appeal, fixed on Hart's face. 'You've got to help me.'

'That's what I'm here for, girlfriend,' Hart said mendaciously. 'Let's just get something hot inside you. You got to think of that baby.'

Thinking of the baby seemed to generate more tears. Hart made a cup of instant with two sugars, slapped some Nutella on the toast – all she could find at short notice – and hustled her patient into a sitting room whose sole beauty was a large window giving a view of a great swathe of sky. Turn your head slightly either way and the sky was hemmed in by tall buildings, but you took what you could get.

On the sofa, urged along by Hart, Liana sipped the coffee and ate a few bites of the toast, and seemed to revive a little. There was a box of tissues on the radiator shelf, and Hart brought them over and got the girl to blow her nose and compose herself. More bites and sips, and she judged her ready to be questioned.

'So, your husband – what's his name?'

'Gary. Garfield Burke. But he's not my husband.'

'I thought you left Wiseman's to get married?'

'No, to move in together. We got the offer of this flat, and I'd seen this vacancy at Translit. We were going to get married some time,' she concluded, and the lip wobbled ominously.

'All right. When did you last see Gary?' Hart had spotted a framed photograph of Liana cheek to cheek with a mixed-race lad with big hair and a chirpy grin. 'That him?'

'Yeah. Monday, when I got home from work, he was here, he was in a temper. He'd found this photograph of Ed I'd kept. He said he was looking for a pen when he found it, but I think . . . I think . . .'

'He was looking for it? Looking for *something*?'

She nodded miserably. 'He's a jealous, suspicious pig.'

'Where was the picture?'

'My bedside drawer.'

Hart mentally rolled her eyes. Really hard to find, then. 'And why do you keep it?'

'No reason,' Liana said defiantly. 'He was a good boss. I liked working for him. Why shouldn't I have a picture of him?'

'Were you in love with him?'

'No!' she said indignantly.

Hart gave her a shrewd look. 'Come on, darlin'. I didn't fall off the last Christmas tree. A girl don't keep a photo of a man in her bedside drawer just 'cos he was a good boss. Were you sleeping with him?'

Liana flushed pink, which showed up all the more because her face was so pale. 'No!' she cried. 'Of course not!'

'You were, weren't you? Oh blimey, you poor kid.' Sympathy made Liana's lip tremble again. The defiance had gone out of her. She watched Hart passively again, glad to have the initiative taken away from her.

Hart was thinking. 'Oh, wait a minute. How long ago did you leave the job?'

'Three months,' Liana whispered.

'And you're four, five months pregnant? Christ, Liana, is it Ed's baby?'

'No!' she cried. And then, blurtily, 'I don't know! I don't think so. We only did it twice. Maybe three times. Or four. It could only be when Amy wasn't there, and she was nearly always there. Ed said she mustn't know. Well, I didn't want her to know. She might have told Gary. She was a jealous, spiteful cow. She was like his mother – she had to be the one to do everything for him, no one else was allowed near.'

'Was that why you left?'

'No, I told you, Gary got the offer of this flat, we wanted to live together. Gary said sharing living costs would be much cheaper, we'd have money left over. We were going to save up for a wedding.' Her mouth bowed bitterly as the present caught up with her. Hart could hear the thought as plainly as if she'd spoken it: *that's all changed now.*

'Did you know you were pregnant when you left?' She shook her head, dabbing dolefully with a tissue. 'Did Ed know?'

'I never told him,' she said. 'I thought it was Gary's. Anyway, Ed always used a condom. It never crossed my mind it might be his. Not till Gary threw a wobbly.'

'And how did Gary feel when you told him you were up the duff?'

'He was a bit worried, because of my job and the mortgage, but we talked it over and we reckoned we could swing it. His mother could look after the baby when I went back to work. Then after that he seemed pleased about it. And we talked about whether we should get married before it came – just a register office thing – or keep saving for a big one later. It was all . . . all . . . lovely, until . . .'

'Until he found the picture? But you said you thought he was looking for it.'

'Well, he'd been a bit more worried about the baby lately. He'd lost one of his customers, so he wasn't making as much, and . . . I don't know.' She sighed.

Hart knew. He was trying to wriggle out of it, and like a fox in a trap, he was willing to bite his own paw off to get out. 'Did he ask you to get an abortion?' she asked gently.

A freshet of hot tears leapt alarmingly from the overworked eyes. 'Not before, only when . . . when he found the picture. Then . . . he said . . . it was Ed's and I was trying to trick him. He said I had to get an abortion. He said . . . he said . . . it was legal until twenty-four weeks!'

The last bit burst out, obviously the worst thing. He had looked into it. She put her hands over her face and cried.

Hart waited for it to ease off, and then said, 'Yeah, that was rotten. But look – he didn't say he was leaving you, you got to think of that.'

Liana raised her sodden face. 'What d'you mean?'

'I mean he still wanted *you*. Otherwise he'd have just said, "Not my baby, I'm off, sort it out for yourself". See the difference? The relationship's not over.'

She contemplated that. 'But then, where is he? Where did he go? Why doesn't he phone?'

That, thought Hart, *was the question.* 'When exactly did he leave?'

'I don't know the time exactly. I got back from work, he faced me with the photo, we had a flaming row, and he stormed out.'

'What did he say when he left?' She bit her lip, and seemed reluctant to answer. 'The exact words, if you can remember,' Hart pressed her.

'He said . . . he said, "I'm out of here," and I said, "Where are you going?" and he said . . . he said . . . "I'm going to sort it out". Or something like that.'

'Sort it out? Or sort *him* out?' She didn't answer. 'You said to me you were afraid he'd done something. What did you mean? What do you think he's done?' Big victim eyes stared. 'You know that Ed Wiseman is dead, don't you?'

This time there were no new tears, only a look of unfathomable horror. 'I read something,' she said. 'On the Internet. It was an accident.'

'Not exactly,' Hart said grimly. 'He was helped on his way. Is that what you're afraid of? You think Gary went over there in a temper and killed him? That's why you haven't been to work. You're scared you're living with a murderer.'

Her lips moved soundlessly, then she managed no more than: 'He wouldn't . . .'

'I think,' said Hart, 'we'd better have a go at finding Mr Gary Burke.'

In the car outside Virginia Foulkes' house, Slider rang Atherton.

'Interesting,' said Atherton. 'She has no verifiable alibi. Do you think she's capable of it?'

'Emotionally, yes. I sensed a lot of jealousy and bitterness. And she's a strong-minded woman who could do it and not fall to pieces afterwards. And there is a state of mind that says, "if I can't have him, no-one shall".'

'Hm. Also, if she thought his infatuation with Calliope Hunt was verging on senile, she might have wanted to put him out of his misery.'

'Well . . .' Slider said doubtfully.

'But physically? Could she have dealt that sort of blow?'

'You don't really have to have great strength, just to get a good swing going.'

'Okay, but bundling him out of the window?'

'Given time. It would be hard, but if someone was determined enough, they'd manage somehow. Once you've got the upper half over the sill, gravity takes over. And I'm thinking the culprit is likely to be someone who knows the layout of the house, and who is intelligent enough to be able to set a scene.'

'All valid points.'

'And we know he was having sex with a woman up there.'

'Bareback sex. And Foulkes is past the menopause, presumably.'

Slider winced. 'Let's not get too personal. But sex was had with someone, and it could be that someone who did it.'

'Or the man associated with her. What did you think about Oliver Knudsen?'

'I only met him briefly,' Slider admitted. 'But he's big, angry, possessive of his wife, and jealous. And makes violent television serials.'

'An episode of which he was filming that evening. Good alibi,' said Atherton.

'If he was *there* all evening. We've been caught out that way before,' said Slider. Someone had claimed to be at a wedding, which sounded like a terrific alibi, until it turned out he'd left before the bride arrived. You couldn't take anything for granted.

'All right, we'll check on that. I saw one of his films once,' Atherton added. 'Very nasty. Sick, even. Smacking Wiseman round the head with a baseball bat would be small beer compared with what his characters got up to.'

'Why a baseball bat?' Slider queried.

'Shorthand for the traditional blunt instrument. He was hit with something, we just don't know what.'

'We don't know a lot,' said Slider, dissatisfied. 'I'm on my way back.'

'What the?' Slider exclaimed to himself as he drove up to Stanlake Road. There was an excited media presence outside the station, and when he drove round to the yard, another one gathered at the electronic gates.

'What's going on?' he demanded as he passed into the back office.

'One of yours made an arrest,' said Sergeant Paxman. 'McLaren. We're processing him now. Name of Langley. A real beauty. Giving us a bit o' trouble.'

'Oh my God,' said Slider, quite mildly in the circumstances, and went to see.

McLaren had half expected Langley to come storming out after him, but he hadn't, and there was no sound from inside as he waited in the street for backup to arrive. When at last the factory wheels came round the corner from the Fulham Palace Road, to McLaren's surprise and concern they were closely followed by a TV van, which scorched to a halt and disgorged reporter, soundman and a bloke with a shoulder-cam.

'Who the hell called them?' McLaren shouted as uniforms Renker and Organ piled out, followed by DC Fathom, who always had difficulty in extracting himself from small cars.

'Dunno!' said Organ. 'They picked us up as we come under the flyover. They must've been coming this way already.'

McLaren cursed under his breath. 'You'd better go and keep them back. Me and Jez and Eric can cop chummy.'

The downstairs neighbour was hovering in the tiny hall as the large and heated presence of Lily Law trampled up the path, but he popped back into his flat like a rabbit down a hole when they reached the door. 'Is that him? You wanted backup for him?' Renker demanded indignantly – though even a medium-sized woman could take four men to subdue her if she was enraged enough.

'Upstairs,' McLaren said economically. They pounded on the door for a bit out of courtesy before breaking the lock, which was pathetically easy. They could hear Langley shouting upstairs, which could be interpreted as a cry for help if anyone objected. But when they galloped up the stairs they found he was standing at the open window onto the street shouting down to the press below.

'How did you know Ed Wiseman, Mr Langley?' someone below was shouting.

'I sent him my book,' Langley bellowed back in a carrying voice. 'It's called *Death Planet*. It's going to be huge. There'll be a movie and everything. *Death Planet* by Brian Langley. Remember that name!'

'Why did you kill him, Mr Langley?'

'Are you being framed, Mr Langley?'

Langley didn't have a chance to reply. Meaty hands grabbed him. There was a bit of struggling and scuffling, but his heart didn't seem to be in the resistance – it was more a show than anything – and McLaren got the cuffs on him with nothing worse than dishevelment. He left Renker to secure the house – 'Make sure you get that baseball bat!' – and with Fathom escorted Langley carefully down the steep stairs and into the street.

A small crowd had gathered, including at least one other

journalist, because two voices were shouting questions, which Langley seemed inclined to answer. McLaren hustled him towards his own car, and Fathom opened the door. At the last moment, Langley made a determined effort and swung round to face his public, and there was a flurry of clicks and a further splurge of questions and an excited babble. Several people in the crowd were holding up smart phones, photographing or videoing it.

'I'm the man who killed Ed Wiseman! Brian Langley, *Death Planet*!' Langley managed to shout before Fathom bent his head under the door frame with such determination he had either to get in, or lose it.

'How did the press get there just at that moment?' Slider asked despairingly.

'I reckon he had to've called them, guv. There was enough time while I was waiting for backup. And as soon as they arrived, there he was at the window telling the tale.'

'But why would he do that?'

'I dunno. Maybe he likes attention. Maybe he reckoned we'd got him anyway, and it was only a matter of time.'

'What did you arrest him for? Not the murder?'

'Course not,' McLaren said, slightly hurt. 'Assault on me, guv. But he was refusing to answer questions, and bad-mouthing Wiseman. Raving hatred for him, he was, which made him tasty for it. So when he swung at me it was a gift. Question him here instead of on his own ground, keep him off balance.'

Slider nodded. It was sound reasoning – and assaulting an officer was ample cause for arrest. 'Do you think he's a credible suspect?'

'Yeah, guv. He really hates Wiseman. And he's violent and unstable. And I reckon I could smell dope in his flat. Unemployed, so he sits there all day smoking weed and weirding himself out with all that sci-fi bollocks, and brooding about how Wiseman done him wrong. And you only got to look at the size of him. Whacking a lanky bloke like Wiseman and chucking him out the window he could do with one hand tied behind his back. And the chucking – it's the sort of thing he'd do to show he was the bigger man.'

'Chest beating, you mean? Yes, I can see that. Well, they're all good points. Anyway, we've got him now, so we'll question him, see if he wants to confess.'

'He done that already. Right to camera.'

'Yes, but I'd like him to do it formally. Find out if he's got an alibi. And meanwhile—'

'Toss his pad. There's this baseball bat up there.'

'Ah, the ubiquitous sports equipment,' Slider murmured. 'Organise it, will you. It would be nice to have something solid to present him with when we go in. You've got time. Processing will take a while, and then I'll let him sweat for a while, think about his sins.'

'Maybe he'll have calmed down a bit by then. He's a big bugger. He took a swing at *me*—'

'So he wouldn't hesitate to clobber *me*?' Slider finished for him. 'Well, I'm afraid he's just a bear I have to cross.'

TWELVE
No Pizza for the Wicked

'This is a mess,' Porson grumbled. He drummed his fingers rapidly on his desk with a sound like horses galloping away. Would they could all gallop away from this one, thought Slider. 'You've stirred up a hermit's nest all right. Bloody press all over it – exactly what Mr Carpenter didn't want.'

'That wasn't our—'

'And this Langley sounds like he's a few bricks short of a picnic. That'll get him sympathy.'

'McLaren doesn't think he's stupid.'

'Oh, McLaren,' Porson said, witheringly.

'He's a good officer,' Slider protested.

'But he's not pure as the driven. Got a few blots on his scuttle.'

'What are you accusing him of, sir?' Slider asked, hurt.

The drumming speeded up. 'I'm not accusing him. Just thinking that now he's nicked Langley, he's got to make it good.'

'Langley assaulted him.'

'So he says.' Porson made a restless movement. 'Well, get him fed and watered. Don't want any complaints in that department.

But nothing fancy – just a sandwich. Don't want him too comfortable. Doctor seen him?'

'Seeing him now, sir.'

'Somebody good?'

'Gill Carstairs. She knows what's what.'

'Good thing somebody does,' Porson said in dissatisfied tones. 'Get her report as soon as poss. And nobody's to talk to the press. *Or* any friendly stranger who just happens to be passing and wants to buy you a drink.'

Slider kept his dignity and didn't respond to that one.

Slider got back to the office and found Gascoyne had gone out and brought in take-away for everyone.

'Who ordered Thai food?' Slider asked.

'I did,' said Atherton. 'I'm sick of sandwiches and pizza.'

'How can you be tired of pizza?' LaSalle said wonderingly.

'I'm tired of life, also,' Atherton assured him.

'Did Langley get fed?' Slider asked.

'Ham sandwich and a cup of tea,' Gascoyne told him. 'Nothing fancy, as per orders.'

It sounded fancy enough to Slider. 'I don't think I even like Thai food,' he complained, peering suspiciously at the containers.

'You've probably never had the good stuff,' Atherton said. 'There's a lot of bad Thai around. This is from the Mamwing Restaurant – traditional Thai cooking, like mother used to make.'

'Ah, you mean old-school Thai?' Slider queried.

'Ho ho, guv. You put the pun in punishment all right. Here – that's *laap*, that's *phat kaphrao*, and that's *kai yang*.'

'Cute names.'

'They're a cute people. Try it with an open mind – you'll love it.'

Slider was doomed not to find out if he loved it, because before he had lifted the first forkful, he had an urgent call, passed on by the switchboard. A very excited man, so breathless he was hard to understand, further rendered himself incomprehensible by babbling about FSFFF, which Slider had not had McLaren's advantage of encountering yet. Once he'd calmed him down and sorted out the acronym, he obtained his name as Derek Horsefall, website builder by profession, and host of the FSFFF chatline by inclination. And he had, he said, very important information about the murder of Ed Wiseman.

They had all been following the Wiseman news online because several of them were engaged in writing SF novels ('Please don't call it "sci-fi"') and posted their success – or more generally, lack of it – in getting their works taken on by agents. In the process, they had all become well-acquainted with the names of agents who accepted unsolicited work, and Ed Wiseman was generally considered to be a king among men for his accessibility and kindness. So the idea that anyone had seen fit to murder him horrified them all.

Slider listened patiently to this not-uninteresting background – anything that helped to flesh out Langley's lifestyle was useful – and brought Horsefall gently round to the purpose of his call.

'Well,' said Horsefall, 'there's news clips all over the web about Brian Langley being arrested. He's one of us – I mean, he posts on our site quite often. And . . .' There was an audible click over the line as he swallowed. 'He's posted a confession. That he killed him – Mr Wiseman, I mean.'

Slider's scalp prickled. 'What exactly did he say?'

'I'll read it to you. He says, "Fellow fans, you've been talking about Ed Wiseman's death, so it's only fair to tell you that I was the one who killed him. You didn't know him like I did. The man was a low life and an impostor. It was pesticide, not homicide. So I got rid of him."' Into the silence as Slider finished writing it down, he said, 'It's awful, isn't it? Really terrible. Did I do the right thing, ringing you? Only, I know he's one of us, supposed to be, but this – well, you can't go round killing people you don't like. Not in real life.'

'You did exactly right. This post is still on your website, is it?'

'Yes, I wouldn't take it down until I knew if I should.'

'And you're the only one that can edit the stream, are you?'

'Yes, only me.'

'But anyone can post?'

'Yes, but you know who it is from the email address. So it was definitely Brian. Or definitely from his computer, anyway. Do you want me to copy and email it to you?'

'I'll look myself if you give me the URL,' said Slider.

'Man,' said Horsefall with profound emotion. 'I've never been mixed up with anything like this. It made my hair stand on end when I read it.'

'Murder is always upsetting,' said Slider.

It turned out that Liana Karev's attempts to find her beloved had been limited to ringing his mobile at frequent intervals.

'So what about friends? Relatives?'

'His mum lives in Brixton,' she said doubtfully. 'He goes to see her a lot.'

'Didn't you try there?'

Liana shrank. 'She doesn't like me. If he's told her this isn't his baby . . .'

'I get it,' said Hart. 'But finding him's a bit more important than that.'

But Mrs Burke hadn't heard from him since the previous Sunday. 'He's off working somewhere,' she said with confidence. 'He's a good boy, a hard worker, wants to make something of himself. Why you looking for him?'

Hart said only that he had quarrelled with his girlfriend and hadn't been in touch and she was worried about him.

Mrs Burke snorted. 'That one! Yes, she would be worried! Never get herself another good man like my boy! Why he picked her I don't know. I've introduced him to lots of good Jamaican girls, who know how to take care of a man. That one – she doesn't even cook, you know?'

Hart extracted herself, and the promise that Mrs Burke would let her know if she heard from Gary. She didn't seem in the least worried about his disappearance, which was either worrying or reassuring, depending on your point of view.

Hart then tried such friends as Liana could think of, and some of the clients identified from a file of invoices, with equal lack of success, before heading back to the station, armed with a photograph of the missing Mr Burke, and Liana's promise to ring her at once if she heard from or of him.

'He left in a temper, swearing vengeance on Wiseman, and hasn't been seen since,' Hart said to Slider at the end of her report. 'Lookin' good, innit, boss?'

'Promising,' said Slider. 'But there has been a development.' He caught her up on the Langley situation.

'He sounds like a right nutter,' she pronounced. 'So if he's confessed—'

'Not to us, yet.'

'Give it time. Then how does Burke fit into it?'

'You'll need to find if there's some connection between them. But first—'

'I gotta find him, yeah,' Hart agreed. 'I've got his laptop. I'm gonna go through his contacts. Ten to one he's gone to ground somewhere wiv a mate. But in case he's wandering the streets, can I send his photograph round the boroughs?'

'Definitely,' said Slider.

Marina Haig, daughter of Simon Haig, was a TV presenter of some note, appearing on such high-minded programmes as *Newsnight* and *Money Mart*, and semi-educational series such as *What The Romans Did For Us*. Atherton acknowledged to himself having fancied her for years – the thinking man's totty, she had been dubbed on one occasion – right up to the point when she had married Ben Dawlish, the retired England rugby captain and current sports presenter. The idea of that delicate gardenia being crushed beneath a meat mountain like Dawlish had quite put him off. But he was not at all unwilling to seek her out for a face-to-facer – just out of curiosity, he told himself.

He caught up with her at BBC Studioworks at the old Television Centre at White City, where she was engaged in recording a new series called *The Year of the Woman*. Atherton received that information thoughtfully. The TVC was only a short distance from Ed Wiseman's house, and if Marina Haig was recording a series, it meant she would be there on multiple occasions.

A production assistant showed him into a dressing room, and said Ms Haig would be with him as soon as possible, and after a ten-minute wait she walked in, dressed in a burgundy power-suit whose severity was mitigated by her trademark curly brown hair, hanging loose past her shoulders. She was taller than he had expected – he'd only ever really seen her sitting down – and had very good legs, and the studio make-up gave her a perfect, enamelled finish which focused attention on her fine bones. She also seemed a bit cross, but was holding it in out of politeness, or professionalism, or something.

'Detective Sergeant Atherton?' she queried, holding out a long hand, tipped with perfect burgundy nails. He shook it briefly – it was warm and damp, probably from the studio lights, he thought. 'I can't give you long, I'm afraid – I've got a studio schedule and guests waiting. Is it about Ed?'

'Why would you think that?' he asked.

She made an impatient movement of her head. 'Please don't play games – I haven't the time. What else would you want to talk to me about?'

'All right, I'll come to the point.'

'I wish you would.'

'I'd like to know what your relationship was with him. I know you were seeing him a few years ago. Were you still close?'

She perched on the edge of a dressing table and folded her arms over her chest. 'Define "close".'

He smiled winningly. 'Now who's playing games? Why don't you just tell me what you were to each other.'

She blinked slowly, thinking. She was immaculately turned out and, as a TV presenter had to be, was wafer thin. Under the make-up, she looked tired. What must it be like to be obliged to keep up that perfect façade all the time? Knowing that the paps would leap with glee on any chance to snap you looking frowsy or awkward, or even, God forbid, human? He felt an old admiration for her reviving itself. And, it had to be said, she had a certain something in the flesh. He wouldn't throw her out of bed for eating biscuits.

'We were friends,' she said, at the end of her considering. 'Once Ed's friend, always his friend. I was madly in love with him once. That passed. But I loved him dearly.'

'The time when you were in love with him – was that the time your father hit him outside the Ivy?'

'Oh, that old incident,' she said wearily. 'Blown up out of all proportion.'

'Why did your father object to your seeing him?'

'I'm not sure. I think he thought it was weird, because he was married to Ed's ex-wife. Incestuous, sort of? I can't really say for sure. On that particular occasion he'd been drinking and . . . well, was probably a bit high as well.'

'Cocaine?'

She shrugged. 'He'd been out for the evening with Oliver Knudsen, and they always behave badly when they're together. It's a thing they do from time to time – go out on the blast – and they behave like absolute idiots. They egg each other on. Anyway, he was with Oliver when he bumped into Ed and me coming out of the restaurant, and he just lashed out. Showing off, probably. There was no real malice in it.'

'There wasn't?'

She looked away. 'I'm sure not.'

Meaning she was sure there was, but she wasn't going to land her father in it, he thought. He saw her glance at the wall clock and hastened on. 'You said you and Ed were friends. Was that friends with benefits?'

It was impossible under all that make-up for her to blush, and perhaps she didn't want to, because after a moment she said steadily, 'We still slept together sometimes. I'm being honest with you, but I hope that won't go any further. I am married, you know.'

'I know. And I've no wish to make trouble for you. When did you last see Ed?'

'Last week. I was recording here and I rang him for a chat and he said come round afterwards for a drink. I was only there for an hour or so,' she added. 'I had a dinner engagement so I couldn't stay.'

'And on that occasion, did you make love?'

Her eyes were hard. 'Yes. If it's any business of yours.'

'I'm sorry. I'm just trying to get a complete picture of his life. And was that the last time you spoke to him?'

'No, I rang him on Monday – this Monday just past. The day he . . .'

'Died. Yes. You didn't appear on his phone log,' Atherton said.

'Well, I rang him,' she said blankly; and then: 'Oh, I remember – I borrowed Erica's phone – my producer. I was in the studio and I'd left my phone in the dressing room. I'd just had a recording cancelled so I was free that evening, and Ed was just round the corner. I thought he might like to get together. He said yes. But later he rang me back and said he couldn't see me after all, he had someone coming round and it was important.'

'Did he say who it was?'

'No.' She met his eyes. 'But I guessed. He was having a fling with a girl.'

'You sound as though you disapprove. I'm sure you knew he had a very active sex life.'

She moved her shoulders, as if shaking off something unwelcome. 'But this was different. All right, I knew I wasn't the only old flame he still saw, but this girl was another matter.'

'We're talking about Calliope Hunt, are we?'

'You know about her. Well, you know, then, that she was far too young for him. It wasn't a normal thing. He was unbalanced about her. And I'm sure she was just using him.'

'Do you know her?'

'I've met her around the circuit once or twice. She presented for local television at one time.'

'So why did you think it was her Ed was seeing on Monday?'

She frowned slightly. 'Because of the way he said it. The tone of his voice. And because he *did*n't say who it was. It would have been natural for him to say, sorry, I've had a call from Gus or John or Martin, sudden emergency so I've got to see them. He knew I'd understand. There was no reason for him to be silly and secretive except about *her*.'

'He knew you didn't approve?'

'I had . . . spoken to him about it,' she said circumspectly. 'Is that all? Because I really have to get back. We can't overrun on studio time, you know.'

'Just one more thing. You didn't go to see Ed on Monday evening. Where did you go?'

You couldn't catch an intelligent person with that question. They would always expect it. And she said at once, 'Home. I had an early night. I don't get many of them.' She was already standing up, to signify his time was over.

'Your husband was at home?'

'No. Ben's in Sydney, covering the Sevens for ITV.'

'So there's no one to vouch for you.'

'My cat, Felix. Why? Am I under suspicion?'

'We just like to be able to cross people off,' Atherton said smoothly. 'It makes life easier.'

She gave an indifferent sniff and left him. How like her, he thought, to call her cat Felix – jokey, referential, modestly erudite, retro-chic. Extremely cool.

And yet another person with no proper alibi. She said she had not gone round there that evening, but supposing she had. Supposing it was while they were chatting in Ed's study that he revealed he was seeing Calliope later on, and she went nuts with jealousy and whacked him, and then had to think of a way to cover her tracks. She was intelligent enough to think of the fall-from-the window scenario, and to make sure she had not left any fingermarks.

Or it could even have been premeditated. That thing about her borrowing someone's phone – had she hoped the contact would not be discovered?

The trouble was, they had no evidence against her, or anyone.

No alibi. And a grudge against the deceased. The same grudge, it seemed, endlessly recycled. All these women, tolerating each other because they had no choice, like cats forced to live in the same house, but each seethingly jealous of the newcomer who was not like them, who might oust them from their precarious perch on top of the bookcase. All of them wanting a piece of Ed. He remembered what Slider had told him Virginia Foulkes had said, that Ed was not the predator, but the predated. He had a certain sympathy now with the idea – and not even because it might give him a good excuse for his own wide-ranging activities.

THIRTEEN

The News, and Whether . . .

Loessop, the least well-known to the press of Slider's firm, had slipped out and had an anonymous word with some of the assorted media hanging around, and got the story.

'Apparently,' he reported to Slider, 'Langley rings the TV news and tells them that he's about to be arrested for the murder of Ed Wiseman. He says the police have come round and threatened to rough him up, but he's managed to barricade himself inside his house, and now it's a siege situation. He says he doesn't know how long he can hold out. So they dash round, because it's too good a story to miss.'

'Of course.'

'And as soon as they get there, he hangs out of the window and says he done it, he killed Ed Wiseman.'

'He also confessed on the chatline,' said Slider.

Loessop tugged absently at his beard plaits. He was good-looking in a piratical way, and cultivated a resemblance to Captain Jack Sparrow, as far as regs would allow. Slider defended him to an extent because it was useful to have a detective who didn't look like a policeman. Most of them were all too obviously Plod, with the Burton suit and the ten quid haircut.

'Yes, sir,' said Loessop. 'I've been looking at that, and the web generally. It looks like others from that chat room have spread the word on their Twitter and Facebook, and it's spreading like wildfire. And there are clips of the arrest from people's mobiles all over the place. It's going to go viral.'

'Is the general conclusion that he did it?'

'All except the usual anti-police element, that assume he must've been fitted up, because it's us.'

Slider nodded. 'Well, keep monitoring, in case anything useful pops up. A confession's no use without some evidence.'

'Renker and Organ are on their way back in from the house,' Gascoyne said. 'Maybe they've got something.'

Gill Carstairs was a tall, big-boned woman, with sleek dark hair today drawn back into a bun, from which strands were escaping to slip over her face. She pushed them back, behind her ear with a gesture so automatic it was almost a tic.

'I found him in a very excitable state,' she reported. 'I did a couple of field tests, and he's positive for cannabis and cocaine. And he may have other substances in there as well, so I'll get a full tox screen.'

'Right. Anything else?'

'No, otherwise he's fit and well within normal parameters – if not very clean. I'd say he hasn't showered or changed his clothes for a good few days. And I can affirm that he has not suffered any recent injuries.' She met Slider's eyes with a faint, ironic smile.

'God knows how. The size of him! How did they get him in without a bruise?'

Slider shrugged. 'He wanted to come.'

It was on the TV news now. Slider joined the group around the TV set. Against the background of the house, taped off with the usual blue-and-white, the woman holding the microphone said, 'And in a surprising development, a West London man today confessed publicly to the murder of literary agent Ed Wiseman on Monday. He has been named as Brian Langley, forty-eight, unemployed. Police are detaining him in custody pending investigation.'

And then they had a clip of the downstairs neighbour peering out of his window from behind the curtains, and ducking back quickly as cameras went off and questions were shouted at him.

'We'd better have him in,' Slider said. 'For his own protection as much as anything.'

'Renker's bringing him in, guv,' Swilley confirmed. 'Along with the baseball bat.'

Renker and Organ also brought good news in the form of three spliffs and a sheet of little white pills they had found in the desk drawer, ample to justify keeping Langley in custody for the time being. There was also a very illegal-looking combat knife and a set of knuckledusters they had found under the mattress.

'And we've got the bat, and his computer,' Renker concluded.

'That ought to get us enough to bring him down,' said McLaren with relish. 'Can I interview the neighbour, guv?'

'Yes, all right. But don't go in hard on him. Remember he's not a suspect. Meanwhile, I think it's time I had a preliminary word with Mr Langley.'

Langley seemed enormous, one of those men that dwarfs furniture. He was sweating nervously, and the smell of his sweat and his feet filled the interview room like an olfactory form of aggression. His big fists clenched and unclenched on the top of the table, and his little eyes darted about – as much as they could, sunk in the meat of his face.

In the absence of Atherton, Slider took Swilley in with him, and selected Dave Bright from the uniforms available, because he was big but also had a calming influence on the intractable.

He was the old-fashioned sort of copper who could defuse a situation just by turning up.

For himself, Slider adopted a cool, official sort of mien, as if this were nothing but a bureaucratic exercise. 'I understand that you've been offered a telephone call, but elected not to make one,' he began.

Langley shrugged. 'I got no one to call.'

'Is there somebody we could tell that you're here? A friend or relative?'

'I got nobody,' he said indifferently.

'And I understand you've waived your right to a solicitor?'

A trace of energy entered him, and made a muscle at the corner of his mouth twitch. 'I don't want one of those bastards! They're all the same. Liars and thieves! They're all out to do you down. Just like bastard agents. And bastard cops. You're all in it together. Establishment bastards.'

'Nevertheless, you ought to have someone to support you,' Slider said, but not with any great urgency. It was always easier if they didn't have a brief to hide behind. What mattered was that he'd said it, and covered himself.

'I said, I don't want anyone!' he said, his voice rising. 'I can speak for myself. What am I, an idiot?'

'I'm sure not,' Slider said soothingly.

'You bring a bastard law-monkey in here, I'll do for him, all right?'

'That's very clear. Have you been properly treated since you got here? You've had something to eat and drink?'

'Yeah, but I want a fag. I need a smoke.'

'I can arrange for you to be taken outside later for a smoke. When we've had a little chat.'

'Little chat!' Langley sneered. 'What d'you think I am, some middle-class ponce like you? I killed Ed Wiseman, all right? I'm a murderer. Whaddaya think of that?' And he sat back with a complacent smile.

'Yes, about that,' Slider said. 'I'd like a few more details, if you don't mind.'

'Well I do mind. I'm not going to do your job for you.'

'*Why* did you kill him?' Slider asked.

'That's my business.'

'Was it because he turned down your book?'

For a moment, red gleamed in the little eyes. Then he stared over Slider's shoulder and said, 'No comment.'

Slider sighed inwardly. They'd all seen that on TV cop shows, the 'no comment' bit. It was more annoying than plain, sullen silence.

'All right, *how* did you kill him?'

'If you don't know, I ain't gonna tell you.'

'How did you get to his house? Bus? Taxi?'

'No comment.'

'How did you first get to know Mr Wiseman?'

'No comment.' Langley's eyes moved from the wall briefly to Slider. 'You may's well save your breath. I've told you I killed him. That's all I'm gonna say. The rest is up to you.' And then he looked at the wall again.

While he was out and about, Atherton thought he'd follow up on a few more things. A telephone call to Stepchange, the independent TV production company responsible for *Brimstone*, confirmed that the schedule showed they had been filming in Lavenham on Monday. So far, so good – but he still had to check that Oliver Knudsen had been there. He asked who had been in charge on the location, and secured an interview with a Verity Tucker, as soon as he could get to their offices in Notting Hill.

Ten minutes later he was shown into a brightly-lit, modern office in a converted factory building, where a skinny, elegant black woman waved him to a seat while she finished a phone call. At last she clicked off, subjected Atherton to a keen all-over glance, and said, 'You were asking about the filming in Lavenham? May I ask why?'

He gave her his best disarming smile. 'I'd sooner have your answer first. You were there? You were in charge of the whole shoot?'

'Yes, I was. What did you want to know, in particular?'

'Let's start with what time it began. What time it finished.'

'It started before dawn,' she said. 'Getting everything set up. You have to work when the roads are quiet. Yes, we had part of Lady Street closed to traffic, but you've got to get all the equipment in.'

'But I suppose the important people don't turn up until later – the actors and director and so on?'

She gave him a shrewd look. 'Who are you interested in? Maybe I can be more help if I know.'

'Just tell me about the actual shooting, when everyone was there.'

'Well, that would have started about ten-ish. And we knocked off at about three, three thirty, because it started to rain and the light got too bad.'

'So everybody went home then, did they?'

'No, most were staying in local B & Bs.'

Damn, thought Atherton. More checking.

'Tell me who you want to know about,' she suggested patiently.

He gave in. 'The director.'

'Oh, Oliver. He went back to London. He wasn't going to be on site the next day – he had something else to do, and we'd got the important scenes in the can. The assistant director was going to cover the rest on Tuesday. There was just a couple of crowd scene retakes to do.'

'So Oliver Knudsen left Lavenham at about three thirty?'

'Or thereabouts. You could ask him,' she suggested.

'I shall,' Atherton said with pleasure.

He tracked him down at the Groucho, at a table in the corner of the dining room, eating shepherd's pie and talking to a tousled young man in a grubby shirt who was taking notes. Knudsen looked annoyed at being interrupted, and rose to his feet, scowling heavily when Atherton murmured who he was.

'What the hell is this? It's bad enough you people invading my house and bothering my wife, but interrupting me here is unforgivable! A man's club is sacrosanct, don't you know that?'

'I just have a few questions,' Atherton murmured. 'Better here than at the station, surely?'

That made him stare. 'Are you threatening me?'

'Is there anything I can threaten you with?' Atherton returned urbanely.

The tousled young man was looking from one to the other. Knudsen seemed to come to a decision. 'Tris, would you mind giving me a minute? Wait in the bar – this won't take long.'

When they were alone, he waved Atherton irritably to the vacated seat, and sat, addressing himself once more to the shepherd's pie. He ate wolfishly, shovelling the stuff in, barely chewing before swallowing. Everything about him, Atherton thought, had an air of controlled violence – though, of course, that could be an assumed persona. With someone so much in the limelight, it was a job to know when you got to the bottom of the pretence. 'Well, what is it?'

Atherton came to the point. 'You told your wife you were filming in Lavenham on Monday evening. In fact, you left there around three thirty. So I need to know where you were.'

'You've been checking up on me?' he said in outrage. 'How dare you!'

'We check everything. We have to. It's our job,' Atherton said, putting a hint of I'm-a-reasonable-man-and-so-are-you into his voice.

'Well, what the hell d'you want to know where I was for?'

'You had a very solid alibi. Now you haven't. And you lied about it.'

'To my *wife*.'

'Nevertheless—'

'Is this still about that jackass Wiseman? You can't possibly think I had anything to do with it.'

'I have to consider every possibility. That's also my job.'

'What if I don't want to tell you?'

'Then I'm afraid I'll have to inconvenience you until I find out.'

There was an instant of tension, and then the heavy scowl melted into a grin. 'That's a bloody good line! D'you mind if I use it?'

'Not at all. As long as you tell me where you were.'

Knudsen sat back in his chair expansively. 'All right – as long as you don't tell my wife.'

'If everything checks out, I won't need to tell anyone,' Atherton said blandly.

Knudsen's eyes narrowed a moment, then he looked away. The fingers of his left hand drummed a little on the table edge. 'I was out on the piss with my old mate Simon Haig, all right?'

'I see. And where did you go?'

'Pubs and clubs up and down the Earl's Court Road. That's where he lives. We do it now and then – sort of a pub crawl. Get a bit pissed. Let our hair down. You have to loosen the bow string now and then, for your health as much as anything. Tension's a killer, long term.'

Atherton nodded receptively. 'And you lied to your wife because . . .?'

Knudsen scowled. 'I wish you wouldn't keep saying I lied to my wife. I didn't say anything to her. There was no need. As far as she was concerned, I was in Lavenham. I don't have to clock in with her day and night like some bloody factory hand.'

'But you didn't want her to know where you were. Why, if it was just a few drinks for the sake of your health?'

Knudsen looked as though he wanted to blow up at this apparent irony too, but he changed his mind at the last moment. 'If you must know, we picked up a couple of tarts. I didn't want her to know that bit.'

'What were their names?'

'Aren't you listening? They were tarts, they don't have names. We went back to their place, partied a bit, paid them, and left.'

'Where was their place?'

'A flat, nearby. Some road off the main road. Penywern, maybe? I don't remember. I was a bit spliffed.'

'And where did you go afterwards?'

'To Simon's.'

'What time was that?'

He looked irritable. '*I* don't know. I wasn't looking at my watch. The whole point of relaxing is that you *relax*. We were with the tarts until the early hours, that's all I can say. I had a couple of hours' kip in Simon's spare room, then went to work. That's our usual routine when we have a night out like that.'

Atherton nodded. 'So you were with Simon Haig all evening and all night. What time did you meet on Monday?'

He frowned in thought. 'It must have taken two, two-and-a-half hours to drive from Lavenham. I suppose six thirty-ish.' He stirred restively. 'Now, can I get on with what I was doing, or have you got any more silly questions? Because, much as I would have liked Ed Wiseman out of the picture, I'm not fool enough to murder him.'

Or at least, Atherton added to himself, not to murder him and get caught.

*   *   *

Langley's downstairs neighbour's name turned out to be Douglas Wortley, and he was also unemployed, having been made redundant with the closing of Young's brewery, where he'd had a clerical job.

'My health's deteriorated ever since,' he complained to McLaren, casting him little peeping glances, as though his frailty might dissuade McLaren from duffing him up. 'I'm of a nervous constitution, always have been, since a child, and it affects my health generally. I'm not strong. I get dreadful neuralgia and toothaches. I should be on long-term disability, but my doctor doesn't understand a constitution like mine, he thinks I'm a lot stronger than what I am.'

'So you're at home most of the time, then?' McLaren pushed him, as gently as *his* constitution allowed.

'Practically always. I only go out for essentials. Noise and traffic, and especially people, make my neuralgia worse.'

'So you'll have a pretty fair idea of your upstairs neighbour's movements.'

Wortley closed his eyes with a martyred air. 'All too well. That man is a monster. I can tell you, my health wouldn't be as bad as it is if I didn't have to live underneath him. I've asked the council till I'm blue in the face to move me, but they won't. What do they care if I'm driven to my grave by that . . . that . . .'

'Monster,' McLaren finished for him with scant sympathy. 'What does he do, then, that annoys you?'

'*Annoys* me?' Wortley was left momentarily speechless by the inadequacy of the word.

'Specifically,' McLaren prodded.

'Well . . .' Wortley looked at a loss to begin, then plunged in. 'The noise, to start with. He walks like a herd of elephants, thump thump thump across the room, thump thump thump back again. Sits down with a crash. Scrapes his chair so the plaster flakes off my ceiling. Banging about all day and into the night. And the typing! On and on for hours . . .'

'You can hear him typing?'

'Have you seen the man? Hands like sledgehammers. When he types he makes the house shake. Rattling like a giant woodpecker up there.'

'Noisy music? Parties?'

'No-o-o,' said Wortley, unwilling to grant his neighbour any virtues. 'He doesn't do that. As far as I know, he doesn't have any friends. I've never seen anyone go up there. He's what you'd call a loner. But he's got a horrible, violent temper. I've been in fear of my life from him, when I've had cause to complain – like with him putting his rubbish in my bin. All I said was he should use his own bin – I don't see why his smelly rubbish should filthy up mine. I keep mine clean and swill with Dettol every week. It was a reasonable request. But his face went all red and he clenched his fists and shouted like . . . like . . . I thought he was going to kill me! I ran inside and put the chain on the door. And that was in the morning when he wasn't even drunk.'

'Does he get drunk a lot?'

'About the only time he goes out is when he goes down the Dunstan, and that's practically every evening. And then he comes back all hours, when I'm in bed trying to sleep, and crashes about, banging into things and cursing a blue streak, and then he's rattling on his computer and thumping back and forth. I tell you . . .' He shook his head with the impossibility of conveying his suffering. Then his expression sharpened. 'And if you ask me, it isn't only alcohol. I've had some very strange smells wafting down from his flat. And I've seen him . . . well, very woozy, in a way that didn't look like drink. I don't know anything about drugs myself,' he added primly, 'but I've seen things on telly.'

'Does he have a girlfriend?' McLaren asked.

'You're joking. Who'd go out with him? He'd squash any normal girl. Like I said,' he added, when McLaren gave him a look, 'he doesn't have any friends, not that come to the house. I'd know if anyone visited him, because I can hear his doorbell in my flat, and I can hear every footstep going up those stairs. I'm very sensitive to noise. It's one of my problems.'

'All right, let's talk about Monday,' McLaren said hastily, before Wortley got off on another organ recital. 'Was he in all day?'

Wortley screwed up his face to remember. 'Monday. Monday. Let me see. Well, that's bin day. I waited in until they'd been, because if they spill something and you don't get right after them, it stays there all week. So they came about half past nine. Then I went down the shops to get my few bits and pieces. I was out about half an hour. He was there when I left and he was there when I got back. In between I can't say. But he doesn't normally go out that early. He's up half the night keeping *me* awake, so he sleeps late. Then I was in all day, and he didn't go out until, it would be, about six-ish. No, make that half past, because I'd just got up from the news to go and make my bit of supper when he went crashing out. Thump thump thump down the stairs, bangs his door, bangs the front door. I looked out the window and saw him walking off down the road, and I thought thank the Lord for that, a bit of peace for a few hours while he's swilling down the Dunstan.'

'And what time did he come back?'

'About eleven. I was in bed, reading.'

'So you didn't see him?'

'Didn't need to. No one else makes that noise. Then he was crashing about upstairs his usual way, and it all went quiet about one o'clock, and I was able to get off for an hour or two. I don't sleep well at the best of times,' he added pathetically. 'If I get two, three hours a night I'm doing well.'

'Did you ever hear him talk about Ed Wiseman?' McLaren tried, though he didn't suppose the neighbours were on terms to have intimate conversations.

'Not till all that business this morning with the press.' He shuddered delicately. 'I don't think I shall ever get over that. To think I've been living downstairs from a murderer all this time.'

'Wiseman was only killed on Monday.'

'Yes, but I bet that wasn't the first time he's killed. He's mad – and violent. He's threatened me often enough. I bet I'm lucky to get away with my life.'

There was considerable satisfaction under the outrage in his tone. How everyone likes to be the centre of attention, McLaren thought. But as far as it went, his witness seemed to be good, that Langley was out of the house from six thirty until eleven, just the right time to be killing Wiseman.

Or, as McLaren had taken to calling him in his mind, Not So Wiseman.

FOURTEEN
On the Trail of the Loathsome Vine

A therton tracked down Simon Haig at home and, fortunately, his wife wasn't there. Haig himself was in the process of changing into dinner jacket for a formal evening do, and Atherton caught him in demi-toilette and a bad temper. His dress trousers were topped with a pleat-fronted shirt, collar open, one cufflink in and one out, and his black tie hanging over his shoulder.

'I hope this is important,' he grumped, fiddling with the second link. 'I'm in a hurry. Literary dinner at the Dorch, and I'm the guest of honour, so I can't be late.'

It was a lot of self-congratulation to get across in one short sentence. Atherton was impressed. The chummy use of 'Dorch' for 'Dorchester' was particularly crushing.

'I shan't take up much of your time, sir,' he said. Only a policeman can make it clear that calling you 'sir' is not a compliment. 'I'd just like you to confirm your whereabouts on Monday evening.'

'Oh Lord, not this again! You're not still on about Ed Wiseman, are you?'

'He *was* killed, sir. It *is* a murder investigation,' Atherton reminded him.

'Yes, but why are you bothering *me*? Just because I married his ex-wife? It's ridiculous. I had nothing to do with the man.'

'I'm not sure that's quite true. You must have met frequently on the literary circuit.'

Haig did the patient exhale. 'Just because we're present at the same event doesn't mean . . . For heaven's sake! There'll be two hundred or so people at the dinner tonight, but I won't know half of them. Or talk to more than half a dozen.'

'Nevertheless, you did know Mr Wiseman. And were known to harbour a grudge against him.'

'A grudge? I didn't like the man, I grant you. He was a wart. An excrescence. But—'

'Your wife still had feelings for him.'

Haig coloured. 'She made a point of getting along with him. That's how civilised people behave. I'm still on civil terms with *my* first wife. But if you're suggesting that Reggie—'

'And he was seeing your daughter. Potentially ruining her life.'

Now Haig stopped, looking at Atherton, weighing the situation. 'That was all over between them, a long time ago. She's happily married now.'

'She's still seeing him. And you know it. And you don't like it. You don't like *him*. You made that very clear when you punched him outside the Ivy.'

Haig made a restless movement. 'That was years ago. And it was nothing. I was . . . we'd had a bit of a heavy evening. Substances were taken. Anyway, it was meant to be a joke – you know, throwing a pretend punch – but my balance was a bit off and I connected when I'd meant to miss. We all laughed about it afterwards. He wasn't hurt. Nobody was upset.'

Atherton continued with the receptive silence into which an interviewee could drop himself.

'Look,' Haig went on, 'Ed and I were friends. There was no bad feeling.'

'Friends?' Atherton said silkily. 'You said you had nothing to do with him.'

'If you're going to jump on every word I say—' Haig began crossly.

'Let's go back to Monday,' Atherton interrupted, now he'd got him off balance. 'What did you do on Monday evening?'

'I don't remember. Nothing. I was at home, I think. Reading a script.'

'So, not out with Oliver Knudsen, then?'

'What?' He looked wary.

'He says you were out together for the evening.'

'Oh. Yes. I'd forgotten. I mean, I thought that was . . . No, of course, it was Tuesday I stayed in reading. Yes, Monday, Oliver and I went out. It's a thing we do from time to time. Memory's a bit hazy – you understand.'

'Boys' night out?' Atherton suggested. 'Drink, drugs, girls? Don't tell the missus?'

He tried for dignity. 'You needn't be facetious. People like us with stressful jobs need to unwind from time to time.'

'That's what Mr Knudsen said. You like to tear one off together. Purely as a health measure, of course.' Haig began to stutter, and Atherton went on quickly. 'What about these girls?'

'Oh, there was nothing in that. A couple of girls we happened to sit next to in the pub. Got chatting, bought them a drink. Nice girls – Australian, I think,' he added on a burst of inspiration. 'Just arrived. Hoping to work over here. Bought them a drink, then moved on. Nothing in it at all. But wives don't tend to understand that, so we wouldn't bother them with that detail.'

'I quite understand,' said Atherton, very man-of-the-world. 'And where *was* your wife on Monday, as a matter of fact?'

'Playing bridge. Monday's her bridge night.'

'She'd have been here when you brought Mr Knudsen home afterwards?'

Haig thought, brows lightly furrowed. 'Um – that would have been very late. Early hours of the morning. Reggie would have been in bed. She and I have separate rooms. And we were quiet, not to disturb her. Oliver bedded down in the spare room, and was off and out before she woke in the morning.'

'You're quite practised at this,' Atherton suggested, not making it clear what they were practised at.

'Well, we do it from time to time,' Haig said uncertainly.

'So, to be clear,' said Atherton, 'either or both of you didn't pop over to Shepherd's Bush during the evening?'

'Certainly not. Why would we?' Haig regathered his indignation. 'And now you've got that cleared up, may I get on with dressing? It would be frightfully bad form for me to be late, given that I'm—'

'The guest of honour. I got that. Very well, thank you, sir, that's all. For now.'

'For now?'

'I might have to come back and clarify a few details. Or ask you to come into the station to do it.'

'I'm a busy man – far too busy for this sort of thing. You know perfectly well I had nothing to do with Wiseman's death. I think you've just been amusing yourself at my expense.'

'I assure you, sir, I didn't find it amusing at all,' said Atherton. And took his leave, before the stink of red herrings could over-power him. The question was, which was covering for which? It would be nice, he thought, if it turned out they both did it.

But of course, important celebrities like them didn't do menial tasks like murdering the man they both hated.

They'd get someone else to do it for them. Someone less sensitive.

Slider took Joanna's car on Saturday morning, and she took his, rather than attempt to move the child seat from one to the other. It had been designed by a sadist with a twisted mind, whose deranged cackles echoed on the ether whenever harassed parents attempted to fit his brainchild in place.

George was stimulated by the change to routine, and chattered to Slider all the way in. He was full of questions, particularly about the girl he was to meet, and since Slider knew nothing about little Ashley he was forced to fall back on, 'She is a really nice little girl' and 'You'll really like her', and then contemplated how frequently one was obliged to lie to one's offspring, while George piled on the agony with questions about Toddletown. Was it like the Lambado? Interrogation from Slider resolved that this was a softplay centre to which Granpa and Granny Lydia had taken him. Slider supposed that it was. So then could he go on the climbing wall? Only Granpa had said he was too young. Slider supposed that he couldn't. George took this philosophically. He waxed lyrical about the delights of the Lambado, where there were big slides and real dodgems and chips in a bucket, and a tea party if it was your birthday, with a tiger that sang a song. Could he have a party there when it was his birthday? Given that it would be many months before George's next, Slider supposed vaguely that he might, and George seemed satisfied with that, and settled to look out of the window, only speaking to comment on dogs, cats, pigeons, big lorries, cranes, buses, and anything else of interest that they passed.

Swilley's Tony arrived promptly to collect George, and introduce him to Ashley, who was as golden and blue-eyed as her mother, and so ravishingly beautiful that George could only insert a finger into his mouth and stare in astonished silence.

'We've got a tea party to go to this afternoon,' Tony told Slider, 'so I can take him with us to that, if you like. I don't mind keeping him all day.' Slider gratefully agreed, and watched his son follow the golden girl out as though attached to her by strong magnets. *Know how you feel, boy*, he thought. *That's how I feel about your mother.*

Atherton arrived late, looking faintly green. 'What's good for a hangover?' he asked.

Slider considered. 'Drinking too much?' he suggested. He surveyed his colleague with scant sympathy. 'You've got a face like a bad kipper.'

Atherton groaned. 'Please don't mention kippers to me. Have you no pity?'

'Not for self-inflicted injuries.'

'All in the course of legitimate work. I was pub-crawling.'

'Ha!'

'But on the trail of a potential suspect.'

He told of his interviews with Knudsen and Haig. 'It was obvious that one or both of them were lying. The questions were which, and why. They both had reason to want Wiseman dead. Was one of them covering for the other while he did it? Or did both of them do it – one keeping nick while the other clobbered, for instance – and they were each other's alibi? I established before-hand from Marina Haig that they were accustomed to go out on a binge together from time to time, so they had an excuse ready-made, as it were.'

'But from what you've said, Simon Haig was a bit clumsy about backing Knudsen up,' said Slider. 'Surely if they'd colluded before-hand he'd have had it down a bit more pat.'

'It could be that he was just taken aback. Didn't expect to be called on it so soon – or maybe at all. Got flustered and didn't do himself credit. Or,' he added, 'he was being even more subtle and knew that a smooth alibi would look false so he deliberately fumbled the pass so as to look natural.'

Slider gave him a look. 'That would be *really* subtle. Suicidally subtle.'

Atherton didn't back down. 'He's a clever bastard who thinks himself even cleverer than he is. He could well over-think it like that. Or, of course, he could just be a bad liar and a general clot. Anyway, I thought it was my duty to hit the Earl's Court Road to try and winkle out some corroboration, or otherwise, for the alibi.'

'And?'

'No soap. The clubs were tight-lipped and slitty-eyed and couldn't confirm that anyone in particular was there or not there at any particular time. And the pubs were cheerfully ignorant. The bar staff are mostly East European, so they're polite and helpful, but they don't know customers' names.' He gave a dissatisfied shrug. 'They chose their alibi well. Impossible to prove or disprove.'

'So you sacrificed your honour, not to say your health, in a lost cause?' said Slider.

'Someone had to do it,' Atherton said modestly.

'Actually, someone didn't,' said Slider. 'If you'd checked in yesterday, you'd have known that we've got a man in custody who's confessed to the crime, twice, and in public.' He explained about Langley. 'And he's a huge man with a violent temper, a grudge, and a drug habit.'

'So my sacrifice was all in vine,' Atherton concluded.

Slider looked askance. 'Please tell me you didn't try to drink *wine* in a *pub*?'

'Hops grow on vines,' Atherton reminded him. 'I stand by my pun.'

McLaren had been jeopardising his own health at the Dunstan, otherwise the Dunstan Arms, a pub on the Fulham Palace Road, just round the corner from Langley's house. Most of the pubs round there had been poncified into theme pubs where young people with money hung out, or turned into pub-restaurants. They had cutesy names like the Pig & Banjo, the Jagged Hare, Truffle Hunter's, Foggy's, the Goose & Grapes.

The Dunstan was one of the last unreformed working-class boozers, and who knew how long it would hold out? The smoking ban had killed the straight-drinking trade, and pubs could not survive any more without offering food. The Dunstan was defiantly drab, of the yellow ceiling and sticky carpet variety, offered no food beyond packets of crisps, pork rinds and chilly pre-wrapped scotch eggs, and was frequently on the police radar for after-chucking-out-time pavement brawls. Atherton had said that a man with nothing else in his life had an inalienable right to his leisure activities: necking eight pints and then letting some blood out of his drinking companion's nose. It was the sort of thing Atherton said. McLaren's opinion of places like the Dunstan was simpler: it was where sad bastards went, and he wouldn't take Nat there.

It was as full of sad bastards on Friday night as it ever would be, and he slipped discreetly between the dreary denizens, trying to question them without alarming them. Most of them just wanted to be left alone with their misery and their pint, and answered him, if at all, in grunts. One or two threw him cautious or even apprehensive glances, and told him in carefully enunciated certitude that they didn't know any Brian Langley, as if they thought Langley might have installed listening devices and would come and get them later. Even the barman was studiously vague. Yes, Langley did drink in there most nights, no, he couldn't be sure he had been there on Monday night, or if he had, for how long, or when he had arrived and when he had left.

A sour old woman at the bar with lank grey hair in a ponytail and the sort of misshapen face that comes either from too much drinking or too many slappings-around, had been listening to this, and gave him a largely edentate grin and said Langley had been in on Monday all right, and what was it worth to him. 'Give us twenty and I'll tell yer,' she suggested.

McLaren ignored the last part of the sentence and asked, 'What time did he come in? D'you remember?'

An old man from a few stools down shouted, 'She don't remember her own name. Right, Maggie? Pissed her brains away. You wanna save your money, tosh.'

'Shut your face, dog-turd!' Maggie shouted back, then leered beguilingly at Atherton. 'Go on,' she urged. 'A tenner, then. I need anovver drink. What's a tenner to you? I seen him. I seen that bastard.'

'I'll buy you a drink,' McLaren compromised, and gestured to the barman, who sighed and poured another Mackeson's. 'Go on, then. Brian Langley.'

She sipped appreciatively, lifted her face with a foam moustache, and said, 'That big bastard? He was in here Monday night.'

'Yeah, but what time?' McLaren insisted. 'Gimme some times, ma.'

'Ma? You cheeky bugger. I ain't your ma.'

'I'll have that Macky off you, if you don't answer me straight.'

'All right, all right, keep yer 'air on. I come in about ar pars five of an evening, he gen'ly comes in a bit later, say ar par six. But he never come in till late on Monday. Ten o'clock time, summing like that.' She drank again, deeply, as if making sure of the stout before he could snatch it away.

'Are you telling me the truth, now?' McLaren said sternly.

'Course I am. 'Ere, you got a fag on yer?'

'No smoking in here,' the barman said sternly, proving he'd been listening.

She ignored him. 'Go on,' she urged McLaren. She winked. 'I'll stick it in me bra for later.' And she went off in a cackle of mirth.

McLaren looked at the barman. 'Is that right, he didn't come in until later on Monday? Come on, now, it's important.'

The barman looked away. 'I couldn't say.'

'He's afraid of getting called up as a witness,' the woman said contemptuously. 'I don't mind. It makes a change, dunnit? Maggie Goss, that's me. You can call on me any time you like, handsome.' She leered again. 'Give us another Macky and I'll give yer a kiss.' And she went off into another peal.

'You know you can get into serious trouble if you're lying,' McLaren warned her through the noise.

She sobered with a few wet coughs. 'If I'm lyin', I'm dyin'. Ten o'clock he come in. You can quote me. I ain't afraid o' that big turd. All mouth and trousers, he is. Yeller trousers!' she added in contempt. 'Who's he think he is with his yeller trousers?'

'So he's missing at the crucial time, guv,' McLaren finished his report to Slider. 'Not at home and not down the pub.'

'Do you think you can trust that witness?' Slider said doubtfully.

'What, Maggie Goss?' McLaren considered. 'She's a typical old bar bag, say anything for a dollar. I dunno that I'd put her up on the stand. But I reckon we can trust her far enough for our purposes. After all, we're not trying to prove an alibi for him. The other way round, if anything.'

Slider took the point. 'Still, we need a lot more for a case.

Confession alone won't cut it with the CPS. We have to present some evidence as well.'

McLaren knew that. 'I don't understand why he's not telling us everything,' he complained. 'Usually they wanna boast about how clever they were. Can't shut 'em up. Why's he saying he did it, and nothing else? I s'pose he's just taking the piss,' he answered himself. 'Trying to make monkeys out of us.'

Slider didn't disagree. 'But he may be more forthcoming today, after a night's stewing. Now his high's worn off, he might start to see the position he's in, and want to co-operate. All right, the next thing is to find out exactly where he was, and when. And I'm afraid that means a lot of hard work for you. He hasn't got a car. It's unlikely he *walked* to Wiseman's house, but it's not impossible, so that means finding out what cameras are on the most likely routes.'

'I know,' McLaren said resignedly. 'Plus buses and taxis.'

'And the tube. Again, not likely, with no direct tube route from Fulham, but we don't know that he wasn't somewhere else first that evening, so you'll have to check the station cameras as well. Get Fathom to help you. Gascoyne, too. The quicker we can get Langley pinned down, the better.'

'Yeah,' said McLaren. 'I won't be sorry to see the back o' this one.'

FIFTEEN

No Stoat Unturned

Langley was fidgety, nervous, a little depressed – probably the consequences of coming down from the cocaine high. It was better than his previous state of self-satisfied elation, at any rate, Slider thought. At least there was a chance he might actually think about the trouble he was in.

The custody officer said he had slept heavily and was eating well, though he was asking with increasing frequency for a smoke. He had also asked for a television in his cell. When that was denied, he asked for a mobile phone, and when that was also denied, for a newspaper – though, curiously, when asked which one, he didn't seem to know.

When he'd had his mid-morning tea, Slider had him taken back to the interview room and went in for another try. This time, he tried a different opening.

'How did you kill Ed Wiseman?'

Langley seemed startled into a response. 'What d'you mean?'

'It's a straightforward question. You say you killed him—'

'I did. He deserved it.'

'So give me some more detail. How did you do it?'

'No comment.'

'What time did you get to his house?'

'No comment.'

Slider stared at him in silence for a long time, trying to spook him. Eventually, Langley said, 'Look, I want a telly. Why can't I have a telly?'

'This isn't a hotel.'

'Well, a mobile phone, then.'

'You were offered a telephone call. You can still have one. You just have to tell us the number.'

'I don't want to ring anyone.'

'Then why do you want a phone?'

He didn't answer, chewing his lip. Then he asked, on the burst, 'Has anyone been asking for me?'

'No,' said Slider. 'Is there someone you want informed of where you are?'

'Everybody knows where I am, all right,' he said, as if it were a boast.

'Who do you think will be asking for you, then?'

He shrugged and looked away uncertainly. 'I dunno. Anyone.'

'Your co-conspirator, perhaps?' Atherton had voiced his idea that the posh guys might have got someone else to do the dirty for them.

'You what?' Langley clearly didn't understand.

Slider dumbed it down a notch. 'Did someone tell you to kill Ed Wiseman? Pay you to do it, maybe?'

Langley thought about that for a long second, his eyes on the top left-hand corner of the wall, before he said, 'No comment.'

Interesting, Slider thought. Why did he hesitate? 'Tell me about Monday,' he resumed, very matter-of-fact. 'Exactly what you did. What time did you leave home?'

Langley's eyes came back, but all he said was: 'No comment.'

Hart had a telephone call from Liana Karev, in an agitated state.

'Gary just rung me!' she cried. 'Oh my God, I can't believe it! I've been so worried, and scared—'

'Where are you?' Hart interrupted, to slow her down with a practical question.

'I'm at home. In the flat. I was asleep and the phone rung and I grabbed it and it was him! He says he's all right. I said, I thought you were lying dead somewhere, why didn't you ring me?'

Hart saw a change in persona since she had spoken to her yesterday. Then Gary Burke had been a jealous, suspicious pig who had told her to get an abortion; now she was the tragic, faithful wife waiting at home for news of her inexplicably missing husband.

'Take a breath, girl,' Hart advised. 'Tell me exactly what he said. Exactly.'

The mental effort required had a calming effect. Liana's voice slipped several harmonics lower, and she said, more steadily, 'He said, Li? It's Gary. I said, Oh my God, Gary, where are you? I've been worried sick! And he said, I had to get away. I'm all right. Are you all right? So I said, I'm all right, as if you care. And he said, Don't start all that. We need to talk, and I said, Bloody right, we need to talk, so come home. Then he said he couldn't come home yet, but not to worry, he was all right. And I said, The police have been here looking for you. What have you done? And he didn't say anything, he was, like, silent – and I said, Gary, you still there? Where are you? What have you done? And he said, Nothing. Don't tell them anything. And I said, I don't *know* anything. And then he just rang off, without a word.'

Hart was impressed with this feat of memory. Evidently every treasured word was burned on her brain. 'Did you try to ring him back?'

'Yeah, but his mobile was switched off.'

'Never mind,' said Hart, 'now he's rung we can work out where he was calling from. He might have moved on, but it gives us somewhere to start looking.'

'Can you really do that?' Liana said tremulously.

'Yeah, I'll get on to it.'

'When you find him – you won't hurt him? Just tell him to come home. Tell him I . . . I miss him. I'm not angry with him. I just want him to come home.'

'Yeah, I'll tell him. And if he rings you again, let me know.'

Now that Gary Burke knew the police had been looking for him, it was important to move fast, before he disappeared again. Hart knew Langley was downstairs, confessing to the killing, but that didn't rule out collusion or partnership between them, and Burke certainly had a much better motive than Langley – at least, in her estimation. She didn't know from first hand how strongly would-be writers felt about their books, but she knew how blokes felt about other blokes fathering kids on their women. It could even be that Burke had some sort of hold over Langley, and Langley was taking the fall for him. That would account for the lack of detail in his confession. All in all, Burke had to be nabbed, and as soon as possible.

It gave Slider a new angle at which to insert the knife and try to lever open Langley's shell. He took Burke's photograph down and showed it to him.

'Who's this?' he asked.

Langley shook his head, but then looked more closely and said, 'I've seen him before somewhere.' He thought a moment, and then said, 'Yeah, I seen him near the house. He was coming along the road, he looked at me—' He stopped abruptly.

'Near the house. You mean Ed Wiseman's house,' said Slider, trying to sound as if it wasn't important. And wasn't a question. Langley was looking at him with an unfathomable expression. It might have been fear, or dismay – it was certainly disconcertitude. 'What time was that? Approximately.'

'I don't . . .' Langley began automatically, and then stopped again. 'No comment.'

'Oh, come *on*,' Slider said. 'You've already said you saw him. What time?'

'I made a mistake. I don't know him. I've never seen him

before.' And he folded his arms across his chest to indicate there would be no more answers forthcoming. But the hands he tucked under his armpits were shaking.

'Interesting development,' said Atherton.

'It is,' said Slider. 'If they were both in Penkridge Gardens at the same time on Monday night, it suggests they were both on their way to see Ed Wiseman.'

'But together or separately?' Atherton wondered. 'And if Burke made Langley take the fall for him, why not simply deny he knew him from the start?'

'Because he's stupid,' said Hart.

'On the other hand,' Atherton went on, 'if there's no link between them, why did he try to cover up that he'd seen him?'

'At the very least, Burke could be a valuable witness,' Slider said. 'So far we've got no evidence that Langley was even there. So find him.'

'On it, boss.'

Hart went out, and Slider looked at Atherton. 'Langley doing the job *for* someone makes a bit more sense of his confession, but not a lot more. There was no need for him to confess at all. And Burke as the mastermind? We haven't met him yet, but surely a mastermind would at least arrange an alibi for himself. I don't think we've got hold of the right strand yet.'

'Hmm,' Atherton said. 'I know we've got Langley downstairs. And Burke has a top-class motive *and* did a runner. But I can't help feeling that Knudsen and Haig are up to something. I'm sure they were involved somehow – otherwise, why are they lying to me?'

'Come on,' said Slider, 'you know better than that. People lie to the police all the time, automatically, for no reason at all. It's just what people do.'

'Maybe,' said Atherton. 'But I'd still like to nail those two bastards. They think because they're rich and famous they can do what they like, and they'll get some kind of special treatment.'

'Privilege,' said Slider, and when Atherton raised an eyebrow, he said, 'That's what "privilege" means. Private law. The privileged have a private law system, and the ordinary one doesn't apply to them. Or so they think.'

'So can I go after them? Pretty please. Hound them and badger them.'

'And fox them. Leave no common British mammal unturned.'

'Humiliate them. Cut them down to size.'

'I can't spare you for a private crusade,' Slider said. 'That would be privilege too.'

'It's not a private crusade. I'm sure they had something to do with this business.'

'But what?'

'Don't know yet. Everybody's lying. Talk about tangled web! This thing is as straight as a ball of wool in a roomful of kittens.' His face lit with a sudden thought. 'You don't think this is going to be a sort of Orient Express job, do you? They *all* did it?'

Slider shuddered. 'Don't even think it. Can you imagine what Mr Porson would say?'

Atherton decided to go for Oliver Knudsen, largely because his office told him Knudsen was going to the States on Sunday night, so his time was limited. And also because Knudsen had been the angrier. Haig had been pissy, but Atherton felt he could take Haig, mentally and physically, with one hand tied behind his back. Knudsen was more of a challenge – and, if you wanted a work-related reason, the more likely of the two to have clobbered Wiseman and chucked him out of a window.

Knudsen was attending a script read-through in a rehearsal room in Archer Street, and when he saw Atherton, he rolled his eyes heavenwards, but he called five minutes. The room broke up in stretches and chatter as Knudsen got up from his seat at the head of the table. Atherton, eyeing the others around it, recognised a couple well-known actors and actresses, though they were all read-through scruffy and un-made-up. Most of them headed for the table at the far end, where coffee and doughnuts awaited, while others lit cigarettes. Private law again, he thought. Only a zealot would want to stop a famous film star smoking. They were special people.

Knudsen actually laid a hand on Atherton, gripping his upper arm to turn him and hustle him out of the room into the corridor, and shut the door behind them. There Atherton took hold of the hand and prised the fingers off ungently. He had quite a lot of

steel in his own mitts, artistic and elegant though they looked (or
so women frequently told him. Yes, and what *was* that, with women
and hands? Why on earth did they notice hands when he had so
many other magnificent features?).

Knudsen dropped his grip, and drew himself up in compensation
to loom as much as possible over his adversary. Atherton was tall,
but lean: in the silverback stakes, he couldn't outweigh Knudsen; but
he had the law on his side. The real law.

'So what the hell do you want *now*?' Knudsen demanded in a
ready-to-bellow-if-necessary voice.

'I want to know where you were on Monday evening,' Atherton
said with maddening reasonableness – he hoped it would madden,
anyway.

To do him credit, Knudsen, who was scanning Atherton's face
with noticing eyes, did not go the 'I've already told you that'
route. Instead, he said, 'Simon backed me up. What's the problem?'

'You've checked with Mr Haig,' Atherton said, not making it a
question. 'Unfortunately for you, I got to him before you did. You
hadn't co-ordinated the story, so his version differed from yours
in several details.'

Knudsen refused to be put out. 'Details,' he said, waving them
away. 'What do they matter? We were together all evening, that's
all you need to know.'

Atherton contemplated him thoughtfully. 'Ye-es,' he said, 'but
you see, that sort of thing doesn't go down well in court.' Did he
flinch slightly at the word 'court'? Yes, perhaps just a bit. 'People
would want to know why someone would change the details of a
story, if it was true. And if it wasn't true, people would want to
know why you and Mr Haig are telling porkies to police over a
matter this serious.'

'Oh, come on! It's not that serious!' Knudsen said
magnificently.

'I'm afraid it is. Ed Wiseman was murdered. You and Simon
Haig both had good reason to hate him, you have no alibi for the
time in question, and now you've lied to the police as well. You
can see how it looks.'

'We have got an alibi,' Knudsen asserted. 'We were together.
On the piss. You don't expect anyone as drunk as we were to
remember every little detail.'

'No one in the whole of Earl's Court remembers you – a bit surprising for two famous men like you, especially if they're acting like idiots.'

He flushed. 'Who said—?'

'Getting drunk, doing lines, reeling about, shouting and mugging – I know how these things go. And what about the girls?'

'The girls?'

'The prostitutes you picked up, who Simon Haig says were respectable Australian job seekers.'

'Oh, look – that's easy to explain. Simon's a bit of a prude. He didn't want to admit we picked up a couple of hookers. He wants everyone to think well of him – even you.'

Atherton shook his head. 'I'm afraid that's not good enough. I'm going to have to ask you to come along to the station and make a statement, and you *will* remember all the details, and we *will* check them—'

'I haven't got time for this nonsense!' Knudsen exploded, making as if to leave.

Atherton moved slightly to be in front of him. 'I know, you're going to the States tomorrow. Which means I'll have to ask you to come with me now. I can't risk having you run away.'

'Run away?' Knudsen exclaimed in outrage.

The door behind them opened, and the young man Atherton had seen with him in the Groucho presented an anxious, humble face. 'Oliver, we really ought to get on,' he began.

'Five minutes!' Knudsen bellowed, and the face disappeared. He looked at Atherton. 'All right. Come with me.'

He led the way into another room, off the other side of the corridor, furnished with a battered table and chairs, brown lino on the floor, walls painted dark green to dado line, dirty cream above. It was just like the other room, but smaller. Knudsen whipped out a chair and sat, and gestured to Atherton to do the same.

'Look,' he said, and sincerity was the facial expression that went with this one, 'I'll tell you the truth, but it's not to go any further.'

'That's not for you to decide,' said Atherton.

'Oh, for God's sake, don't be such a jack!' Knudsen said impatiently. 'I didn't kill Ed Wiseman – though I've often wanted to – and nor did Simon. Simon's a rabbit. He couldn't kill a wasp at a picnic. He wouldn't even send back a corked bottle of wine until I put some spine into him.'

'So why all the lies? Where were you on Monday night?'

Knusden made a spreading gesture with his hands. 'It's a thing Simon and I do. We worked it out years ago. If either of us needs an alibi, we quote each other, and it's always the same. We were out on a bender down the Earl's Court Road. That way, we don't have to check with each other on what to say.' His eyes shifted away. 'I'm afraid I got a bit carried away and embroidered a bit, with the two tarts. Caught old Simon on the hop.' He tried a rueful grin. 'It's all the scripts I get involved with. I'm always trying to improve the story, make it more realistic.'

'More dramatic,' Atherton suggested, tonelessly.

'Well – if you like. It's just a habit of mine. I look for stories everywhere. It's the job.'

'Lying to the police is a serious matter.'

'Oh, come on!' He appealed. 'No harm done, eh?'

'Police time was wasted checking on your lies. It could be construed as attempting to pervert the course of justice. And I still don't know what you *were* doing.'

'I don't see why I should tell you,' Knudsen said. He seemed sullen now.

'Because I will keep asking until I find out.' He locked eyes. He could do this all day.

At last Knudsen sighed. 'There's a girl. I was with her all evening and all night. But obviously I don't want my wife to know. And it would be like you lot to go prancing round there and asking her about it. So I used the Simon story, knowing he'd back me up. And before you start pontificating about "lying to the police" again, it's none of your damn business where I was on Monday. I wasn't out killing Ed Wiseman, that's all you need to know.'

Atherton listened to this impassively. 'Name and address, please.'

'Oh come *on*!'

'I have to check your story.'

'I don't want her bothered.'

Atherton gave him the steely look, straight into his eyes. 'Mr Knudsen, your wife told us that she is very well aware of your sexual activities, and she told us, moreover, that you *know* she knows – that it is an agreement between you that you both see other people. So saying you're worried about your wife finding out doesn't hold water. You will give me the name and address of the person you claim is your alibi, or I will arrest you for obstruction. *And*,' he continued, seeing some bluster on the horizon, 'I must warn you that if I check it out and it proves to be false, I can still arrest you for obstruction. One of the definitions is "where the offender's actions result in a significant waste of resources". In fact,' he concluded, getting to his feet, 'considering the time I've already wasted on you, I'm minded to nick you anyway, right now, and be done with it.'

Knudsen surged to his feet too. He was angry, but thoughtful. He said, 'I've got a reputation to maintain. My career could be ruined. You don't know what it's like, always being in the public eye. The press would have a field day – they follow you like ravening hyenas, just waiting for you to slip. Look, I'll tell you, but you mustn't let it get out.' He was pleading now. 'For God's sake – there's no reason to ruin me, just because . . .! Swear to me you'll keep it to yourself.'

'Whatever your alibi is, I will have to check it.'

Knudsen shook his head, goaded. 'I didn't kill him! You've got no reason on earth to think I did.'

'Only the lying. And the obstructing.'

Knudsen sighed, looked down at his hands, and then shrugged. 'All right. I suppose I let myself down. But I swear to you, if this gets out, I'll know who spread it.'

'You really don't want to be threatening me,' Atherton began.

But Knudsen said, 'Oh shut up,' not violently, but wearily. 'I was at a club, a special club I go to. In Soho. They cater for people with special tastes. You can check with them. They'll confirm I was there. And that's all you need to know. Do *not*,' he concluded, trying for menace, 'let this go any further. If it gets out, I know it won't come from them. They know how to be discreet – they have to.'

SIXTEEN
White Vin Man

It turned out to be surprisingly easy to trace Gary Burke from his telephone call to Liana, because he had made it from a landline, and unlike mobile phones, landlines can't be switched off. Hart snorted at the clever-cloggsery that had missed something so obvious. She snorted again when the landline came back registered to Mrs Abigail Burke with an address in Brixton. Gary Burke had gone running straight round his mum's. The address proved to be a flat in one of those 1930's LCC blocks, just like those in White City; and like those in White City, they had been sold off by the council into private ownership.

This being Brixton, there were not a lot of white faces around, so Hart fitted right in. Certainly when the door was opened to her ring, the woman before her showed no concern or alarm until she said, 'Mrs Burke? Police, love. Can I come in and have a word?' She held up her brief, and there was an instant of panic in Mrs Burke's eyes, and the brief contemplation of a slammed door, before wisdom overtook, and she said, 'He's not done anything, I can tell you that now for nothing!'

'That's good,' said Hart. 'Then it won't 'urt to 'ave a chat, will it?'

Mrs Burke sighed and yielded. She was a short, stout woman in her fifties, well-corseted and neatly dressed, with a fair amount of gold about her, enough make-up for self-respect, and a hairstyle done at a salon – a puffball on top of her head which the stylist had probably told her would make her look taller. She was achingly familiar to Hart, who had older female relatives galore who looked just like that. The layout of the flat was also familiar, for all these estates were much the same – she could have found her way about it with her eyes shut. She knew exactly where the sitting room was, and it was in the sitting room that she found Gary Burke, in grey tracky bottoms, T-shirt and bare feet – no surprises there – though all three elements were clean, which made a nice change.

He was sitting on the sofa, staring at the football on the television. At the sight of Hart he jumped to his feet and cried a protesting, 'Mu-u-um!'

But Mrs Burke said, 'They were bound to find you sooner or later, baby. You know that.'

'But Mum!'

'You haven't done anything,' Mrs Burke said sternly. 'You talk to this young lady and clear it all up. I told you from the first to do that. Get it over with now, Garfield, or you'll have me to answer to, so I warn you. I'm not going to hide you anymore.'

He subsided onto the sofa again, and ran his hands through his hair distractedly. He looked as though he hadn't been sleeping well.

'Yeah, get it off your chest, Gaz, mate,' Hart added her two cents. 'Poor old Liana's been dead worried about you, y'know.'

Mrs Burke snorted audibly. 'That girl,' she muttered disapprovingly. 'What *she* got to worry about?'

'Look,' said Gary in desperate tones, 'I didn't *do* anything!'

'Can I sit down?' said Hart. 'All right, so tell us, then, why did you run away?' He didn't seem to know how to start. Hart, who had taken the armchair catty-corner to him, leaned forward, elbows on her knees, and said kindly, 'You had a big fight with Liana Monday night, right?' He nodded reluctantly. 'About the baby.'

Mrs Burke jumped in. 'That's not Gary's baby! She's not a good girl, that Liana, and he doesn't have to worry 'bout her when she does a thing like that. I didn't like lying for him when you rung up before, but I'm telling you, he's better off out of it. He doesn't have to go back to her after that.'

Hart threw her a minatory look. 'How about making Gary a cup o' tea? He looks like he could do with it.'

Mrs Burke gave her a suspicious look, but after a hesitation she stalked away. Hart turned back to Gary, urgent to get it done before she came back. 'You had a big row with Liana about the baby,' she urged. 'You thought she'd been messing around with Ed Wiseman.'

'Well, she had. I know it in me guts,' he said.

'You guts might've lied, did that ever occur to you?'

He hunched up his shoulders defensively, looking like a bedraggled owl. 'It's not my baby. We used condoms.'

'So did he.'

'Sometimes they don't work,' he said uncertainly, as though realising where that argument trended.

'Well, it probably is yours,' Hart said, 'and there's ways to find out. But that's not the point, is it? The point is you had a big row, you said some 'orrible things to Liana, and then you run out the flat in a temper and went straight round to Ed Wiseman's.'

He stepped straight into it. 'But I never *done* anything!' he wailed. 'I went round there but I never went in. I rung the bell but no one answered.'

Inside, various bits of Hart slumped with relief that he had admitted it. Outwardly, she was unmoved. 'What'd you go round for, Gaz?' she asked. 'Have a little word with him?'

'I wanted to know if it was true. If he'd – you know – with Li.'

'And if he said yes, what then? You got a bit of a temper, haven't you? You was gonna bash him up, wasn't you?'

She thought he would cry *no*, protest, deny it, but he only looked sullen. 'Blokes like him, they think they can do whatever they want and get away with it. They think no one can touch 'em. Yeah, I'd have given him what was coming to him. But I tell you, I never got in the house. There were lights on inside, but no one answered.'

Hart shook her head. 'I think you did get in. I think he let you in, and you went upstairs to talk. You lost your temper, hit him too hard, found you'd killed him, panicked, and had to cover your tracks. Isn't that what happened, Gaz, old mate? You can tell me.'

'No!' he cried. He leaned forward, pushing his face at her, jaw gritted. 'I'm telling you the truth. I went round his house, but there was no one in. I rang and knocked but no one answered. So I went away. I was still mad, so I went and had a few drinks, and walked about a bit. I didn't want to go back home. I was mad at Li, I was afraid I might – you know . . .'

'Hit her?'

He scowled. 'I've never hit her in my life. But I was mad at her. So I came over Brixton, had a few more drinks with some mates – I know a lot of people round here—'

'Which pub?' Hart slipped in.

'The Prince Albert,' he answered without hesitation. 'Used to be my local. Then I come here to Mum's to sleep. I was pretty ratted, so I slept late, and by the time I got up it was all over everywhere about Ed being murdered. Then I got scared.' He raised brown eyes to Hart's like an apprehensive puppy. 'I thought you'd think it was me. I thought someone might've seen me.'

'Someone did,' said Hart.

He looked startled. 'What? But – who? Where?'

'In Penkridge Gardens. On Monday evening. At just about the right time – the time when Ed Wiseman was killed.'

'*I didn't do it!*' he wailed. 'I didn't do *anything!*'

Hart got out a mugshot of Langley and pushed it at him. 'Who's this, Gaz? Your partner in crime? Maybe you were in it together. Did you keep nick while he went in? Or was it the other way round?'

Burke stared at the picture at first blankly, and then with vague recollection. 'I think I've seen this bloke before. Is he big – really big?' Hart nodded. 'I passed him,' said Burke. 'I was going towards Ed's house and he was coming the other way. But I don't know him. Never seen him before that.'

'So why did you look at him?'

'Wouldn't you?' Burke said. 'Bloke that size, that face. And he was wearing yellow trousers. I mean . . .' A thought crossed his face. 'Wait!' he said. 'He was coming from that direction. Maybe *he* did it.' A huge relief came over his face. 'Yeah, he looked like the sort, rough as a bagful o' spanners. He's the one you want, not me.'

'I dunno, boss, I kind of believe him,' Hart said reluctantly. After some more questions she had brought Burke in to make his statement. 'It makes sense the way he tells it. He lay low until it was on the news about Langley being arrested, then he felt safe to ring Liana. But she said the police had been round looking for him, so he rung off again in a panic.'

'But all that would fit just as well if he and Langley had been in it together,' Slider mused.

'No, because he wouldn't know what Langley'd said about him. He'd have kept his head down, in case Langley'd shopped him. But anyway, I've been through his emails and his phone log and I can't find any contact between him and Langley. I'd like to do him for something, but I think he's just a stupid git.' She watched Slider's thoughtful face for a moment, then said, 'I could check up whether he *was* at the Prince Albert that night.'

'But by his own admission, he went there *after* Wiseman's, so it wouldn't be an alibi.'

'No, s'pose not. But if he was there, witnesses might say what sort of a state he was in.'

'What did he say about Langley? Did you ask him how he seemed?'

'Yeah, boss, but he said he didn't notice particularly. It was just a glance as the bloke passed.'

'And Langley's face doesn't show much anyway,' Slider said. 'Or at least, it pretty much always looks the same.'

'If Burke was guilty, he could've said Langley was in a state, or covered in blood – tossed him overboard. He's stupid enough to've. You know how hard it is for 'em not to say too much, if they're hiding something.'

'Yes, I get it. You believe him.' Slider ran a distracted hand backwards through his hair, leaving the front sticking up. 'The time he said he was in Penkridge Gardens – around half past eight?'

'Between eight and eight thirty, but it's a guess. He never looked at his watch. It makes sense from Liana's story, with her coming home from work, them having a row, and him having to get to Shepherd's Bush from Wandsworth.'

'But Langley left home around half past six. So if they passed in the street, he must have gone somewhere else before going to Wiseman's,' said Slider.

'Another pub'd be my guess,' said Hart.

'Mine too,' said Slider. 'He'd want to prime the pump. I'll see if I can get him to say where – otherwise we'll have to try all the likely pubs in between, and that's a lot.'

Hart nodded. It didn't help that they didn't know how he'd made the journey, or by what route. Still, she thought, given that his local was the Dunstan, he would probably avoid the more trendy places, which would cut it down quite a lot. 'What'll I do with Burke for now, boss?' she asked.

'Let him go,' said Slider. 'We know between a guess or two where he'll be.'

'Yeah, and I've got his laptop,' Hart said. 'He's not going to do a runner and leave that as a hostage.'

She had only just gone out when Tony Allnutt came in, carrying George. One look at his son's eyes showed Slider he was ready to drop off right there and then, exhausted by an excess of pleasure.

'Ashley's visiting with her mum for a minute,' Allnutt said, 'but I'm taking her home now. It's been quite a day. What would you like me to do with this little tearaway?'

Slider stood up, and George gave him a weary smile and held out his arms for the transfer. 'Come here, you sybarite. Did you have a nice time?' Slider took the warm weight of him onto one hip. George nodded, too tired to speak. 'Say thank you nicely.'

''nk you,' George managed. The heavy head came down on Slider's shoulder.

Tony Allnutt regarded Slider with a slight tilt of the head. 'What'll you do?' he asked quietly. 'I know there isn't a crèche.' He would know that, of course. It was a problem. You couldn't have little children littering up a police station. 'What time's your wife home?' he asked helpfully.

'Ten thirty-ish,' Slider said hopelessly. 'I suppose I'll have to take him home myself.' And stay there – knock off early. But there was so much he needed to do here. And what sort of message did that send the troops? It was unprofessional. He had a moment of resentment against Joanna. If she'd only given him more notice! But of course, it was he who'd had the last-minute call-in. He realised, his normal sense of fair play restoring itself, that she must have to juggle with this problem all the time. It had never arisen with Irene, because Irene didn't work.

And he didn't want to think of his son as a problem.

While he struggled with his thoughts, Swilley appeared at his door, carrying Ashley, drowsy and with a thumb in her mouth, and took in the situation at a glance.

'Tony'll take him, boss,' she said. 'You can fetch him on your way home. We only live ten-fifteen minutes away.' She looked at her husband. 'Pop him into bed with Ashley, darl.' And at Slider again. 'He'll have got well to sleep by the time you come, so he'll probably just drop off in the car again.'

'Thanks,' Slider said profoundly. 'You're a lifesaver.'

She looked at him curiously. 'You need to get a deeper backup list. Mine goes to five, but they'd be no use to you – too far away.'

'Normally I have my dad on hand,' Slider explained.

'Never hurts to have backup,' she insisted.

Atherton came back in high spirits. 'I love my job!' he exulted, grinning like a maniac.

'What are you so chirpy about?' Slider asked.

'I'm chirpy, I'm cheery, I'd chortle if I knew how. Oliver Knudsen's got an alibi.'

'And that's a cause for celebration?'

'I haven't told you what it is. He was at a club – no, wait for it! It's in Wardour Street. The ground floor is a cocktail bar called The Gin Factory, with burlesque shows on Thursday, Friday and Saturday nights. Downstairs, in the basement, there's a private member's club, officially called the 221, but the members themselves tend to call it Spankie's.'

'Oh,' said Slider. And then: 'Really?'

Atherton's grin reached not only from ear to ear but for some distance on either side. 'Bondage and S & M. All perfectly legal, of course – all consensual. But the media-consuming British public tend to frown on that sort of thing.'

'Those clubs don't like to reveal their membership,' Slider pointed out. 'Are you sure Knudsen wasn't just giving you another alibi you couldn't check?'

'He didn't volunteer it. He really didn't want to tell me, until I threatened to arrest him so he'd miss his plane.'

'But you checked?'

'Hey, it's me! Of course I checked.'

'And?'

'The club didn't want to tell me anything, of course, but I told them I'd confiscate their security tapes, which would mean I'd see who *else* was there, not just our Ollie.'

'You're larging on the threats today.'

'Sometimes you just feel like being pissy,' Atherton said airily. 'Anyway, they confirmed he was in on Monday night, arrived about ten o'clock and stayed until two. Better still, Monday nights is dressing-up night. Imagine what the press would make of it if they discovered that the great Oliver Knudsen, director of such iconic films as *Six Million* and *Rachel's Promise*, likes to dress up in Nazi uniform and beat people on the bare bottom with a leather swagger-stick!'

'Did Knudsen tell you that?' Slider said in surprise. 'Why would he volunteer something so damaging?'

'No, he didn't tell me that bit.' Atherton dialled it down a notch. 'I don't know that *he* dressed up, or what as. But I spoke to one of the barmen, and he said Nazi uniform is one of the favourites, along with Ivan the Terrible and Headmaster Whackem. Catwoman and the Biker Queen are favourites among the women – anything in black leather, really.'

'Even being present when that sort of thing was going on would be damaging,' Slider noted.

'Quite. The barman said Knudsen was a long-standing member – I wasn't sure if that was a pun or not. Came in as often as his filming schedule allowed. Always drank white burgundy – strange choice that. I'd have thought champagne would fit the image better. He was very discreet, the barman, and wouldn't give me any more intimate details. He said their clients had to feel safe, and the staff had to be watchful for secret filming and undercover journalists. But I couldn't help wondering whether the white wine was code for something else. I mean, who drinks white wine? Women,' he answered himself. 'I'm imagining Oliver Knudsen in a silver lamé evening gown and bouffant wig – think Priscilla Queen of the Desert – sitting cross-legged on a high stool sipping Puligny Montrachet. It's a stretch,' he admitted, 'and it gives me a headache, but I can just manage it. Not quite as incendiary as an SS leather greatcoat, but still.'

'If you've finished burbling,' Slider said, 'I'd like to point out that that isn't a full alibi. If he left Lavenham at three thirty, got back to London, say, six'ish, that still leaves him ample time to kill Ed Wiseman.'

'Except,' Atherton answered, 'that he dined lavishly at the Quo Vadis beforehand – which they confirm – arriving about seven thirty. And since Amy Hollinshead didn't leave Wiseman until around six thirty, I'd suggest it would be a bit of a squeeze for

Knudsen to murder him and get back to the West End in one meagre hour.'

'It could be done,' Slider acknowledged, 'but it probably wasn't.' He frowned unseeing at the papers on his desk. 'You've gone to a lot of trouble to clear Knudsen. Why?'

'I was hoping *not* to clear him,' said Atherton.

'So I gather. But much as I want to encourage your private fetishes, we've got Langley downstairs under lock and key, and this helps our case – how?'

'You always say, "clear as you go". And anyway, he could still be behind the murder. Langley could just be the paid assassin. In that case, Knudsen would go to a lot of trouble to establish himself an alibi – which he has.'

Slider looked up. 'I think you *must* have a headache. Why would he give himself an alibi like that, that would put him in danger from the media if it got out?'

Atherton sighed. 'All right I suppose it does tend to put him in the clear. It's a pity. I'd so like to see him wriggle.'

'Well, make sure none of this goes any further,' Slider said sternly. 'If there's a leak, you'll be the prime suspect.'

'I shall keep my Chardonnay imaginings to myself,' Atherton promised. 'What now?'

'I have to go home. Swilley and her husband are holding George for me, and it isn't fair to lumber them. Once I've reported to Mr Porson, I'll be off.'

'I'll buzz off too, then. They're showing *Barton Fink* at the Electric tonight. You don't get many chances to see that. Then a nice little supper at Assaggi, I think.'

'On your own?' Slider asked casually.

Atherton gave him a sphingine look. 'You know that Emily's away,' he said, and swung out.

That was not, Slider realised a moment later, an answer. And, he acknowledged, he had no right to one.

SEVENTEEN
Con, Descending

Porson was seated, hemmed in by documents, and looked up wearily as Slider knocked delicately on the open door and stepped in. He didn't look as if he'd be heading home for some time.

Slider caught him up on the day's developments, such as they were.

'And Langley?' Porson asked.

'Still no-commenting. I had another chat with him just now. He's looking a lot less confident. I think by tomorrow he'll be ready to talk.'

Porson pursed his lips and dug the cap end of his biro into the lower one. 'You'd better hope he does. Unless you get enough to charge him soon, we'll have to chuck him back in the water.'

'We've placed him at the scene at a suitable time,' Slider reminded him.

'You think Burke is a reliable witness? Well, maybe. But you need a lot more than that for the CPS. You're trying to trace his route?'

'Yes, sir, but it takes time, of course. My team's coming in tomorrow to keep on with it.'

'And the baseball bat?'

'No report back on it yet.' Of course, it might not have been the baseball bat that Langley used, Slider thought, but he didn't say that. It was not a thought to comfort. If it came up negative, they were left looking for an offensive weapon, which could be anything, and could have been dumped anywhere. A length of metal pipe or rod, say, when you were next-door to a building site. Needles and haystacks didn't come into it.

'Hmm. Well, we've got him for ninety-six hours, if I put in for another extension. Goose up forensics. Have another good go at him tomorrow. For Gawd's sake get me something to tell Mr Carpenter.

He's still chuntering – worried,' he corrected himself hastily, 'about
the effect on this girl's career, his wife's niece or whatever she is.
Chockfull of talent, apparently, some sort of child progeny, and he
doesn't want her chances spoiled by association with a nasty case.'

'Yes, sir,' Slider said as neutrally as possible.

Porson took that for a disparagement. 'What?'

'I had a look at her on the Internet,' Slider admitted.

'So did I,' said Porson. 'Can't see it myself. Still, beauty's in
the eye of the tiger, I suppose. You going home now?'

'Yes, sir.'

Porson grunted. 'All right for some.'

Unfortunately, a few hours' sleep in Ashley's bed had simply
refreshed George, and instead of clinging to the cobwebs he
propelled himself to full wakefulness as Slider carried him to the
car, and kept up daytime conversation all the way home, mostly
about an imaginary pet dinosaur that he kept in his bedroom. He'd
had to take the roof off, he assured his father, because it had such
a long neck, and you could see it looking out right from the end
of the street. It lived on banana sandwiches and it liked rice pudding
and boiled eggs with soldiers but it didn't like fishcakes or stewed
apple – in which its tastes closely matched its master's.

By the time they got home, George was so lively that Slider
had to bring him down by reading to him in bed, which took a
great many repetitions of Ferdinand Fox. George asked for *The
Gingerbread Man*, but Slider vetoed that as too stimulating.

When he was finally settled, Slider got himself a sandwich and
a malt whisky – Scapa – and was asleep in front of the news when
Joanna got home. She woke him to tell him she was going up to
bed, and she moved so quickly that by the time he had pottered
about, switching off lights and checking doors and windows were
locked – including Dad and Lydia's – she was in bed, on her side,
with her bedside light off. He finally crept in beside her and,
wondering if she was still annoyed, murmured, 'Do you want to
talk?'

She grunted a 'no'. *Thank God for that*, Slider thought. He
spooned up behind her, and it was a close run thing which of them
was asleep first.

*   *   *

Joanna woke him by getting up. She went out of the bedroom without a word, and he heard her go into George's room, their murmuring voices, and then their slow descent of the stairs, to the accompaniment of one of George's monologues. He wondered if it was still the dinosaur. His imagination was intense but wide-ranging. Last weekend he had told Slider all about the garage he owned and the cars he mended in it, some of which could fly.

Slider went and abluted, and got dressed, wondering about Joanna's mood. Normally she woke him – if she woke first – with a kiss and, if there was time, a snuggle. He knew she had been angry about his working yesterday, but he had coped with the situation, hadn't he? He'd looked after George all right, so there should not still be any case for resentment. He descended cautiously, like a man stepping down into a bath, testing the temperature. She didn't look round at him as he came into the kitchen – bad! – but she said, 'What do you want for breakfast?' in a normal voice, which was good.

'I'll have what you're having,' he said, to be obliging.

She gave him a pinched-lipped look. 'That's a really annoying answer.'

Slider cut to the chase. 'Look, Jo, it wasn't my fault. I *had* to work.'

'I know,' she said.

'So why are you mad at me?'

'It's just your blithe assumption that childcare is my responsibility and mine alone.'

'I'm sorry about that,' he said, meaning it. 'I'll try to be more helpful in future.'

'There it is, you see!' she said in exasperation. '"Helpful".'

'What's wrong with "helpful"?' Slider asked, bewildered.

'You're generously offering to *help* me with *my* problem over childcare.'

'I didn't mean it like that,' he said. This was a minefield – and before breakfast, he thought resentfully. A man shouldn't be expected to boogie between hazards on an empty stomach.

'I know you didn't,' she said. But she still looked gloomy. She thrust the piece of bread she had just buttered into George's fingers. It went automatically up to his mouth, but his eyes were going back and forth like someone watching a tennis rally.

'We're both in this together,' Slider tried. 'It's both our respon-sibilities.' What an inelegant locution that was. 'I know you have a job and your job is important. It was unfortunate, that's all, that Dad was away. And,' he added before she could speak, 'I was clumsy in suggesting you should have had the answer. I'm sorry. I won't do it again.'

She sighed. 'You can stop apologising. It's the way things are.' She raised her eyes to his. 'My generation grew up believing we could have it all. But we just can't. Men can have children without any effect on their career, because they can get married and have a wife. When we get married, all we get is a husband. Even if we're rich enough to afford a full-time nanny, it's still us that have to take the time off work for childbirth. We'll never change that until we can find a way to fit men with wombs.'

He thought it a good moment to get in his bad news. 'I have to go in again today. Langley's on the clock, and—'

She laughed. 'You're such a clot, Bill Slider! Here I am debating a deep and painful philosophical issue—'

'I thought I'd get all your pain over with at once,' he said, relieved at her reaction.

'You didn't. You just blurted out what was foremost on your mind, like a typical man.'

'Ooh, gender stereotyping!'

'If the jockstrap fits.'

'You can't say that to me.'

'I just did.' She reached over and pushed George's hair back off his forehead, and he looked up at her over a moustache of buttered bread. It looked like foam. 'And I *want* to spend time with my child. But I love my job, too.'

There was nothing he could say. They were both in the same boat, and someone would have to compromise: realistically, it was always going to be her, and that wasn't fair. Not fair at all.

'Boy and I are going to have porridge and prunes,' she said, breaking into his thoughts, 'but if you want me to do you an egg, being as you're the lord and master . . .'

'I love porridge and prunes,' he said. 'And I'll try not to be too late home today.'

'You've got your job to do,' she said, turning away to the stove. And he saw, as she turned, that the smile fell off her mouth, and her eyes were still – what? Not sad, exactly, but tense and troubled.

But he really didn't know what he could do about it – whatever 'it' was.

Langley was a very different person on Sunday morning from the man they'd arrested on Friday. He looked worn, depressed and nervous, and not all of it, Slider felt, could be put down to coming off the jollies. He started up when Slider and Gascoyne came into the room, but remembered of his own accord and subsided into the chair without being told. His eyes were fixed on Slider's face, while his fingers twisted about each other nervously. Every now and then one of them made a bolt for his mouth, and got worried by his teeth. He fidgeted in his seat, and the chair groaned a little under his weight.

Slider started off with the usual questions about his well-being and his resolve not to have a lawyer present, but he could see Langley wasn't listening. As soon as he stopped talking, Langley said, 'I need my phone. I need to get on the Internet. I got to find out what they're saying about me.'

'Who? What who's saying about you?'

Langley didn't answer that, his brow creased, his eyes fixed, as though he was trying to do mental arithmetic. 'Have they been asking for me?' he demanded. 'People have been ringing up, asking for me, right? You've got to tell me if they have, right? It's my rights, right?'

'I've told you what your rights are. They don't include having me act as your social secretary.'

'Eh?'

'I don't have to pass on messages to you,' Slider translated.

'But there've *been* messages, right? They've been ringing for me?' Langley urged.

'No one has made any enquiries about you,' Slider said. 'Who were you expecting to call?'

'Well . . .' He hesitated, his eyes flitting; but then they fixed urgently on Slider's face, and he said, 'Like, agents, and publishers, and that. They'll be after my book, now I'm in the news. I mean, arrested for murder – they'll all want it now. I told them about it, the news people, when I got arrested. My book, *Death Planet.*'

A horrid feeling, like a cold crawling on the skin, came over Slider. 'Your book,' he said flatly.

'It's great publicity,' Langley said urgently. 'Wiseman turned down my book, so I murdered him. It's all over the Internet, bound to be. Now they'll all want it. They've got to!'

'Nobody's talking about your book,' Slider said.

Langley searched his face. 'You're lying!'

Slider shook his head. 'Nobody's interested in your book. I promise you. Not one word. And they're not talking about you. All the talk is about Ed Wiseman. He's famous, you see. You're nobody.'

'No! I'm the man who killed Ed Wiseman! That Chapman bloke, that killed John Lennon, he was famous!'

'He did it in public, in full daylight. Everybody saw. You haven't even told me how you did it.'

'But you know,' Langley said uncertainly. 'I mean – you must.'

'I want to hear it from you,' Slider insisted. 'How did you do it?'

'Well – I chucked him out the winder, didn't I?'

Slider nodded patiently. Langley stared, clearly out of his depth. Slider encouraged him. 'Did he cry out as he fell?'

'I dunno. He . . . yeah, he yelled. Like a big baby. Like, "Help! Help!".'

'I see. What else?'

'What else what?'

'What else happened. What else did you do?'

Langley was so far out of his depth now, there were barnacles on his behind. 'I dunno what you mean,' he said.

'You just picked Ed Wiseman up and threw him out of the window? Was it open?'

'Course it was,' Langley said helplessly.

'It was very cold that evening. Why would the window be open?'

'Maybe he . . . Maybe I opened it first.'

'What was he wearing?'

'I – I dunno.'

'You don't *know*?'

'Look—'

'Did he struggle?'

'No. Yes. A bit. Not much.'

Slider stared at him for a long time, and Langley shifted nervously. His Adam's apple moved visibly up and down his thick throat. 'You see,' Slider said at last, sternly, 'I don't think you did kill Ed Wiseman.'

'I did! I did!'

'Because he didn't die from being thrown out of the window.'

'But it said on the Internet . . .' he began fatally, and stopped.

'He was dead before he went out of the window.'

Langley was tortured with thought. 'Well, I killed him first. I forgot.'

'How?'

'I – I poisoned him.'

'Nope,' said Slider.

'No, I stabbed him. With my combat knife.'

'Nope.'

'I – I—'

'You didn't kill Ed Wiseman. You can stop lying to me now and tell me the truth. I know you went to his house that night, because you were seen in the street, but the street is as close as you got, isn't it? You're not a murderer, and nobody's going to publish your book. You're a nobody. Aren't you?'

Langley's face wasn't built for expressing emotions, but Slider thought for an anxious moment that he was going to cry. 'I could've,' he said feebly. 'I could've killed him.'

'But you didn't,' said Slider.

'No,' said Langley, hanging his head. He looked so defeated, Slider almost felt sorry for him.

Atherton had just arrived when Slider got back upstairs. He heard him talking to Swilley in the outer office.

'Well, you *look* like crap,' Swilley was saying.

'It was a heavy evening of sex and debauchery,' Atherton replied. 'Can I help it if every female is mad for my body?'

'Not *every* one.'

'Even excluding you, Norm, it's still a heavy responsibility. It takes its toll, satisfying all those women.'

'Never mind, a couple of days on your feet and we'll have you back in bed in no time,' said Swilley.

Slider diverted a few steps to go in that way. 'What's going on?'

'I think Jim feels the need to compete with Ed Wiseman,' Swilley said. 'Chest beating, horn clashing – that sort of thing.'

'You're in early, guv,' Atherton said, to divert attention.

'I've just been hearing Langley's confession,' said Slider.

'Heard it already,' said Atherton.

'Not that one. The new one. He's confessed he didn't do it.'

He went through the interview for their benefit.

'Bugger,' said Atherton mournfully. 'The retraction of a confession is the limbo dancer under the lavatory door of life. Just when you're nicely settled and getting on with your business—'

'We get it,' Slider assured him hastily.

Gascoyne commented, 'It was funny, really, seeing him come down like a deflated balloon. He went all the way to rock bottom. Pathetic, after all his hard man pose. He was giving himself such airs before, with his "No comment", and "I'm not doing your job for you".'

'So what was he doing in Penkridge Gardens?' Swilley asked.

'He'd wound himself up all day, thinking about his wrongs,' Slider said. 'He set off from home at half past six to go to the pub as usual, but changed his mind and diverted to Shepherd's Bush to have a stern word with Wiseman and possibly threaten him with violence. He admits that, though he says he didn't take a weapon with him. He was going to use his fists.'

'Much more satisfying,' Atherton agreed.

'Besides,' said Gascoyne, 'taking a weapon along would mean planning. He's not a great thinker, in my view.'

'He stopped on the way, at the Richmond, for a pint or five,' said Slider, 'thus winding himself up further. But by the time he'd walked round to Penkridge, I suspect the brew was starting to have a somnolising effect, because he said he knocked at the door but there was no answer, so he went away.'

'Which was when Burke saw him,' Atherton mused, 'making it eight to eight thirty – about right, given the stop at the boozer. So that fits.'

'Why did he do it, boss?' Swilley asked. 'The false confession?'

'He thought the notoriety would make publishers eager to publish his book.'

'Now that's *really* pathetic,' she said.

'I don't know,' said Atherton. 'Sillier things have happened. A lousy book can still succeed if there's a good publicity hook to hang it on.'

'I mean,' said Swilley scornfully, 'that it's pathetic to want to go to jail for life just to get your book published.'

'He was intending to withdraw the confession as soon as he got his book deal,' Slider said.

'He thought he just had to say he didn't do it after all, and he'd get off scot-free,' Gascoyne added.

'The plonker!' said Swilley.

'He was very crestfallen when I told him he'd still go to jail for perverting the course,' Slider said. 'He tried to rally and claim that he could handle himself, and that he'd be a big man inside. He wilted again when I pointed out that he wouldn't be a murderer or a novelist, just a dope who'd messed up his plan, and everyone would laugh at him.'

McLaren and Fathom arrived together at that point, and the story had to be told again.

'So what happens now, guv?' McLaren asked at last.

'He can stay where he is for a bit,' said Slider, 'until we decide what to charge him with. Wasting police time, at least. We have to discourage false confessions, or we'll be up to our knees in 'em.'

'Yeah, but I meant what happens with the investigation?' McLaren said. He brightened. 'I s'pose we don't have to go on looking for Langley's route, that's one thing.'

'There'll still be plenty of searching,' Slider said. 'But for different people.'

'What if this climb-down is false?' Swilley said. 'What if he *did* do it after all?'

'That's an unwelcome supposition. I don't think he did it, but it's possible. We know more or less where he was before Penkridge, but there's the period between half past eight, and ten o'clock when he turned up at the Dunstan. A witness for that period might have something to say about the state he was in, and what he said.'

'That's a lot of work, for someone you've ruled out,' Atherton complained.

'I just said, it's possible,' Slider pointed out. 'And as of this moment, we don't have a hell of a lot else.'

'As in, "nothing else at all",' Atherton muttered as Slider walked away to his own room.

Behind him, he heard McLaren say to Atherton, 'You look a bit knackered this morning. What you been up to?'

And Swilley answered for him, 'Training for the Ed Wiseman stakes.'

EIGHTEEN
A Quiche is Still a Quiche

Porson wasn't due in, but he came in anyway, as was frequently his habit when there was a big case on. His beloved wife had died a couple of years ago, his only daughter was married and lived in Swindon, and he had nothing much to stay at home for. He didn't play golf or fish, his garden was a fifteen-by-twenty patch of grass, and his local pub had been turned into a Thai restaurant called the Tamarind. Once he'd ironed his shirts for work, Sunday yawned unfillable. It could not compete with the siren call of work.

He received the news that Langley had retracted his confession with stoicism. Slider would have preferred he blew straight away. At least you knew where you stood. Or rather, cowered, whimpering.

'Nothing on the baseball bat?' Porson asked, drumming his fingers on the desk.

'No, sir. Not likely to get an answer today – you know what they're like.'

'I'll see if I can use a bit of leverage. Better to know, one way or the other.' He shot Slider a keen glance. 'But do *you* think he didn't do it?'

'That's my feeling. It's making sense now, all his actions. The fact that it was *him* called in the media. The reason he wouldn't elaborate on the murder – you know how they usually like to boast once they've confessed. And,' he added, a little reluctantly,

'Loessop's had another look at the online confession, looking at the timing, and he posted it *after* his visit from McLaren. He must have made his plan there and then.'

That got a reaction. 'Bloody hell!' Porson stamped up and down a bit. 'Couldn't have found that out sooner, could you?' he demanded.

'In fairness, sir, we weren't looking for the confession to be false.'

'Well maybe you should've been,' Porson snarled. 'So now our whole case has gone Capone – what've we got?'

Slider was about to say that Langley was unemployed, so probably didn't pay tax, when he realised the Old Man meant *kaput*. 'We've got a lot of people with a grudge against Wiseman. Oliver Knudsen, Simon Haig. Regina Cantor and Virginia Foulkes possibly – sexual jealousy. Ditto Marina Haig. Marina Haig's husband – we haven't considered him. If she was still involved with Wiseman, he could have been angry about it.'

'All the little angels,' Porson muttered. 'All those people without alibis.'

'Except for Oliver Knudsen. He's pretty much covered. Unless—'

'Unless?'

'He paid someone else to do it.'

Porson rolled his eyes. 'Don't start down that corridor. What about Burke?'

'Yes, there was time for him to have done it. But I don't think it was him. His story rings true, and he admitted freely that he went round to Wiseman's house. I think if he'd done it, he'd have been a bit more cagey – he wouldn't have volunteered that. And maybe he would have worked out an alibi. He'd had four days to think about it.'

'So that leaves us where? With nothing.'

There was a silence. Then Slider said, unwillingly, 'The one person we haven't spoken to is Calliope Hunt . . .'

Porson's head snapped round. 'Oh no you don't!'

'She rang him, that last day. She might well have visited him. Marina Haig said he told her someone important was coming round, and she suspected it was Hunt. Virginia Foulkes thought he might have been seeing her that evening. And she said Hunt's book was full of violence. A nasty sadistic streak, she said. There could have been a lover's quarrel.'

Porson moved impatiently. 'Suppostition.'

'It's all we've got,' Slider said.

'Then get something else!'

'Sir, even if she didn't do it, she would be an important witness if she *was* there – to his state of mind, to who else might have been coming to the house – to give us timings, at least. All we know is that he was alive at six forty-one when the last phone call ended.'

'You can't talk to Calliope Hunt,' Porson said. Slider gave him a long, level stare. 'Not until you've got some reason – some *proper* reason,' he deflected a repetition. 'And if you do get a reason, I'll have to square it with Mr Carpenter first, *before* you talk to her.'

'Sir . . .'

'You know about the cuts, I presume,' Porson said impatiently. 'You might have noticed Carver's whole firm has gone. Nobody's job is safe – and you've got a habit of getting up people's noses, Slider. *And*,' again he forestalled interruption, 'what you don't know, because I haven't told you, is that Carpenter's hinting about seconding you to SCD9.'

Slider boggled. That was the Human Exploitation and Organised Crime Command. It was the branch of the Specialist Crime Directorate responsible for investigating human trafficking, but also for policing prostitution, nightclubs, casinos, and obscene publications. What used to be called the Vice Squad – or occasionally, when spirits were really low from hiding in lavatories and taking covert photographs, the Cottage Industry.

'*Me*, sir?' Slider managed at last to squeak. 'Why me?'

'He said they could do with a senior officer who got on well with prostitutes,' Porson said, his face a perfect blank. 'You could take that as a compliment.'

'I—'

'I'll make that an order. Take it as a compliment. Otherwise we'll have to start wondering what our illustrious senior brass have got against you. And look here, Slider, I don't want to lose you, even if my loss would be obscenity's gain, so I'm telling you again, get something concrete on this case before it's too late, and *don't go talking to Calliope Hunt without permission.*'

Slider had got as far as the door when Porson added, 'Oh, and you can chuck Langley back, but charge him with something – assaulting a police officer, wasting police resources, possession of class A drugs – whatever. All of them, if you like. I don't want that little toe-rag boasting down the pub that he got away with it.'

The troops were assembled in the outer office talking quietly and drinking tea. They looked up enquiringly at him, like dogs hoping to be taken out for a walk.

'Right. What lines can we follow up?' he asked briskly. 'And before anyone brings it up, I don't want to hear the word Calliope. She's off-limits.'

Atherton spoke. 'Well, there's Simon Haig. He and Knudsen were supposed to be each other's alibis, but now that Knudsen's blown, it leaves Haig wide open. He's got nothing but, "I was at home reading scripts".'

'I can't really see it being him,' Swilley said. 'He comes across like a real wuss. Some nancy-boy novel writer?'

This was meant as a direct provocation to Atherton, who read books, but he swallowed it nobly. 'The enraged can be possessed of superhuman strength,' he said loftily.

'Why don't you talk like a normal person?' Swilley complained.

'And he lied to us,' Atherton went on. 'And he's got form – he slogged Wiseman once before.'

'All right,' Slider said. 'That's one.' His mind offered him the old song, *All the little angels, they rise up, they rise up*. He wished one would rise up head first, with his hand up saying, I dunnit! 'What about Marina Haig's husband – what's his name?'

'Ben Dawlish,' Swilley supplied. 'He's gorgeous,' she added free of charge.

'If you like good-looking, fit, buffed men with denim-blue eyes,' Atherton said dismissively. 'But he's out of it, anyway. He was in Sydney covering the rugby sevens.'

'Have you—?' Slider began.

'I checked up on it, guv,' Loessop put in. 'He really was there.'

'Leaving Marina Haig without an alibi,' Gascoyne said. 'And she was supposed to have been visiting Wiseman that evening.'

'But she volunteered that – why would she tell us that if she was guilty?' Atherton objected.

'In case we found out anyway,' said Swilley. 'You don't want it to be her. Is that just general chivalry on behalf of all women – or are you on a promise with her?'

'All we've got left is women,' Slider pointed out. 'All the jealous women, they rise up, they rise up. Foulkes and Cantor and Haig.'

'And Calliope Hunt,' said McLaren.

'I told you not to mention her. And then there are person or persons unknown.'

They looked at him glumly.

'Surveillance cameras,' McLaren said after a silence. 'But there's no cameras covering the house. The nearest is on the Green, might just about cover the end of Penkridge Gardens. And there's the bus camera in Holland Road, that covers the end of Penkridge Road, if anyone went in or out that way.'

'Which you might if you were going east or south,' Loessop interpolated.

'But—'

'I know,' said Slider. 'If it was person or persons unknown, how would we know to look at them? But we're at the bottom of the barrel. We'll have to try and spot someone we know heading towards the house or coming away from it. Look at the tube station, and the bus stops on the Green and in Holland Road. Look at the traffic cameras and see if any number comes back to anyone we know. Let's get a list of everyone we know who knew him more than casually, find out if they have cars and get the indexes. And let's put out a call to the cab companies – anyone who set down or picked up in Penkridge, or in the immediate area.'

'I'll do taxis,' offered Gascoyne. 'But we don't have a time limit.'

'It's going to have to be between six thirty and, say midnight,' Slider acknowledged. 'A big margin. It's going to be a long haul,' he concluded.

An exhausting trawl, probably resulting in nothing, as he didn't add. But it had to be done.

'Loessop,' he went on, 'keep scanning the Internet, see if anyone's said anything useful to us. A confession, a suspicion – and anything about anyone we know. And Swilley, how are you getting on with the phone logs?'

'I'm following up the calls on the last day, but they're all turning out to be straightforward so far.'

'Keep at it. And finances?'

'He didn't seem to be in any trouble. Mostly his outgoings were restaurants and clubs, plus recently quite a lot spent on women's clothes and jewellery. Assuming he wasn't cross-dressing, I'm guessing they were presents for girlfriends. But even with that, he wasn't broke. With no mortgage, no kids, and not being house-proud, his day-to-day was well within his income.'

'Right. Well, let me know if you come up with anything anomalous. That goes for all of you. And now I'm going to deal with Langley.'

'Charge and chuck?' McLaren asked.

Slider nodded. 'A man must have some pleasure in life.'

Having dealt with Langley and the associated paperwork, Slider left his troops toiling at their thankless tasks and went home to spend the rest of Sunday with his wife and son.

He could tell Joanna was still not back to normal. She wasn't ratty with him, but she was unsmiling, and disinclined to talk. Using his finely-honed forensic skills, he deduced that she had something on her mind which, for the moment, she did not want to share, and he decided that the best thing was to leave her alone to work it out – which happily coincided with his own wishes. She would tell him when she was ready, he reassured himself.

As it was fine and unexpectedly warm, they were out in the garden. Slider's father, who lived in the granny flat with his new wife Lydia, usually did the basic maintenance, but since they were away, Joanna volunteered to mow the lawn, which involved a soothing and, in particular, solitary walking up and down, and then went indoors to do some practice.

Slider did a bit of desultory work on the borders. He liked the idea of a garden, but there was never enough time to create anything much. He had at least managed to get some bulbs in last autumn, which meant there was a cheery display of daffodils, lifting their ecstatic faces to the hazy sky. He settled down comfortably now to divide the clumps of spent snowdrops and replant them.

George helped him by digging. Not digging anything in particular, just digging wherever there was a bare spot – or a spot that could be encouraged to be bare with a bit of covert defoliation. He had his own trowel and a child-sized watering can, and carried out some important research on the effect of different quantities of water on the consistency of mud, and how far the resulting product could be spread over the young male physique.

It was just starting to get too cool for comfort, and Slider was finding his thoughts turning to a gin-and-tonic before supper, when Joanna came out.

'That was Jim on the phone,' she said. 'He wants to come over and talk to me.'

'To you?'

'He said, specifically, to me.' She shrugged. 'Maybe he wants relationship advice. He can't talk about that sort of thing to you.'

'Not if there's a door in the room I can fit through.'

'If you'd sooner I didn't get involved . . .'

'I wouldn't deprive him of the comfort – as long as you don't mind,' said Slider, absently picking up George, who'd been tugging at him, and receiving a benison of Chiswick loam to his hair and clothing. 'Invite him to supper.'

'I did. I've got that egg-and-bacon flan of your dad's in the freezer – that's big enough for four. And there's salad and new potatoes.'

'Fit for a king,' Slider said, managing to kiss her sad cheek as she withdrew. 'Isn't it a quiche?' he called after her.

'Your dad doesn't call it that,' she replied without turning. 'And Jim laughs at the word.'

'I expect he could do with a laugh,' Slider replied, but she'd gone too far to hear.

'Is Granddad home?' George asked.

'No, but we've got some of his cooking for supper. Bath time for you, I think. You are one very muddy boy.'

George laughed, and placed a muddy hand square on Slider's face. 'Squish,' he said.

'Likewise squelch,' said Slider, removing the hand and kissing George's cheek, which was more responsive, though muddier, than his mother's.

'What's squelch?' George asked as they headed for the house.

'Same as squish. Or egg-and-bacon flan. You must remember this, a squish is still a squish.'

'Don't sing, Daddy,' George said imperiously.

'I'll have you know I have what's known as a pleasant tenor.'

'You can sing when I have my barf,' George allowed graciously. 'Can I have bubbles?'

'What's a bath without bubbles?' Slider said, and kissed him again.

Atherton arrived while the bath was still in process, which gave him Joanna to himself. He sat at the kitchen table while she prepared salad, having made them both a gin-and-tonic.

'Hair of the dog,' he said.

'Not for me,' she said. She glanced at him. 'Have you been on the razzle?'

'Last night,' he said. 'And then again this morning.'

'Are you drinking to forget?'

'I've got something on my mind,' he acknowledged. 'It's about Emily.'

'I can't tell you what to do,' Joanna said quickly. 'And remember, Emily's my friend, so don't put me in a position of conflicted loyalties.'

'I've got no one but you to talk to,' he said, which she thought rather mournful. 'I don't suppose it's news to you that Emily wants to get married and have a baby. Or at least have a baby.'

'I suspected. She's seemed a bit broody around George. What's the problem?'

'Oh, you know. The whole settling-down thing. We men are known to have difficulty with it.'

'You men!' she snorted derisively at the expression.

He looked away. 'Swilley said something the other day. It made me . . . uncomfortable. She said I was like Ed Wiseman, but she said it as though it was a bad thing to be.'

'I can see similarities – the dilettante lifestyle, the perpetual bachelorhood.'

'There it is, you see – the note of pity,' he said with faint annoyance. 'But most men would think he had just about the perfect lifestyle: no responsibilities, no one to answer to, all the guilt-free hot sex he could handle.'

'Look at it another way: he lived alone, his kids were halfway across the world and he never saw them, he didn't seem to be able to sustain a relationship. Sounds pretty bleak to me.'

He thought for a moment, sipping slowly. 'So you think I should get married and have children?'

'I can't make your decisions for you,' she protested, bringing the salad bowl and the bottle of vinaigrette to the table. 'Dress that for me while I check the potatoes.'

'All right. But tell me *something*.'

'I can tell you what Bill's dad would say. He'd say it's what life is for. He'd say, what else is there?'

'Lots, I should have thought.'

'He'd say do you want to lie on your deathbed and look back at a job you stopped doing years ago and the names of a string of women you'd once had sex with; or at a life shared, and children and grandchildren?'

'And you think that's right, do you?'

She gave him something of an evil smile. 'I'm not sure one ought to live one's life on the basis of how one's going to feel on one's deathbed.'

'Oh, thank you!'

'On the other hand, it's as good a yardstick as any. I think the chances of getting things right is pretty slim. Most of us just do what seems to work at the time, and muddle along with the consequences.' She turned off the gas under the potatoes. 'They're done.'

'So it's marriage and parenthood that really matter, is it?'

'Doesn't matter what you call it. It's meaning something to another person or persons. I suppose if you wrote symphonies or built cathedrals, you would mean something to a lot of people, and that might be enough. But most of us don't have those outlets.'

'You're not helping,' Atherton said.

'Look,' she turned to face him. 'I love my job, and I resent like hell that I can't have that and a family in the seamless way you bastards can.'

'Coppers?' he asked, startled, looking up from the salad.

'Men. But if you put a gun to my head and said I absolutely had to choose, I could be the world's most renowned fiddle player but I'd have to give up Bill and George . . .' She shrugged.

'You'd choose them.'

'I'd have no choice. Once I might have chosen to be Paganini, but not now. They're my hostages to fortune, you see.' And now she looked sad again. She took the potatoes and the colander to the sink and drained them. 'You're not there yet,' she said through the steam. 'Your wife and children are only potential. You can still choose – and you should think carefully before you hand over hostages. Be sure what you really want.'

Atherton frowned, putting down the spoons. 'But isn't that the opposite to what you said before?'

'I told you I wasn't going to tell you what to do. I can't give you advice. I only know what I'd do if I were in your shoes.'

'And what would that be?' he asked, trying to sound casual, to trap her.

'Make up my own mind,' she said cruelly. 'It's all ready. I'll go and see if Bill and George are done.'

'Something smells good in the oven,' Atherton said. 'Is that quiche?'

'We don't call it that in this house,' she said, exiting stage left.

NINETEEN
All the Little Angels

The painstaking work, the tedious work, occupied them. Endless viewing of security tapes. Trawling through reports. Following up statements. None of it was glamorous. And it was disheartening when all you could expect at the end if you were successful was the elimination of another suspect.

Regina Cantor was the easiest. She took it in good part: the idea that she even needed to be eliminated tickled her. 'It's the first time I've laughed since poor Ed died,' she told Hart. 'Look at me! I'm a plump middle-aged woman with arms like spaghetti. I never exercise. Do you really think I could heave my ex-husband, who was twice my height, out of a window – even if I wanted to? Which I didn't. Ed and I were all right. He was hell as a husband, but as an ex-husband he was genial and easy and occasionally quite generous. I could live with that.'

She supplied the name and address of the friend who had hosted the bridge evening, and the names of the other players, and at the end of that particular piece of plodding, Hart was able to report to Slider that Cantor was playing bridge from seven thirty to ten thirty, and had taken a minicab home from a local Earl's Court firm. 'I've only got to get hold of the driver, to make sure every end's tied off. I just wish we knew what time Wiseman was killed,' she grumbled. 'If she's covered until eleven, say, does that do it?'

'He was alive at six forty, and Doc Cameron gave us twelve to eighteen hours, which puts it anything up to ten forty. Obviously that's not exact,' said Slider. 'It could be up to midnight, or even the early hours at a push.'

'That's not much bloody use,' Hart said, frustrated.

'But I think we can rule her out. I can't see her going back out after a night of bridge to bump him off. Unless we get a sighting from one of the taxi firms – and she'd hardly go by public transport at that time of night.'

'Simon Haig's got a car,' Hart pointed out.

'And we're checking that.'

The trouble with trying to trace the journey of a car through London was that while there were ANPR cameras at some major junctions, and traffic management cameras on various roads, there was a maze of lesser streets, and from any point A to any point B there was almost an infinity of routes that could be taken. London drivers, indeed, often prided themselves on never taking the direct line, and always knowing 'this little back route that misses all the traffic'. So the fact that Simon Haig's car did not trigger any cameras on Monday night didn't necessarily mean it wasn't out. He had a resident's parking permit and parked it in the street outside, but there were no cameras covering that street, so it was impossible to say whether it had been stationary there that evening.

'He was in and she was out and he's in love with her but she's in love with him,' said Atherton happily. 'I want Haig. We've got to have Haig. I don't like his books and I don't like his intellectual smuggery, and he's got two reasons to hate Wiseman – his wife and his daughter.'

'You're cheery again,' Slider remarked. 'Your little talk with Joanna must have done you good.'

'Not really,' said Atherton. 'But Emily's coming home tonight. Now, apart from beating a confession out of him, in a manner largely viewed as unacceptable nowadays, how can we nail Simon Horrible Haig?'

'I leave that to your ingenuity,' Slider said. 'I've just got the report on the baseball bat – negative.'

'Well, we weren't expecting anything from that, were we?' said Atherton. 'Now we've struck off Langley?'

'You might consider, in your contemplation of Haig, what he used as a weapon. In fact, the same with any of the suspects. And what he did with it afterwards.'

'Yes, it makes a difference,' Atherton agreed. 'If it was something they took with them, that makes it premeditated. I can see that working for someone like Haig, but not for one of the women. It would more likely be an impulse thing with them.'

Marina Haig lived with Ben Dawlish in a flat in a modern luxury block in the St John's Wood area. Loessop went round to inspect it and to try to find neighbours who might or might not have seen Marina Haig on the Monday evening. It was not such a luxury block that it had a porter on the door, and unfortunately it did not have security cameras either. 'How come?' he asked a maintenance man who was working on one of the two lifts.

'Lot of slebrities live in these flats,' he said. 'They don't want their comings and goings on record. Supposing some journo was to get hold of it?'

'Oh, they get up to stuff, do they?' Loessop asked innocently.

'They might or they might not,' he replied with a shrug. 'But they don't want anyone to know either way.'

It did turn out, though, that they had modern key cards rather than an old-fashioned Yale to get in and out of the front door, which news put joy into Loessop's heart. A laminated card screwed to the wall inside the door gave the security company's name, and even more fortunately their offices were in Edmonton, off the North Circular Road, and not in South Wales or Sweden.

Once there, and having proved his credentials, it didn't take him long to get a printout of the key activity for Monday. It took a little more persuading to get the match between the key codes and the individual flats. The technician, a young man with an ambitious hairstyle and an unsuccessful moustache, looked with admiration at Loessop's dreads and beard plaits, but still objected. 'I can see why you want to know about the one you're interested in, but why do you need the other residents?'

'In case the suspect used someone else's key,' Loessop explained. 'If they were trying to avoid detection, and they understood how the keys work, they might either borrow or steal someone else's card for the evening to avoid leaving a digital trail.'

'Oh!' he said, enlightened, and impressed by the language. 'I wouldn't have thought of that. Yeah, s'obvious.'

The activity list, fortunately, wasn't as long as it might have been. Of the twenty-six residents of the block, six were away, and eight others seemed happily stay-at-home. And Marina Haig's card showed she had come in at six thirty-four and not gone out again until the following morning at eight fifteen.

However, there was key activity for eleven other flats that Monday evening, and he needed to check up on all of them. It was going to be a long job. He stuffed the printouts into his pocket and headed back to St John's Wood.

Fathom was toiling over the ANPR and other cameras, while McLaren looked at public transport. During a break to rest his eyes and, possibly, brain, the latter found Hart at the coffee area waiting for a new brew to filter through. One hand clutched her personal coffee mug at the ready while the other clapped her mobile to her ear, and she was saying 'yes', 'no', and 'I know' at regular intervals. She rolled her eyes at McLaren to register his presence in the queue; finally said, 'Yeah, all right, Mum. Love you,' and rang off. The coffee maker emitted a final borborygmic gurgle. 'All right, Maurice, it's ready, keep yer 'air on,' she said prophylactically, turning to him fully, to find his face frozen in thought.

'Wassup?' she asked. Whatever it was, it was coming through as slowly as the coffee. 'Come on, Mo, you look as if you're having a bowel movement.'

'I've just thought,' he said.

'I tried that once. Didn't like it.'

'Shut up. Haig's mobile record will show if he was at home that night.'

Hart considered. 'Unless it was turned off. Or he didn't make any calls,' she amended.

'I bet he did,' McLaren said. 'He's the kind of up-himself ponce that never stops talking.'

'Worth looking into,' Hart said. 'Have a gold star.'

'I'll—' McLaren began, brightening.

'No, I'll get on to the provider. You got public transport to do,' said Hart. She smiled inwardly as his face slumped and he trudged away, forgetting all about coffee in his disappointment.

Every time a person made or received a call, the mobile service provider logged the time, date and duration of the connection and, because the call went through a network of towers, the device's location, arrived at by triangulation of signals. In addition, the modern smartphones carried a GPS capability which pinpointed the device's actual position on Earth. Luckily, most people thought of their phones as part of their bodies – or rather, thought about them as little as they thought about their own liver or pancreas – rather than a surveillance device aimed at them.

Fortunately again, these records were held for a year and it only took a warrant for the police to obtain them. Hart went off to follow it up.

On Tuesday morning, in mid-toil, Atherton appeared in the doorway. 'Phone call for you,' he told Slider, with a raised eyebrow of interest. 'Murray Pauling, CEO of New Avalon Publishing Group. Otherwise known as—'

'Gus Pauling, founder member of the Claret Club—'

'And secret lover of Ed Wiseman.'

Slider frowned. 'They didn't—'

'Lover as in he loved him. According to Virginia Foulkes. Not that they actually bumped bodies. Although—'

'I'll take it,' said Slider quickly. 'I'll take anything that could possibly provide a new insight.'

'I wonder if he's rung up to confess. That'd be fun,' Atherton said as he disappeared.

A moment later, Slider had Pauling's deep, handsome voice in his ear. His first words eliminated the possibility of confession, because he said, 'I've just got back from two weeks in Australia and the Far East. Of course, I heard the terrible, terrible news when I was over there, but I haven't heard if there have been any recent developments. And I thought I'd call and offer any help I could give, to do with background and so on. I've known Ed since we were teenagers. We were very close.'

'That's kind of you, Mr Pauling,' Slider said. 'Of course, any details of his current life could be useful. I'm afraid there's no substantial progress to report. These things take time.'

'And I gather there's really no forensic evidence to go on,' he said with audible sympathy. *Where did you gather that*? Slider wondered irritably. 'It must make things difficult.'

'What did you know about Mr Wiseman's current life?' Slider asked, to cut to the chase. 'Did he have any enemies, anyone who had issues with him?'

'I can't imagine anyone wanting to harm Ed,' said Pauling with a quiver of emotion. 'He was a lovely, lovely man. Everyone liked him. Of course,' his voice became brisker, 'he was also a businessman, and every business treads on toes now and then. We are accustomed to talk about agenting as a cut-throat business, but we don't mean it literally. Agents don't like other agents poaching their talent, and agents sometimes resent publishers for not valuing their clients as they should. And writers always think they're not paid enough or given enough publicity. But none of that feeling is strong enough to lead to murder.'

Gus Pauling, Slider decided, liked the sound of his own voice, and had no useful information to give. He began, preparatory to ending the conversation, 'So you don't—'

Pauling hurried on, as if he knew he was being dumped. 'But this was a transition phase for Ed. He'd been thinking of getting out of the business for a while, but it kept calling him back – it's something of a drug. There's always the irresistible lure of that exciting new book just over the horizon, you know?' His tone asked for an understanding smile from Slider. 'But I do know he'd finally decided to sell.'

'Sell his business?'

'Yes. Just before I left for Australia he told me he'd got a buyer lined up.'

'Nobody else has mentioned this,' said Slider, wondering how it changed things.

'I don't suppose he told anyone else. These things are delicate until the sale is actually closed – the wrong word and it could vanish in a puff of smoke. And we're all such frightful gossips in the publishing world! There's often a non-disclosure agreement, and if there is, it's easier to say nothing to anyone than to filter out what you can and can't say, and to whom. But Ed told me more than other people. We were close. I was his sounding board, if you like.'

'Who was he selling the company to?'

'Ah, he didn't tell me that. That *would* have been indiscreet. I *am* in the business, you know,' he added with a little laugh. 'But if he was selling up – and he was – it meant that he was contemplating a big change in his life. Something cataclysmic. I wondered if he was emigrating, actually – starting a new life somewhere overseas. Or going off in a completely new career direction.'

'Perhaps he was just retiring,' Slider suggested.

'Retiring?' Pauling said with huge disbelief. 'He wasn't ready to retire! Besides, if that's all it was, he would have told me. No, I could hear in his voice he had something exciting up his sleeve. But he didn't offer to tell me, so I didn't ask. I respected his privacy. He'd tell me when it was all settled, I knew that. Except,' his voice became dull, 'he didn't have the chance.'

'What about the women in his life?' Slider asked. 'Why wouldn't he have told them?'

'Oh, he always had lots of women around, but they weren't important to him. Apart from Reggie, his ex-wife – and he knew from the start that was a mistake – he was never committed to any of them. Long-term relationships stultified him. He was a free spirit, and it was necessary to him to remain free, or he couldn't function. He loved women, of course – as I do – but as lovely desirable objects to admire, not to collect and keep. He was a connoisseur, yes, but one who liked to visit art galleries, if you like, not bid at auctions.' He laughed a little awkwardly, as if he knew the metaphor had not quite worked.

'What about Calliope Hunt?' Slider asked quietly.

There was a slight pause, and when Pauling answered, his voice was different, flat and unmusical. 'Oh yes, I knew about her. There was nothing in that.'

'I've been told he was desperately in love with her.'

'Who told you that? No, no, he was sometimes overtaken by

enthusiasm at the beginning of a relationship – we all are, aren't we? The excitement of the new – until it wears off. But he wasn't "in love" with her.' His voice put the inverted commas around 'in love' as though it were a rather distasteful concept. 'It was just another of his little adventures. It meant nothing. She was nobody, I assure you. I believe it was already cooling off, as a matter of fact.'

It was a lot of words to dismiss something unimportant, Slider thought. 'You think he might have been considering a new career?' he said. 'Any idea what? What other interests did he have?'

'Oh, he had many, many interests. He loved the theatre, especially musical theatre. He might have invested in a show. He loved sailing, though he hadn't done any for a long time, but he could have bought a boat and sailed round the world. That was just the sort of adventure that could fire his enthusiasm.'

'But he didn't, in fact, mention any project to you?'

'No, sadly, he didn't.'

'How much would he have got for his business, can you give me a rough idea?'

'I'm really not the right person to ask, but I'd have thought – a million, two million, perhaps.'

A big difference between the two, Slider thought. One was enough to sail round the world, two perhaps to start up a new business. But if he had meant to do either, surely he'd have mentioned at least the possibility to someone – to his ex-wife perhaps, or one of his collection of women. And yet, why else would he sell? Swilley had said his income was adequate. Blackmail? But those being blackmailed are usually anxious and unhappy, and everyone who spoke to him that last day had said he seemed cheerful.

'Well, thank you, Mr Pauling,' he said. 'You've given me some things to think about.'

'My pleasure,' said Pauling. 'And if there's anything else I can do – any way I can help to bring whoever did this to justice . . . Ed was my dearest friend,' he concluded, and the quiver was back. 'Life without him is going to be . . .' A pause for collection. 'So black and white.'

Atherton came in, having been listening on another phone. 'There's a little cauldron of unsatisfied desires,' he said.

'It was only Virginia Foulkes's opinion that he was in love with Wiseman,' Slider checked him.

'Hm. But you notice how he downplayed the part of any women in Ed's life. I'm surprised he didn't hint that one of *them* must have killed him. Karma's a bitch. He who lives by the sword, and so on.'

'He who lives by the sword generally gets shot by he who doesn't,' said Slider.

'So what do we make of the fact that Wiseman was selling his business?'

'Not fact – idea. And I don't know.'

'If he sold – if it is true,' he inserted, to placate Slider's stern look, 'it might have resulted in a few peeved writers. They might not like being transferred like parcels without being asked.'

'Virginia Foulkes didn't mention it, and she's one of his big names, so presumably he didn't tell her, and if they didn't know, they couldn't have been peeved enough to murder him, could they?'

'True,' said Atherton, disappointed. 'This needs thinking about.'

Hart came to the door. 'Boss, I've got Simon Haig's mobile log from the phone company,' she said. 'He was home all evening.'

'Damnit!' said Atherton. 'Let me see.'

She handed over the sheets and Slider put them on the desk so they could all look.

'My God!' Atherton breathed. 'That man could talk. Look at this! And this! There's only about ten minutes of the entire evening when he's not jabbering.'

'Exaggeration,' Hart said. 'But he doesn't half bunny, all right.'

'Wait a minute – there's nothing after eleven-oh-five,' Atherton pounced. 'He could still have gone over there and done it.'

'But his wife came home around eleven,' Hart pointed out. 'Unless they were in it together.'

'I don't think she was,' Slider said. 'But in any case –' he turned to the next page – 'even if he went, his phone stayed put.'

'And he's not the sort to go out wivout it,' Hart said mournfully.

'And the killing more likely took place earlier in the evening. We're pushing it, really, taking it up to midnight. I think Simon Haig is off the hook.'

*   *   *

Loessop came in looking worn. 'I managed to get most of 'em,' he said. 'All legit reasons for going in and out. Of course, I haven't checked they really went where they said they went, but . . .'

'But that's a lot of work,' Slider agreed. A lot of work to establish the alibis of people who had nothing to be alibi'd for, in order to prove that Marina Haig was at home when she said she was.'

'There's two I couldn't get hold of yet, but they don't live on the same floor as her, and from the ones I spoke to, nobody really knows anybody else in that block. One or two mentioned Mikki Yamamoto – you know, that model who used to be married to the Arsenal striker, what's his name – but nobody even mentioned Ben Dawlish, never mind Marina Haig. I got the impression they didn't want to know their neighbours. Privacy and that. So there's really no reason,' he concluded wearily, 'to think they'd lend their card.'

'Quite,' said Slider. 'Well, unless we get any evidence from other sources that she was out and about, and specifically in Shepherd's Bush, I think you can leave it at that for now.'

Porson scratched the top of his strangely bumpy dome. 'Which leaves – what? You've got all these people, innocent as the day – proved at great expense of time and effort, I might add – and no leads left to follow up.'

'Except for Calliope Hunt,' Slider said.

'Oh, get off it. You can't have her. What have you got – a death wish?'

Slider rummaged through his head with an effort. 'We haven't cleared Virginia Foulkes.'

'She was another one alone at home, wasn't she?'

'Yes, but I really don't think she did it.'

'You're not paid to think,' Porson said incautiously. 'All these women – hotbeds of emotion. No knowing what they're capable of. What do they say – the female of the specious? They've got a lot of rage these days, women. Gender pay gap, glass seagull – hating men is second nature to 'em.'

'I'll check on her,' Slider said morosely.

'Well, you've got nothing else to do, have you?'

It was unkind, but Slider guessed it was to keep his mind off the forbidden fruit of Calliope Hunt.

Slider went home, to take over the bridge from Joanna, who had a session. He took the file with him and spent the evening reading his notes, worrying about the danger of being transferred to Vice, and wondering about Joanna's state of mind. One bright spot on the horizon was that Dad and Lydia were coming home tomorrow. He realised – not for the first time – how lucky they were to have them living downstairs.

TWENTY
Notting Hell

S lider had another early-morning meeting, this time with a consortium of community leaders worried about knife crime, of which Shepherd's Bush had relatively little. They were asking for intelligence-led action, without precisely knowing what that meant. Slider answered the questions directly put to him, but kept his mouth shut otherwise. Most of the complainants had grown up in a society unimaginably different from the way it was now, and were naturally disturbed by not understanding any more the land they had always lived in. It was hard enough for the police to keep up with the changes, let alone civilians only marginally involved. He sympathised, but there was nothing he could tell them that would have reassured them.

As he was leaving, he saw Lily Saddler lurking at the back of the room. He tried to shuffle out in the crowd, but she moved with surprising agility and accosted him, drew him to one side with a claw-like hand dug fast into his forearm. Her first words, however, surprised the hell out of him.

'Well done,' she said.

'Uh?' Slider managed.

'The Wiseman business,' she whispered. He thought it sounded like a Simon Haig thriller. 'It's going dead – lost all traction on the web.'

'Oh,' he said. And that was good, was it?

'It's what we wanted,' she went on. 'Keep it all low-key. Zero public interest. Dave's satisfied with the way it's going.'

'I thought he'd have wanted it cleared up,' Slider said suicidally. Internally he slapped his forehead and said, D'oh!

'Oh yes,' she said, as if that were a given. 'But without publicity. No sensationalism. Above all, not involving *a certain person*. Well done. Keep it up,' she concluded, and slithered away through the press of bodies to annoy someone else.

The Wiseman file, when he got back to it after attending to some other matters, still offered him no new thoughts. He was actually glad when the phone rang.

'Call for you on the other line,' said McLaren. 'Female, says she's Mary Wiseman.'

'We don't know any Mary Wiseman, do we?' Slider objected.

'Nah, guv, but she says it's about Wiseman and she can't talk to anybody else except you.'

'Oh well, put her on. I haven't had a good laugh yet this morning.'

'Right-oh.'

A click, and then a young female voice saying, 'Is that Chief Inspector Slider?'

'Speaking,' he said.

'Look,' said the voice, 'I've got to talk to you, but it's got to be private. Is anybody else there?'

'No, I'm alone. Who is this?'

A pause, and then, on a downward cadence, 'It's Callie.' Slider didn't immediately twig, and the voice went on, impatiently, 'Callie Hunt.'

'Oh,' he said, enlightened.

'I'm not supposed to talk to you,' she went on. 'Dad would literally kill me, but I've got to. It's killing me, not knowing. Can you meet me? Phones aren't secure – you never know who's listening.'

Well, at the moment it was McLaren, of course, as per SOP. 'When and where?' he asked. It all seemed a bit melodramatic, but he didn't want it known he had spoken to her either. It would be bound to get back to Mr Carpenter.

'Do you know a café in Portobello Road called the Good Earth?'

'I'll find it.'

'I'll be there in half an hour. But just you – don't bring anybody else. And don't tell anyone. If I spot a pap I'm not coming in.'

'Got it,' Slider said. She rang off. He went through to the outer office.

'You going, then?' McLaren said.

'Yes, but let's keep this under wraps,' he said. 'If anyone knows, eventually everyone knows.'

'I won't say anything,' McLaren said. 'What do I tell anyone who's asking for you?'

'Tell them I've gone to see a man about a dog,' said Slider, and left.

Portobello Road on a weekday was much less crowded than on a Saturday, with fewer tourists, the market mostly dedicated to fruit and vegetable stalls, and the locals, released from their weekend purdah, pottering about like extras in a Richard Curtis film.

The Good Earth was one of those tofu-and-wheatgrass places dedicated to clean eating and moderate celebrity. It had a bare wooden floor, wooden tables and chairs, terracotta-coloured walls, and a great many handwritten notices, to give the impression the place was run by volunteers with no desire to make a profit. There was no sign of any media or paparazzi types hanging about outside. Slider went in and sat at a table at the back and waited. After a bit, he realised it was counter service only, so he went up and asked for a cup of tea. This was not the simple process he had hoped for. There were dozens of fruit and herbal infusions on offer, but nothing he recognised as even coming close to normal Builders, so he settled at last for green tea. And it came in a pot.

'Anything to eat?' asked the girl behind the counter, in an achingly posh voice. She was wearing pure unbleached linen, and her hair was so clean and shiny it slithered about all on its own like a restless pedigreed horse.

'Cake?' he said hopefully.

She opened her mouth to ask another raft of questions, then shut it as she examined him, and without another word shovelled something onto a plate and pushed it across to him. It was a wedge of cake all right, but unadorned and brown and bumpy. It looked as though it would be good for his bowels.

'Thirteen ninety-five,' she said.

He flinched, paid her, and sloped back to his table, reflecting that not being interested in profit must be very good for business. You could get a meal for two people at McDonald's for that. A covert glance at the few other people in the café, however, suggested none of them had ever set foot in a McDonald's, and that north of a tenner for tea and cake would not cause them pain – or indeed be likely to rouse them from their intellectual reverie. Most of them were reading very old, creased Penguins.

He settled to consume his order as slowly as possible. He didn't want to have to go back. She came in twenty minutes later, and despite the sunglasses and the floppy linen hat pulled down over her brow, he recognised her instantly, though he had only seen pictures of her before. She was wearing taupe linen capris, a teal silk shirt plungingly open, wedge-heeled sandals that looked so uncomfortable they *had* to be designer, and a vast handbag slung on her shoulder in soft coral leather with gold chain decorations. She paused in the doorway, as though making an entrance on stage and allowing the adoring fans to register her. So much for subterfuge.

Having scanned the room, she settled on him, lowered her sunglasses halfway to look at him, and when he nodded, she slank slinkily over to him and threw herself into the seat opposite.

'Chief Inspector Slider,' he said quietly, to reassure her.

'Thank God! I was afraid I'd get here before you and have to sit alone, with everyone looking at me.'

She dumped the bag on the floor with a thump that suggested she had brought a steam iron and a full set of plumber's tools with her, removed the sunglasses and whipped off the hat. The dozen bracelets she was wearing rushed first down, then up, then down her arm with a noise like an entire percussion section falling downstairs. Her hair, released, swished down dramatically – the usual silky, glossy, streaky-blonde mane, as straight as a yard of tapwater and reaching halfway to her waist.

Nobody in the café had looked round. Presumably they were locals, and were used to this sort of thing.

Slider waited for her to begin. She seemed to be waiting for him, and finally said, 'Aren't you going to get me something?'

'Oh. Yes, of course. What would you like?'

'I'll have a kale smoothie and the indigo seaweed biscuits.'

When this unappealing snack was before her, Slider had the opportunity at last to study her. He knew she was twenty-two, and she still had the firm contours of cheek and lip of a girl even younger; but in other ways she looked older. Under her make-up, her skin was not good, and there were dark shadows under her eyes. She was thin – where her shirt was open at the neck, he could see her upper ribs, and her arms and legs were twig-like. She fidgeted her fingers all the time. Either extreme dieting, or a coke habit, or both, he thought. But her eyes were sensational – smoky blue and beautifully-shaped. She spoke in the clear, imperious tones, and with the accent, of someone from a wealthy home and a private education. And she had the basic animal attraction of youth and health and self-assurance. He could see why any man – except McLaren, who liked well-padded women who played darts – would want her.

'You wanted to speak to me,' he said, to get the ball rolling.

'Yes,' she said. She leaned forward a little, and said in a semi-whisper, 'Have you solved it yet – the case? Do you know who did it?'

'We're following up certain leads,' he said. She was silent, seeming to digest this. 'Is that all you wanted to say?' he prompted her.

She made an impatient movement of her hand, silencing him – evidently used to that working. 'I can't talk about it at home. My mother and father are furious about the whole thing. They've been trying to stop it becoming a story. They *never* approved of Ed and me. Old people just don't understand. I mean, they don't realise that publicity is a *good* thing.'

'Some publicity. Not all, surely,' Slider said mildly.

She shrugged. 'You can turn things round if you have a good publicist. Mine is totally *pants*. If Dad would only spring for a better one, I wouldn't be having to slink around and practically be a prisoner in my own house. That's why I wrote the book – to get my name in front of the public again. But Dad disapproved of it.' She gave him a challenging stare. 'Because it had sex and violence in it. I mean, what did he think? I was going to write *The Wind in the Willows*?'

'Surely not,' Slider murmured.

'Ed understood that,' she went on, nibbling at a black biscuit that seemed to have the consistency of a roof slate. 'You have to hit the zeitgeist or . . . forget it!'

'So he was helping you get it published,' Slider suggested.

'Yes – well, everybody said you had to have an agent. I couldn't see the point myself. I mean, I already had a name. I thought I'd just give it to some publisher and they'd be grateful. But everyone said it didn't work that way.' She shrugged. 'So I was looking around for one when I met Ed at a party, and I knew straight away he was the one for me.'

'You fell in love?' Slider suggested.

'I mean, I knew he was the *agent* for me,' she said impatiently. 'He was so dynamic, and he knew *everyone*, all the important people, and he went to all the right parties. I didn't want some fusty old fossil smelling of mothballs and living in the nineteenth century. So I just went right up and asked him, and he said yes.'

'So this book of yours,' Slider said, 'it was the next step in your career? You weren't intending to be a writer for ever?'

'God, no! Well, I didn't mind the idea of doing the odd book now and then if I had time, but it was TV and films I wanted to get into – or back into, I should say, because I've already been a top-paid presenter. On TV. I'd like to get into films, and Ed knew a lot of people in that circle, too, so he'd be useful to me. Writing books all the time would be too much like hard work – and nobody *sees* you while you're doing it. God! Think of sitting alone in your house day after day just pounding a keyboard! I'd die! But I thought if I could make a big splash with the one book, I could get someone else to write them for me afterwards. I mean, everybody knows none of the really big authors write their own books.'

'Is that a fact?' Slider asked.

'Obviously. They're out doing publicity. They'd never have time.'

'I believe Ed was helping you with rewriting the book, wasn't he?'

'Tightening it up, not rewriting it,' she objected. 'It was pretty good as it was, but of course he knows what publishers want, so he was suggesting a few little improvements here and there.'

'And in the course of going through that process with him, you must have become very close.'

She fidgeted, and looked away for a moment. 'I wouldn't say that exactly.'

Slider tried the direct route. 'You did sleep with him?'

Her eyes came back. She shrugged. 'Well, he wanted me – of course. And I thought it would concentrate his mind. He had other clients, and I didn't want him wasting his time on them when he should be working for me. So I slept with him a few times.'

'More than a few, I think. And you went out with him – to restaurants and clubs.' He wanted to clear that point up.

'I thought it would be a good idea to be seen with him. We went to a lot of parties, too, and premieres and awards dinners. Actually, that part was fun. Like I said, he knew all the right people.'

'And he bought you presents?'

'Yah, he bought me some nice things. Why not? Shoes. And clothes. He had a great eye for clothes. Jewellery. He was very generous. If I said I liked something – wham, he went straight in and bought it. He bought me these earrings.' She tilted her head towards him so he could admire them.

'Sapphires?' he hazarded.

'He said they brought out my eyes. But then my parents started to get all heavy about it.' She shrugged again. 'And, frankly, I was beginning to get a bit bored with Ed. I mean he talked a big talk, but he wasn't getting anywhere with my book. And he was . . . getting a bit intense. A bit clingy.'

'Did he say he wanted to marry you?'

She looked down at her hands – modesty, or embarrassment, he didn't know which. 'Yah,' she said at last. She looked up. 'I mean, I never said I would. I never said yes. He never asked me, really, he just sort of assumed.'

'But you didn't make it clear to him that—'

She looked annoyed. 'He was still trying to get my book accepted. I wasn't going to mess with that. But he ought to have known – I mean, ok he was fit and everything, and good fun, but he was *old*. I've got my whole life ahead of me. I'd never marry an old man like that. He should have realised.'

'Yes, he should,' Slider said. He felt sorry for Wiseman for a moment. 'Tell me about that last day – Monday of last week. You rang him in the morning, didn't you?'

'Yah, when I woke up. We had a long chat. He was great on the phone – very loving and sexy, and funny as hell. He made me laugh. He always made me feel good.'

'And you made plans for later?' he said hopefully.

'He told me he was going out to lunch with some publisher woman who had a lot of clout, and she was going to get my book taken, and not only that, she could get all sorts of other things like foreign deals and movie deals. It all sounded brilliant. And he asked if I'd come over that evening and hear all about it. So I said yes. He said he'd have something very important to tell me. A big plan for me, he said.'

'This "something important" – did you think that was about the book?'

'No, I think it was something else. To be honest with you, I half thought he was going to propose to me – you know, officially, the kneeling down and the ring and the champagne, the whole cheesy bit.'

'And what would you have done?'

'Well – gone along with it for a bit, I suppose. Until the book deal was done. Look,' she added, as though he had said something, 'I *liked* him, don't get me wrong. And he was terrific in bed. And he was mad for me, so it wouldn't have hurt him if I went along with it for a while, would it?'

'So,' said Slider, as casually as he knew how, 'did you in fact go round that evening?'

'No,' she said, with the ease of truth, 'because I rang him in the afternoon to find out how this meeting had gone, and he said this woman had said no. So then I thought, well, he's not going to make it happen, is he? Despite all his talk. He said not to worry, he had plenty of other people to go to, and this woman might still change her mind, but it wasn't what I wanted to hear, frankly. I was disillusioned with him. And, like I said, he was getting too clingy, and my dad was kicking up at home about the whole thing.'

'So you ended it?'

'God, no. He might've still come through – I wasn't going to burn my bridges. I just let him think everything was fine. I mean,

I hadn't actually decided at that point not to go round, but I was thinking I might just not show.'

'So you ended the conversation on good terms?'

'Yah, of course. He said again not to worry, my book was going to be a huge success, and I said I wasn't worried, and we talked a bit more and he said see you later and I rang off.'

Slider digested this. 'Then,' he said, 'if you didn't go to Ed's house that evening, where did you go?'

She examined him frankly, and then giggled. 'You mean, have I got an alibi?'

'If you like.'

'You haven't been thinking *I* killed Ed?'

'I don't think anything, I just collect evidence.'

'How boring for you,' she said scornfully. 'As a matter of fact, I have got one. I was at Annabel's, with Ollie Brent. Do you know him?'

'Not personally,' said Slider. Ollie Brent was a newish film star – a baby-faced actor who was probably older than he looked. He'd had what Slider believed was called a break-through part in a thriller last year. On the way up, Slider supposed – as opposed to Ed Wiseman, on the way down.

'I didn't mean personally. Where would *you* meet someone like him? He's just been signed for a major Tony Gilroy film, a thriller. It's going to be a box-office smash. We've been seeing each other a lot.'

'But Ed Wiseman didn't know about that?'

'What are you, the dating police? No, I didn't tell him, obvs. But I decided that if he didn't come up with something pretty soon, Ed, I mean, I'd go all out for Ollie, because he could be a lot more useful for me, especially with this new film.' She must have thought she saw something in his face – though he was sure he hadn't shown anything – because she said, 'Look, I liked Ed. I liked him a lot more than Ollie, if you want to know. And Ollie's no good in bed. He takes too many drugs. He's all gong and no dinner. But that's not the point. Your career has to come first. You've only got so much time to catch the train, after that you've had it. Maybe one day I'll want to get married, maybe have kids, but that doesn't fit in with my career trajectory right now. If you want to make it big you've got to be dedicated – ruthless, if you like.'

Slider considered. 'Can you tell me of anyone who might have wanted to hurt Ed? A business rival, a personal enemy – someone jealous of your relationship with him?'

'No, no one. I've been thinking about that, natch, but, no. We didn't talk much about his business. And as far as I knew, everyone liked him. I suppose my dad was the person most angry about our relationship, but you can't suspect him. He's, like, mega-respectable. And look,' she added, leaning forward again, 'can you please not tell anyone what I've told you? I mean, that I was going off Ed. Because when you catch the murderer, it's going to be all over the papers, and as the woman he loved, I'll get a lot of publicity out of it. It might make all the difference to my book and my career.'

'How will Ollie Brent feel about that?' Slider asked.

'Oh, he'll understand. So, you won't tell anyone? And . . .' She reached down with another set of tumbling cymbals and grabbed something out of her bag – a small leather card-case. Fumbling in it, she took out a visiting-card and held it out to him. 'Will you let me know when you catch the right person, give me a heads up that there's going to be an arrest, so that I can make my plans? Please?' She smiled prettily. 'It's what Ed would have wanted,' she added, with a sincere look. 'He loved me very much.'

'I'm afraid I'm not allowed to do that,' he told her politely. 'But you'll read all about it in the papers.'

'I don't read *papers*,' she said, as though the very idea was ridiculous. Then she shrugged. 'It doesn't matter, anyway. I expect Dave will tell me. He's my godmother's cousin's husband. You know Dave Carpenter? He and Dad are tight. He didn't approve of Ed either, so he'll be happy to tell me that everything's wrapped up and finished with.'

'I expect he will,' said Slider.

TWENTY-ONE
Love, Actually

'And for the moment,' said Slider, 'this is strictly between us – you, me and McLaren. If it gets back to Mr Carpenter . . .'

Atherton pursed his lips in a soundless whistle. 'And you really think nobody saw you two together? In Notting Hill, the starlets' playground?'

'Even if they recognised her, they wouldn't have known who I was,' said Slider.

'I can see the headlines now – TV POPSIE'S MYSTERY NEW LOVE.'

'Popsie?' Slider queried in a pained voice.

'Well, you know I won't talk. And McLaren's sound. But I bet you anything *she* tells. She'll start off with little hints – "you'll never guess what happened to me the other day" – and the next time she's drunk, or high, it'll be "you must promise not to tell, but . . ."'

'Oh well,' said Slider, 'we must hope the case is stitched up by then, so it won't matter.'

'And you want me to go check the Annabel's alibi?'

'Better you than McLaren. You won't stick out so much.'

'Hmm. So *who* went round there that night? Which of his many popsies popped into the love-pad for a quickie?'

'We know he had sex with someone. But not that the someone killed him.'

'True. There could have been the popsie, followed at a later time by an angry man.'

'Which only makes it worse. Two people to find instead of one,' said Slider.

'And everyone's got an alibi. All we've got left is – what? Virginia Foulkes?'

'I don't think she did it,' said Slider.

'You don't want it to be her. You like her.'

'Assessment of character is part of a detective's skill,' said Slider. Atherton raised a Vulcan eyebrow, and he said, 'Hart is checking her phone records. If she received or made any calls at home that evening, she's clear.' He stared out of the window for a moment. 'But I think I'll have another talk with her, all the same.'

'Sucker!'

'I'll do it over the phone,' Slider said with dignity. 'Meanwhile – why don't you have another talk with Cathy Beccles? She's the other one with no alibi for that evening.'

'Oh, I'm sure she didn't do it,' Atherton protested.

'You don't want it to be her. You like her,' Slider gave him his own words back.

'She loved him,' said Atherton.

'All the more reason. Love unrequited, love gone sour. It's behind a lot of murders, when you think of it, actually.'

'When good love goes bad – sounds like a country and western hit,' said Atherton. 'Stand by your man – and stab him.'

'And,' Slider went on, ignoring him, 'she's had time now to think about it. She may have some new ideas, or have remembered something that could help.'

When Virginia Foulkes answered the phone, Slider began, 'It's Chief Inspector Slider from Shepherd's Bush. We spoke previously . . .'

'Of course I remember,' she said at once. 'Slider – that's a name it's not easy to forget. Actually, I wish I'd thought of it for my lead character in my Regency mysteries. Inspector Slider has got a nice, old-fashioned ring to it, don't you think? I suppose I can't borrow it, can I?'

'I think if you did I'd have to sue,' Slider said. 'Wouldn't it be breach of copyright?'

'You can't copyright names or titles. If I made my character anything like you, you could sue me for libel. But don't worry, I won't use it. You're quite safe with me.'

It seemed possible from the purring quality of her voice that she was flirting with him. Well, it made a nice change from spitting and swearing at him, in the habit of the criminal classes. Or regarding him with a mixture of curiosity and wariness, as if he were an unknown species of insect, like the rest of humanity.

'I wonder,' he said, 'if I'm not disturbing you – if I could run a few more questions past you?'

'I'm just taking a lunch break. Good timing.'

'They may seem rather random questions . . .'

'Haven't got anywhere with it yet?' she said in sympathetic tones. 'I guessed as much, or there'd have been something in the news. Don't mind, ask me anything. I know all about writer's block. Sometimes you've just got to put words down on the page, however random, and unconnected they seem, and eventually something goes pop. So just talk to me. Use me as your sounding board.'

Definitely flirting. 'Thanks,' he said. 'I was wondering, that last day, when you phoned him in the evening, why you used the landline instead of your mobile.'

'Oh, I always used the landline if we were going to have a long chat. Ed did the same. Those mobiles are so uncomfortable to hold for any length of time. And there was a fuss a while back about the microwaves they emit, do you remember? I don't think it can be good for you to have one jammed against the side of your head for long periods.' She drew a breath. 'God, I miss him! For the talk, more than anything else. Do you have anyone like that, that you just chat to – not about anything in particular, but just whatever comes into your mind?'

'My wife, I suppose,' he said.

'You're lucky, then, to have that sort of relationship,' she said. 'Ed was mine. I suspect you only get one – and it doesn't have to be the person you marry. Rarely is, I imagine. What is it the girls say nowadays? Ed was my BFF.'

Slider knew what that meant – he had a teenage daughter. Though in her case, the 'forever' bit tended to be a bit more flexible. There were photons that had taken longer to travel a Planck length than some of Kate's friendships had lasted.

'You said, in the course of that conversation, that he talked about Calliope Hunt. Can you remember more about what he said about her?'

'Not the actual words. It was all about how wonderful she was.'

'But did he actually say he was going to marry her?'

'Oh yes, he was clear about that. He said, I'm going to marry that girl, Ginnie. She makes me feel young. He said she had a

wonderful career ahead of her. And that he was going to be there
to see it, or make it happen, something along those lines. He said
he had great plans for her.'

'You didn't ask what those plans were?'

'Didn't want to know, as a matter of fact,' she said shortly. 'It
was bad enough having him drivelling on to me about that wretched
girl, without encouraging it. Oh, no,' she recanted, 'I don't mean
that. He could tell me anything. I was just worried she was taking
him for a ride. But there's a moment to tell a person that sort of
thing, and that wasn't it – not when he was in full flood. He said
they were going to start a new life together, I remember that.'

'But nothing about what those plans actually were, or what the
new life entailed?'

'No. It was just general mushy stuff,' she said. 'Is there something specific you're asking about? Have you found something
out?'

'No. I don't know.' He thought a moment, grasping after ends.
She waited patiently. '*If,*' he said, with careful emphasis, 'it wasn't
Calliope who went round there that evening, have you any idea
who it might have been?'

Tactfully, she didn't follow up the 'if'. 'Now you're asking!'
she exclaimed. 'I didn't keep up to date with all his little
adventures. It could have been anybody.'

'So he wasn't faithful to Calliope?'

'Faithful!' she chuckled. 'Well, he was a very faithful man, but to
more than one person at once. He wasn't exclusive, put it that way.
And, seriously, I doubt that Calliope was, either. It doesn't always
mean these days what perhaps it has meant in the past – sex. It's
more a sort of shorthand. But as to naming any women he might
have been romancing – no, I couldn't tell you. I'm sure his playlist
changed from day to day.' She heard his silence and said, 'That's not
very helpful, is it? I can tell you it wasn't me.'

He didn't say, we're in the process of confirming that. Instead,
he struck off in a different direction. 'Did you know he was
selling the business?'

'What? No!' There was a pause, in which she breathed hard
through her nose. He took it for annoyance – possibly anger. 'Who
told you that?' she went on, sharply.

'Murray Pauling,' he said.

She laughed, but slightly brittly. 'Oh Gus! Well, you don't always want to take what he says as gospel.'

'I would imagine about business matters he's quite reliable,' Slider said mildly. 'He has built up a large business empire.'

'Yes, of course, and I didn't mean to . . .' She breathed again. 'I spoke to him yesterday, and he didn't say anything about it to me. What did he tell you?'

'That Ed had confided in him that he was selling the business, nothing more than that. I suppose it would affect you, as a client of his, wouldn't it?'

'Yes, of course, and I would have expected, as one of his oldest clients, as well as a friend, that he would have warned me.'

'Mr Pauling said something about a non-disclosure agreement.'

'All the same . . .' She was silent a moment. 'Why would he tell Gus and not me? Oh, I suppose because of the business side of it. Still, I must say I'm pretty annoyed about it.'

'He's known Gus a long time,' Slider suggested.

'Not *much* longer than me,' she said. 'I met him in the third term at Oxford, he and Gus went up together. I suppose there was that man-thing, that they played cricket together. That forms a bond.'

'They played cricket at university?'

'They were good. They both played in the Varsity Match at Lord's. Gus is more of a sportsman than he looks, though he gave it up when he went down, and Ed didn't.'

'Cricket was a passion of Ed's, wasn't it?' Slider said. 'I've seen those souvenirs of his in his study. Memorabilia. Whatever they are.'

'Souvenirs? Oh, you mean the old cricket balls and the bat. Not particularly attractive as interior design, but he loved them. The balls were from his school and university matches, the important ones, and the bat was from a charity celebrity match he played in, a fundraiser – oh, quite a few years ago. The autographs are all the people who played in it. I think Geoff Boycott's on there somewhere. And David Gower. Michael Parkinson. Michael Jayston. Oh, and Ian Botham. He loved telling people how he hit a six off Ian Botham. I expect Botham went easy on him,' she said with twinkle. 'But, to be fair, Ed was a pretty fair batsman.

I think hitting that six was the proudest moment of his life. He adored that stupid bat.'

Luckily, he had a question ready to cover his reaction. 'It would be worth a bit, I suppose?'

'What, you mean on the *Antiques Roadshow*, or something? Well, I suppose a real cricket nut might give a hundred pounds for it, but it wasn't a Ming vase or anything. Why do you ask?'

'Oh, we always have to consider burglary. Was there anything else of worth in the house, do you know?'

'Nothing I can imagine anyone breaking in for,' she said, sounding puzzled. 'He didn't keep large sums of money hanging around. As far as I know, he didn't even have a safe. And if he was selling the business, maybe he wasn't making large sums of money. But he never said he was in financial trouble, and I'm sure that's the sort of thing he *would* tell me about, if he were. But then he didn't tell me he was selling. Oh, Lord, I wish *you* hadn't told me. It's bad enough losing my agent in the first place, without discovering that he was about to sell me to someone else like a heathen slave.'

'I'm sorry to have upset you,' Slider said, 'but it has been helpful talking to you.'

'I can't think why. I haven't told you anything.'

'But it's like you said, just talking can help unblock the mind.'

'Well, I'm glad I helped. You'll let me know – won't you? – if and when you – what do you say? – solve the case.'

'I will let you know as soon as I am able to,' Slider said, thanked her again and got off the line. Things were turning and clicking in his mind like tumblers in a lock. 'Swilley!' he bellowed. 'In here!'

Swilley appeared, politely enquiring. 'Boss?'

'You're still working through all the phone calls.'

'In and out. There were a lot of them.'

'Business ones as well?'

'I'm just asking them if they made the call, was it business or personal, and if it was personal, do they know of anyone who wished him harm,' she said, surveying his face for clues. 'Minimal approach. If there's anything worth following up, I'll follow it up, but there hasn't been yet.'

'The last call he took – it was on the landline. I think you said a solicitor?'

'That's right. Duncan Grieves.'

'Did you ask what it was about?'

'No, just was it business, and he said yes.'

'Wiseman was selling the company.'

'Yes, so you said, so that could be what it was about. But I didn't know that when I checked him out.'

'I'm not blaming you, I'm thinking aloud. And just before that, he had a long talk with Virginia Foulkes.'

'S'right. She rang off just before the Grieves bloke rang.' Swilley looked puzzled. 'What's this about, boss?'

'Get on to Grieves now and ask him what the call was about. And send McLaren in, will you?'

She departed, and McLaren took her place in the doorway. 'S'up, guv?'

'Forget everything else. I want you to concentrate on the CCTV tapes at the tube station. Get Fathom to help you. And Gascoyne – this is urgent. You're looking for Amy Hollinshead going home on Monday evening. Find her going in to the station, and anywhere else inside. See if you can get a good image of her on one of the cameras.'

'The Hollinshead? What's that about, guv?' McLaren asked.

'She said she left to go home around six twenty to six thirty,' Slider said. 'I want to see if she did.'

McLaren, like a good subordinate, did not ask any more questions, but his face was alive with speculation.

Swilley was back first – of course she was, since checking the camera recordings, even when you know what you were looking for, was a time-consuming job.

'I spoke to Duncan Grieves. It *was* about the sale. He rang Wiseman to say that he'd just got agreement on the sale from the purchasers, and that now it was only a matter of signing the papers. Wiseman was going to go round to his office the next day and sign them. And apparently he said to Wiseman – joking, sort of – that he could tell people about it now, if he liked and Wiseman said that was all right, there was only one person he wanted to tell. Wiseman asked how soon the money would come through. Grieves said it sounded as though that was a crucial bit, so he told Wiseman he would get it as soon as possible, and asked if there was a problem. Wiseman said no problem, he was getting married, that's all. Grieves asked, anyone I know, and Wiseman said you will know her, when it goes public. And he laughed, and sounded very cock-a-hoop.' She fixed her large blue eyes on Slider. 'And that's all he remembers. What is it, boss? What's McLaren looking for?'

'I'll let you know as soon as he finds it.' He stirred restlessly under his churning thoughts. 'There's got to be some evidence before I go round there.'

'Round where? To Hollinshead's? Why her? Are you thinking *she* did it? Or was she in it with someone? Or she just knows something?'

He looked at her sharply, coming out of his reverie. 'Don't go anywhere. I shall need you to come with me. If it comes to it.'

With three of them on it, and now they were only looking for one person, it was at least quicker than Slider had feared. His afternoon cup of tea had not long gone cold on his desk when McLaren appeared, and said, 'Got her.'

'Got her?' Slider queried, half glad, half apprehensive.

'She didn't go home at six thirty, like she said,' he elaborated. 'We've got her going into the station entrance at eight thirty-five.'

Slider was startled. 'That's late! That's too late.'

McLaren frowned, not understanding his objection. 'Well, maybe she went somewhere else first. Went for a drink. Met a friend. Did some shopping. There's Westfield right next door.'

Slider shook his head. 'No, she said she went straight home. Did you get any clear shots of her?'

'Yeah. I've got 'em cued up. D'you wanna look?'

'Yes, of course.' Slider heaved himself up from his desk. 'Probably not too late,' he reassured himself. 'There's no knowing when it happened. And there was the sex.'

'Sex?' McLaren's ears pricked up automatically at that word.

'In Wiseman's bedroom. Sex was had. We don't know when.'

McLaren sat in front of his screen, and Slider leaned over his shoulder. Gascoyne was still working at his machine, but Fathom came and stood by.

'There you are, guv, there she is going in. There's the time.'

Gascoyne looked round. 'I'm looking for her at the other end, sir,' he said. 'At Lancaster Gate.'

'Good lad,' Slider said absently.

He was staring at Amy, in black and white, walking into the station, wearing a coat over trousers and ankle boots, handbag slung over her shoulder, her hair in a ponytail hanging down behind. Walking – wasn't she? – a little rigidly. Her face told nothing, her eyes were fixed straight ahead. No doubt, like everyone else, she knew there were security cameras everywhere. Like everyone else, she might not think about them; or she might know that looking at them conveyed a guilty appearance. But he needed more.

'Keep going,' he said to McLaren.

'Here she is crossing the concourse. Here she is at the barriers. Here she is going down the escalator. Here she is, crossing the lower hall – and going onto the platform. They're good ones, there was nobody walking right in front of her.'

'Freeze it. Show me. And the next. Freeze it.'

Yes, they were good ones. They showed that oddly rigid posture for what it was. Her handbag was slung on her right shoulder, where most right-handed women wore it on the left shoulder to give the right arm free movement. Her left elbow was tucked in to her side and her left arm and hand were pressed across her front at waist-level.

Slider was suddenly calm. And sad.

'Does it look to you,' he said, 'as if she's concealing something under her coat?'

TWENTY-TWO

The Long Day Closes

'Should we just bring her in?' Swilley asked, clattering down the stairs behind him.

'No. I want to do it at her flat. I think she'll open up there, tell us everything.'

'But will it stick, boss?' Swilley said anxiously, glancing at the grim set of his face. 'I mean, without the proper procedures.'

'Once she's told us, she won't take it back,' he said.

'You don't know that. You don't really know this woman.'

'I know her. Leave it, Norma,' he said wearily. 'Just . . .'

Atherton pushed in at the door from the yard as they were about to push out. Slider went past him without a word. Atherton, startled, met Swilley's eyes and she mouthed a name at him, causing his eyebrows to shoot even further up. And they were past and gone before he could speak.

'What if she's not in?' Swilley muttered as they reached the car.

'She'll be in,' Slider said sharply; and then, relenting slightly, 'Where would she go?' Like a hunted fox, she would have gone to ground. Only in this case, it was she who had been hunting herself.

She had been so calm and collected, he thought as he drove. She had played the part exactly right, behaving as an innocent woman would have. Had she sat up all Monday night, going over every possibility, trying to foresee every question? Or had it been more like method-acting – putting herself into the mindset of the secretary who knew nothing about it, and playing it by ear? It had been masterly, he thought, but for one – no, two – tiny errors. And one unstudied reaction she probably couldn't have helped – though even then she had covered so well. Did she think about them now, was she aware of them, or had she not realised? But she must know, she must know eventually she would have to answer. If not to him, to another authority. And, as a thinking woman, perhaps she longed for that – for it to be over, at least. The thinking, the wondering, must be agony.

He rang the bell, and for a moment wondered if Swilley was right, that she might have run. But there was a husky noise from the intercom and a female voice – he could not have recognised it – said 'Yes?'

'It's Bill Slider,' he said, without knowing he was going to use that form until he said it. But yes, it was right – he wanted to encourage, not intimidate her. 'Can I come in and talk to you?'

And there was a moment of wondering whether she would admit them, but she buzzed them in, and upstairs opened the flat door to them. This was not the Amy Hollinshead of a week ago. She had aged shockingly – she now looked all her years and more. Her eyes were ringed, her un-made-up face pale, her cheeks hollow. She wore a long grey dressing-gown under which pyjama trousers showed, her feet bare. Her hair was no longer glossy and neat but dull and unbrushed. The contrast was shocking. It emphasised for him how strongly she had been holding it together when he first saw her on the Tuesday morning. Now she had fallen apart. It was all to the good for his purposes, but he felt an unwelcome surge of pity – as when you saw a dead fox at the side of the road. You might not like foxes, but it was sad to see that sleek, swift, perfectly designed creature brought to ruin.

He said his name again and introduced Swilley. She did not react. Her eyes had that thousand-yard stare. He tried to engage it. 'You knew I would come,' he said.

'I suppose so,' she said at last. Her voice sounded rusty with disuse. She turned and walked away from him, into the flat, and he followed, Swilley closing the door behind them.

And this was not the same flat. The neatness, the almost obsessive tidiness, was blurred, things had not been put away, mugs not washed up, items of clothing had been discarded at random. The cat came straight towards Slider, but with what sounded like an anxious mew. He wondered if she had remembered to feed it.

She sat heavily on the sofa, hands clenched in her lap, a defeated slump to her shoulders. Slider pulled the armchair round and sat facing her. Swilley, in whom she had evinced no curiosity, stood behind the sofa, where she could see her in profile.

Slider leaned forward, elbows on his knees, hands dangling loosely between them, making himself unthreatening, someone to talk to. 'You knew I would come,' he said again, gently. 'You knew I'd find out. Do you want to tell me about it, or shall I talk?'

She barely shrugged. 'I don't know what you want from me.'

The cat jumped up onto the sofa as if heading for her lap, but stopped as if prevented by an invisible barrier. Probably the smell of her distress. It mewed, and jumped down again, and walked away. Its unsatisfied prowlings made the background to Slider's interview with Amy Hollinshead that afterwards he always remembered.

'Let's talk about that Monday,' he said, to get her started. 'When Ed came back from lunching with Cathy Beccles. Were you jealous of her?'

That got through. She looked surprised. 'Cathy? No.'

'They slept together, didn't they?'

'A long time ago. Not for years.'

'You're sure of that?' She shrugged indifferently. 'There is a certain kind of man,' Slider went on, 'who gets amorous when he's had a bit to drink. I'm guessing Ed was that sort of man. He arrived back from lunch a bit lit up, and wanted you to go upstairs with him.'

Amazingly, tears stood in her eyes. He'd have thought she'd be cried out by now. 'You don't understand,' she said. 'I loved him.'

'I know that.'

'And he loved me,' she added fiercely. 'We were lovers.'

'I know. So you went upstairs. Had a glass of wine together. Talked a little, perhaps.'

'A lot. Ed loved to talk.'

'And made love.' She assented with a slight nod. 'In his bed, in his bedroom.' She squeezed her eyes shut. 'After that – perhaps you lay in his arms for a while, talking. Or did he fall asleep? He'd had rather a lot of wine.'

She nodded, staring at the blank air. 'I went downstairs and got on with some work. He never slept for long – just a short nap. Always, after sex. Always a nap. He was very energetic. It took a lot out of him.'

Sometimes Slider regretted his vivid imagination. He saw this picture all too clearly. He even saw her fond glance at the sprawled and sleeping Wiseman as she dressed and padded out – the faint smile of the work-wife who, for the moment, had everything she wanted. Asleep, after sex with her, he was hers entirely.

He had felt it himself, God help him, with Joanna sometimes, when she slept after love-making: Joanna the sleek and beautiful and independent, the musician with the incomprehensible talent, the never entirely possessable.

He went on. 'So he woke up after a bit, dressed again, and

came downstairs and carried on with his own work. Everything was just as normal?'

'Normal,' she consented, but as though it was a word in a foreign language, whose nuances she might not understand.

'Then it was time for you to go home. You'd tidied up, ready to go,' he said, remembering her neatness, imagining her putting papers away, slipping the dust covers over the screen and keyboard. 'But just after six, the phone rang.' She closed her eyes and nodded. 'Why did you listen in?'

'I always did, when it was the landline,' she said automatically. 'In case it was something he'd want me to deal with.'

'But when you heard it was Virginia Foulkes . . .?'

'When she called it was always a long one. I wanted to go up and say goodbye to him before I left. I didn't listen to all of it. I just went in on the line after a few minutes to see if it sounded as though it was near the end.'

He suspected this was not the truth. He suspected she listened to it all – perhaps not with any sense of urgency, but just waiting impatiently for it to be over so she could go up to him again. He saw her seated, leaning her elbows on her desk, the receiver to her ear, half bored with the old-friends chat, only half attending – until something made her sit up sharply.

'And then you heard Ed say that he was going to marry Calliope Hunt.'

He saw enlightenment flicker across Swilley's face. She was quick on the uptake when it came to human relationships. She would not need to have it stressed how important that was.

'He said . . .' Amy began miserably. She hardly wanted to say the words aloud, but they forced their way out. 'He said she was everything to him.'

'But you'd known about her for a long time.'

'I knew he had a crush on her. But it'd happened before. He got these silly . . . enthusiasms. They never lasted. They burnt out, like paper. That's all she was, a paper cut-out, no substance.'

'But this time it was serious. He really was going to marry her.' She said nothing. 'The call ended at last, and you were going to go upstairs, but it rang again immediately.'

'I thought it was Virginia again,' she said. 'So I listened.' He waited, to make her say it. 'It was Duncan. The solicitor.'

He saw the deep-down flicker of anger that had not been entirely burnt away. That was good. He fanned it. 'Was that the first time you'd heard that he was selling the business?'

'Yes,' she said. 'He hadn't said a word.'

'It must have been a shock.'

'Not – a – word,' she repeated. 'I didn't see how I could not have known about it. When the call ended, I rushed upstairs, but he wasn't a bit remorseful. He was happy. He laughed, as if he'd been very clever, keeping it from me. He said he'd had the due diligence done when I was out of the office. I remembered he'd given me the day off one day, saying he didn't feel like working, and he was going to visit some friends in the country. I didn't think anything of it, because he'd done that sort of thing before. Due diligence doesn't take long with a small outfit like ours – they could do it in one day.'

Slider noticed, with an inward wince, that she had said, 'ours'.

'But to trick me like that – to keep me in ignorance, after all I'd done for him!' The words poured out now, on a flood of indignation, hurt and anger. 'I asked him why. *Why*? He said he was selling up and marrying Calliope Hunt, and investing the money in her career. He'd get her stupid book published even if he had to pay for it. He'd spend on publicity for her. He'd be her agent as well as her husband. They were going to start a whole new life together. He looked – lit up! And it was all about her. All those years I'd helped him build up the business, but I didn't count a bit!' She clenched her hands together. 'I said, what about me? What about my job? And he said I'd soon get another one. He said . . . he said he'd give me a good reference.'

It was hard for her to say the last bit. It was the final insult, Slider saw: a reference was what you gave to a mere employee. She had been so much more than that. 'That was cruel,' he murmured.

He didn't know if she heard him. She cried out in pain, 'Thirteen years! For thirteen years I was like a wife to him, more than a wife! I did everything for him. We were so close. He told me everything – he never made a move without me. He loved me – I know he loved me. And then . . . this!'

'It was more than you could bear,' Slider suggested.

'I screamed at him. How could he do this to me? How *could*

he? And with *her* – that – that *trollop*! That painted airhead! She couldn't even write! I practically re-wrote that book for her, when Ed got bored with it. He was throwing me out like a stray dog, for *her*?'

They had come to the delicate bit. No wrong moves now. 'He was sitting down at his desk,' he suggested quietly.

But she was on a roll, her eyes fixed on the replay of the scene, her jaw clenched with the remembered fury. 'Swivelling back and forth in his chair, the way he did, looking self-conscious, like a kid who knows he's done wrong but won't own up. And then he put his glasses on and pulled a manuscript towards him as if he was going to work on it, and he said, "Get used to it, Amy. It's happening." He was dismissing me! And he said, "You'd better look for another job." Without even looking at me, he said that. "Look for another job".'

'So you grabbed the cricket bat off the wall.'

'That *stupid* bat! I *hated* it!'

'And you hit him.'

Now she looked at him. 'I didn't mean to hurt him. Not really hurt him. I was just so mad at him, and he was pretending to ignore me. I had to make him notice me, pay attention to me. So I just – sort of – lashed out at him.'

'You play tennis,' Slider said sadly. 'You have a good, strong swing.'

'It felt good,' she whispered, as if to herself. 'It felt good when I did it. He looked so surprised for a second: oh, stupid Amy, the dogsbody, the nobody, she'd actually stood up for herself! So I hit him again.' She closed her eyes for a second, and Slider heard with her the crunch of the connect. She opened them and went on. 'He fell out of the chair onto the floor. I wanted to laugh, he looked so . . . undignified. Not like Ed at all. Ed was always so together. You could never imagine him tripping or falling over or anything like that. And there he was looking ridiculous, lying on the floor like a bundle of clothing.' She swallowed. 'But he didn't get up, he didn't move, and I realised – I realised I must have hurt him after all.'

'The side of the skull is quite fragile, where you hit him. If you'd hit the back of the head, he probably would have had a nasty bump, but maybe nothing more.'

'I'd killed him,' she said, staring at nothing again, speaking to herself. 'I'd really killed him. It was . . .' She didn't seem to know what it was. Terrible? Slider wondered. Wonderful? At last she said, on a breath of a voice, 'Unreal. It still seems unreal.'

Swilley made tea, and put a mug into Amy's hands, which were trembling now. And at a gesture from Slider, she put some food down for the cat, which ate as though its life depended on it. Perhaps it did.

Bit by bit, Slider got the rest of the story.

She had sat, frozen in shock and horror for a long time – an hour, maybe more.

'You didn't think of ringing for help – police, ambulance?'

'I didn't think of anything. I *couldn't* think. I was numb. I couldn't move or think or anything.'

It was the front doorbell ringing that jerked her out of her trance. It rang long and loud and angrily. She jumped almost out of her skin, her heart pounding with fear, realising the full horror of her situation. Here she was in the room with the body of the man she had killed. Slider, unwillingly, could imagine her agonised fear. Suppose the bell-ringer didn't go away? Suppose they had a key and came in? Or knew someone else who had one? Suppose they guessed something was wrong and called the police? She listened, attention straining, frozen in panic. She was just beginning to think the danger had passed when the bell rang again.

Slider glanced at Swilley, who nodded slightly. These must have been the attempts, first by Langley and then Burke, to visit their tormentor. It was good corroboration – it would help their case when they came to present it.

She waited a long time, but there was no more sound from downstairs, and now she had to move. She knew the trouble she was in, and looked round for inspiration, her trapped mind running back and forth, searching for a way out. The darkness outside made her think of the workings next door. Ed had been looking out of that window one day and had made a joke about making sure not to fall out because there would be no soft landing. It gave her the idea. With scaffolding and heaps of bricks and concrete mixers and all the rest of it, there was plenty down there to account for a head wound if someone did fall. Slider imagined the flood of adrenaline as she thought she might somehow get out of this horrible mire.

She had switched off the light, pushed the window up, and heaved the body up by the armpits until it was hanging out from the waist up over the sill. Ed, though tall, was lean, and she was tall for a woman, and strong – and was made stronger by sheer necessity. Finally, having got the body into position, she lifted the legs, changing the balance, and pushed it out, head first.

She closed her eyes at the memory. 'I heard the thud,' she said.

Then it had all been about covering her tracks. She switched the light back on; had enough wit about her not to close the window again. Arranged the scene, with the desk lamp on, and his papers placed so it would seem as though he'd been sitting there working. Poured a brandy and set the glass on the desk. He had got up for some reason, to look out of the window, overbalanced and fell.

'What did I forget?' she said to herself; and then she looked at Slider, and said it again. 'It looked good. What did I forget?'

'His glasses,' said Slider. 'You had to throw them out with him because they were broken. But if he'd been working, and got up to look out, he'd have taken them off and left them on the desk.'

'Oh,' she said. And then: 'Yes. I see that.'

'And being so very, very tidy in everything, you pushed his chair in under the desk.'

She frowned, remembering. 'Did I? I suppose I did. But what was wrong with that?'

'If someone gets up for a break from work, they shove the chair backwards to get up, but they're coming back again, so they don't usually push the chair in.'

'I would,' she said blankly.

'I know. But would Ed?'

She mulled this over, and then, looking at him properly, seeing him perhaps for the first time as a real, present person, she asked, 'Is that *it*? Is that what gave it away?'

'Partly. The first thing was that when I talked about his bedroom on the top floor, you started. You'd already told me you never went up there.'

'I didn't want you to—'

'To think that you would know anything about his bedroom, I know. You were just the secretary, nothing more. But you'd just remembered you'd left the wine glass up there, the one you'd been drinking out of.'

She bit her lip. 'How could you know that?'

He didn't answer that. 'The final thing, that clinched it, was the cricket bat.' She winced at the word. 'I could see there was a space on the wall, that something was missing, but I didn't know what. I found out later. But when I spoke to you about the cricket memorabilia on his study wall, you talked about the cricket balls, but you didn't mention the bat. An innocent person would probably have mentioned the bat before the balls: with the signatures, it was the more interesting object. And the more important to him. But you didn't dare draw attention to it. Or perhaps you just couldn't bear to speak about it.'

'You're clever,' she said dully.

'You didn't dare leave it in Ed's study. You couldn't put it back on the wall. The murder weapon.'

'Don't,' she winced.

'You'd heard of all the wonderful forensic tests we have now. You had to take it away and get rid of it. So you hid it under your coat and took it home. But then you couldn't think of what to do with it. If you tried to dispose of it, someone might see, you might be caught on camera, it might somehow be traced back to you. You just had to keep it.' He met her eyes. 'Hateful, horrible thing, reminding you every minute of what you've done. It's somewhere in the flat now, isn't it?'

'In my wardrobe,' she acknowledged on an outward sigh.

Slider nodded at Swilley, and she loped quietly out. With the bat, and the lip print, and the CCTV evidence, he had enough now to back up her confession. Hollinshead remained staring at nothing, in a daze, until Swilley came back in and nodded to Slider, it's there all right. Now they could get SOC in to officially find and secure it, and her clothes as well, because there might be blood or matter on some of them.

He stood up. 'Well, that's it,' he said. She looked up at him. 'You had better come with me now to the station, and make your statement.' For a moment she didn't move. He encouraged her like a child. 'Come on now. Up you get. The worst is over. DC Swilley will look after you. She'll help you get it all written down.'

Hollinshead stood up, but didn't seem to know how to move.

She looked around her, and Slider almost *saw* her waking up, saw her face sag with realisation. Now, at this moment, she understood the ruin of her life, of her entire being. It was finished. It was over. This was the end of everything.

'What will happen to me?' she asked Slider, her voice seeming far away. He imagined her receding, blown helplessly backwards away from the warm precincts of the cheerful day, and into the blank chill of process: trial, imprisonment, oblivion.

'You must expect a custodial sentence,' he said. 'But there are discounts for pleading guilty and possibly because you are not likely to kill anyone else. With good behaviour you will get parole. But you should expect to serve at least eight years.'

She said, 'Eight,' but not with any emphasis. The length of time was secondary to the understanding that she would actually go to prison. He had seen it before – that to the respectable middle classes, prison itself was a thing of utter terror, a deterrent as it could never be to the criminal classes.

Although, in the moment of red-hot passion, nothing really deterred, did it? And Ed Wiseman was dead. He must never allow his empathy with the cornered fox to seduce him into forgetting that.

Swilley came up behind her, to urge her into movement. She started forward, then remembered something. Her eyes widened in alarm. 'My cat. What will happen to my cat?'

'We have an arrangement with an animal shelter,' Slider said. 'He'll be well cared for. Eventually, he'll be rehomed.'

She squeezed her eyes shut for a moment, at this further reminder that she would not be coming back. She opened them and looked at Slider. 'I wish you could take him,' she said. 'He likes you. I don't like to think of him being shut in a cage wondering . . .' She stopped, perhaps thinking of her own cage.

The cat was sitting at the junction where the vinyl flooring of the kitchen area met the carpet of the lounge area, its tail curled neatly around its feet, watching the action uncomprehendingly. When Slider looked at it, it purred.

TWENTY-THREE
Gone to Ground

Hollinshead had a cat basket, a tunnel-shaped wicker thing with a cage door to the front, and when the first reinforcements arrived, Slider saw the cat put in it, in case with all the door openings and comings and goings, it got out and was lost. It went in without a fuss, but while he was giving instructions to his team he could hear it in the background, mewing. Not a mew of anger or protest, just an intermittent small sound that seemed to say, 'You won't forget I'm stuck in here, will you?' His empathy circuits had had a real workout today, and it was almost the last straw to be having his heart tugged by a feline. He couldn't cope with kitty-pity on top of everything else. He felt exhausted.

'Make sure the animal shelter sends someone straight away,' he told D'Arblay, one of the uniformed help. 'I don't want it frightened and knocked about by big trampling boots.'

'I'll see to it, sir,' said D'Arblay, with almost too much sympathy in his face.

Am I that obvious, Slider wondered. He had to pull himself together. 'Right,' he said brusquely. 'Let me know when it's been picked up.'

And if it sounded as if he didn't trust him, Slider couldn't help that.

'Sir,' said D'Arblay.

The scowl of furious thought was Porson's default expression, but his brow was so furrowed you could have grown radishes in it.

'Another confession?' he said when Slider stopped. 'Are you sure this time?'

'I'm sure,' said Slider. 'We've got the murder weapon, the CCTV, the lip print, hopefully traces on clothing. And her account fits all the known details – including the visits of Langley and

Burke, which she couldn't have known about if she hadn't been there.'

'Point,' said Porson. Fair play to the old boy, he always managed to keep all the aspects of a case in his head while it was going on.

'The timings fit. It all makes sense,' Slider concluded.

'And plenty of motive sloshing about,' Porson mused.

'Sexual jealousy always goes down well. You don't have to get a psychologist in to explain it to the jury.'

She had talked again in the car, admitting that she had got rid of Liana Karev, who she felt had been getting too close to Wiseman. She didn't know there had been sexual activity between them, but she feared it was heading that way. So she'd told him there was not really enough business for two assistants, and that he ought to be saving money where he could. He had taken the bait – of course, she didn't know then that he had another use planned for his cash, and economy was an argument he was ready for.

'Well, that's all good, then,' Porson concluded. 'And you did it without involving the Hunt female.'

The truth about meeting her bustled up behind Slider's teeth, hesitated, then shuffled off unspoken. He had done nothing wrong, he reasoned. If it came out of its own accord, so be it, but there was no need for him to volunteer his head for washing. What was it his mother used to say? Never trouble trouble, till trouble troubles you. He gave Porson an intelligent, receptive look, and said nothing.

'Mr Carpenter's going to be happy about that,' Porson went on. 'Pleased as a dog with two willies, he'll be.'

'I'm always glad when he's happy,' Slider murmured.

Porson gave him a sharp glare. 'You needn't look as if career means nothing to you. The Job's a job, as well as a vocation. And you've not always been flavour of the month. There was that Gideon Marler business . . .'

'Sir,' Slider began to protest. He didn't want all his sins trotted out again.

Porson lifted a hand. 'I know, I know. Old history. We've all passed a lot of water over the bridge since then. I'm just saying, there's no harm in doing yourself a bit of bon when you can. Looking out for number one doesn't mean you can't still be the capped crusader.' He turned away, to signify the subject was closed.

'So she's in custody now?' he said from a new position by the filing cabinets.

'Being processed, sir, then we'll start taking her statement.'

'That'll take a while. And then there's the paperwork.' He gave Slider an appraising stare. 'You look knackered, laddie. You could go home, take a break.'

'I'd sooner do it in—'

'One foul sweep.' Porson nodded sympathetically. 'Quite right. You can forget things with a night's sleep in between.'

Before plunging in, he rang Joanna.

'It was the secretary?' she marvelled when he had told her, in précis.

'Assistant,' he corrected. 'She was much more than a secretary.'

'Evidently,' said Joanna.

There was a lack of sympathy in her voice. He supposed that was the woman's take on it – the old, clichéd rivalry, wife versus secretary. Of course, having a career of her own, Joanna wasn't so susceptible, but his first wife, Irene, who had been a stay-at-home, was always suspicious of any female at work that he mentioned.

But then Joanna jumped straight back into his heart by saying, 'I suppose she was the work-wife. Poor cow. Must be a rotten position to be in.'

'Could I just mention that I love you?' said Slider, not caring who could hear him.

She laughed. 'It's all right, I haven't got a jealous bone in my body. I'm sure you're not having a hot fling with Norma Swilley. I suppose you're going to be horribly late home?'

Anxiety again. 'I *really* can't help it,' he began.

'Relax, your dad and Lydia are home, remember? Fortunately, since I've got a concert. When will you be back?'

'There's eight hours of paperwork to do,' he said. 'I don't have to do it all tonight, but I'd sooner get it out of the way.'

'Go to it, my lad,' said Joanna. 'I'll expect you when I see you.'

She was about to ring off, when, with one of those tricks of the aural memory, he heard the cat mew again.

'Wait – Jo?'

'Yes?'

'How would you like us to adopt a cat?'

'Dunno. Do you feel that's something we're likely to do?'

'Seriously.'

'Well, George would love it, of course. And it's good for children to grow up with animals. We've got a garden. And it's not as much trouble as a dog – you don't have to take it for walks.' She paused. 'Is this really the moment you want to talk about it?'

He smiled, though she couldn't see him, of course. 'I've got to go. Hot statement waiting. I just wanted to warn you I'd be late.'

Released in the hall from the basket, the cat crept out, and began exploring, a little wary but mostly curious.

'He's not frightened,' Slider noted, pleased. The cat seemed to be following a pre-arranged trail down the passage and into the drawing room, as if he'd been here before.

'He can smell *you* in the house,' Joanna said practically. 'He's met you at the other place. It's a link for him. What do you call it – continuity of custody?'

'You could be right.'

George was entranced. 'It's a cat,' he observed. No getting anything past that one, Slider thought.

'You must be very quiet and gentle,' Joanna warned him. 'With all animals, but especially cats.'

'Don't go after him,' Slider warned as he started towards it. 'You'll scare him. Let him come to you.'

George squatted in that effortless way children have, and watched the cat ambling back and forth, wiping its face on the furniture legs. After a moment it came stalking by and cheek-swiped him, too, and he lifted a face to Slider transformed by wonder and excitement. 'He likes me!' he whispered rapturously.

'What shall we call him?' Joanna asked.

George gazed at her, slightly open-mouthed. There hadn't been much naming of things in his life up to now.

'It's a stripey cat,' Slider said, to help him along. 'What else is stripey?'

George thought furiously. 'A onion,' he said at last.

Slider blinked. He supposed it was, in a way. There was always a new way to look at things to be learned from little children. 'But you can't call a cat Onion,' he decreed. 'What else?'

More thought. Then George's face cleared. 'A jumper. I've got a stripey jumper.'

Joanna was laughing. 'He has,' she said. 'It's his favourite.'

'Jumper's a good name,' Slider said. He supposed it was appropriate, remembering how it had jumped lightly up onto the balcony rail in another life.

Later, with George in bed, he and Joanna had supper at the kitchen table, with Jumper still restlessly exploring. It would wander off for a bit, then come back to brush against Slider's leg; pivoting its journeys round the one familiar thing in the new order.

'He's not used to so much space,' Slider commented. 'It was quite a small flat.'

'He'll go nuts when he sees the garden, then,' said Joanna.

'We'll have to keep him indoors for a while, so he doesn't wander off.'

'How long is a while?'

'A week should do it. Luckily he's been an indoor cat up till now.'

'Luckily he's already discovered the litter tray,' Joanna said dryly. 'And I suppose it'll be my job to clean it out.'

He looked up from his plate, wondering if this was a test. 'My job too. Whoever's at home at the appropriate time.'

'You're a new man,' she marvelled.

'I used to change nappies,' he pointed out. 'Anyway, I brought the thing into the house, so it's my responsibility.'

'Yes, why did you?' she asked. 'Not that I mind – he's a very nice cat, and George is crazy about him already. I'm just wondering.'

'He looked at me,' Slider said.

'He – or his owner?'

'She wasn't that sort of girl. She was a one-man woman – in spades.'

'I suppose she loved him,' Joanna said doubtfully. 'Ed Wiseman, I mean.'

'I don't know,' Slider said. 'It started with love, certainly. By the end it was obsession, passion, possessiveness, jealousy. And . . .'

'And,' she prompted when he didn't go on.

'She didn't have anything else in her life. That's never healthy.'

She surveyed him curiously. 'Are you sorry for her? Or for him?'

'That's a funny question.'

'I just want to know where your sympathies lie. You have an awkward habit of seeing both sides of everything.'

Slider thought, watching the cat ooze back in from the hall, and across to the food bowl by the pantry door, to see if it had magically refilled itself. Life, for cats, was full of magic: the way food appeared, the way doors just opened.

'They were both pathetic,' he said at last. 'But he's dead.' Ed Wiseman had gone to ground, and he wasn't coming back. 'One day, she'll have the chance to rebuild a life.'

'Without him?'

'Point. But a chance, at least.'

So much crime came from thwarted passion, from sexual jealousy, from misplaced possessiveness. And it was none of it to do with love, as was generally claimed by the perpetrators. It came from the lack of love – or the fear thereof. It was so important, he thought, that small, banal thing of having someone to love who loved you: so universally desired, so simple in song and story, so fiendishly tricky to achieve in real life.

It made the world go round. At present, however, industrial-strength tiredness was making his go round. He hadn't slept for two days. 'I'm bashed,' he said.

'I know. You go up. I shan't be long behind you.'

Perversely, as soon as he lay down, sleep rushed away from him like a teenage fan spotting a boy band, leaving him stranded – sleepless, but too tired to do anything, get up, read, even really think. He listened to the soft sounds of Joanna making ready, checking on George, in and out of the bathroom. She had seemed normal all evening. Perhaps whatever had been troubling her had gone away. He'd like to ask her what it had been, but he didn't want to stir anything up. She'd tell him, eventually, he supposed.

She turned out the passage light and padded across to the bed, leaving the door open, as they always did, so they could hear if George called out. One day, he thought, they'd have to start closing it so that he couldn't hear them. She climbed into bed, and inserted herself into his arms. He closed them round her, kissed the top of her head, and as if in response to that, she said, 'I've been ratty lately.'

'No.' He murmured an automatic denial.

'Ratty,' she asserted. 'I know you noticed. I was worried about something.'

'You could have talked to me about it,' he said. 'You can always tell me anything.'

'I know. But I didn't know how *I* felt about it. I missed a period, you see. I thought I might be pregnant.'

He waited, cautiously, not sure what so say at that juncture.

She went on. 'There's my job, you see. I'm just really getting back into the swing of it. I'm on all the fixers' lists, and there's plenty of work coming in. And I love it. I love playing. I'd have to take a big step backwards if I had another baby. At my age, I might never get back onto the A lists again afterwards. And then there's money. It would be really tight without my income.'

'We'd always manage,' he said. 'We've got no mortgage, that's the main thing. With a roof over our heads, and enough to eat . . .'

'You're such a Pollyanna!'

'I've always thought of myself as more of a Micawber. My goal is staying sixpence ahead, not universal happiness.'

She turned over, and made the delicate backing movement – he always thought it of as *docking* – into the spoons position. He locked his arms round her again. The conversation felt unfinished. He waited a while, but she didn't speak.

'But you're talking now. So you're not worried anymore?' he tried.

'I'm not worried any more,' she said. He gave her a little squeeze of acknowledgement. 'But I am pregnant.'

'Oh,' said Slider. He would have said more, but such a rush of emotions fountained up in him, it took his breath away.

'Oh?' she queried. 'I need a little more than that. Use your words, Bill.'

He sought for them amongst the sparklers and Golden Rain going off inside him. Someone to love, who loved you. It was the whole thing, wasn't it?

'I'm the luckiest man alive,' was what he said, eventually.

She gave a little snort of laughter. 'I suppose that'll do. For a start. So you're all right about it?'

'All right? Children are tax deductible! Are *you* happy about it?'

'It wasn't in my plans. But it will be good for George to have a sibling – I have worried about that sometimes. And . . .'

'Yes?'

'I've always been glad you feel the same way about abortion as I do.'

He thought of Liana Karev, and the cruelty of her boyfriend looking up the law. The very word *abortion* was a shadow, and he did not want it cast, like the uninvited fairy's wish, on his unborn child. 'I'm very happy about it,' he offered.

'You're not Pollyanna, you're just polyphiloprogenitive.'

'But we make such pretty babies,' he protested.

'You're a remarkable man, Bill Slider,' she said.

'In so many ways,' he agreed. 'Go to sleep now. Everything will be all right.'

And he felt her fall almost instantly, in that way she had, into deep sleep in his arms. She was tired, too.

He lay, not thinking much, just feeling great warm blankets of contentment wrapping round him. Pasithea tiptoed closer, drawing Hypnos after her by the hand. Take me, chaps, I'm yours, he thought. Don't be shy. There's plenty to go around.

He was almost down when there was a soft thud on the end of the bed, followed by a placatory purr. Jumper had found his way upstairs. He felt the hesitant, heavy footsteps come up the bed, the pause as the cat found the backs of Slider's knees, then the two-and-a-half turns and the perfectly-judged flop into the curve of them.

The purring increased in volume for a moment.

We should have called him Harley, he thought. And slept.